C000147340

THE BOYS

A NOVEL

MICHAEL HARNETT

Hark Press

Copyright © 2011 Michael Harnett.

First Published in Dublin by:
Hark Press, Tirim House, Jamestown Business Park,
Jamestown Road, Finglas, Dublin 11, Ireland
Tel: (01) 834 2700. Fax: 834 2912. E-Mail: harkview@gmail.com

The right of Michael Harnett to be identified as the author of this work has been
asserted by him in accordance with the Copywright, Designs and Patents Act,
1988.

This is a work of fiction. Names, characters, places and incidents either are the
product of the author's imagination or are used fictitiously. Any resemblance to
actual persons, living or dead is entirely coincidental.

ISBN: 978-1-906027-93-3

Printed and bound in Ireland by eprint limited www.eprint.ie

to

JENNY

Remembering 'The Boys'
in particular
Frank Hennelly (1948 – 2009)

THE BOYS

CHAPTER ONE

DUBLIN 1967

Everyone had heard the story of the woman at the window; the one with the enormous boobs, the one who went to bed just after ten. But few had seen her in the flesh. Rumour had it that Finnegan, the chemist's messenger boy, had seen her. The story spread that Finnegan had watched from the lane at the back of her house as she peeled off her clothes down to her nip before admiring herself in the mirror.

'You'd want to have seen her. And the size of them,' teased Finnegan.

The boys decided that this free show had to be seen. This was a golden opportunity for sixteen year old impressionable eyes to see the real thing instead of the usual fantasies which occupied their fertile minds. Sex was something they thought about a lot. They talked about it too, always adopting an air of bravado when they spoke. Each wanted the other to believe that there was little they didn't know about the female anatomy.

They had gathered in the back lane behind the woman's house - Hackett, Brennan and the Scout. They were waiting for the light to come on in the woman's bedroom overhead.

It was a clear crisp November evening. Already the reflection of the moonlight glistened on the frost that had fallen in the lane. It was cold, bitterly cold. The warm breath from their mouths became bursts of fog in the winter air. They were anxious. They were nervous. They wanted the show to begin.

'What time is it?' asked Brennan.

'No watch,' answered Hackett.

'Almost ten to,' whispered the Scout.

'Finnegan did say ten o'clock? Didn't he?' Brennan's anxiety was beginning to show.

'That's what he said. Ten o'clock every night,' said Hackett fishing a cigarette from his top pocket and striking a match against the wall. The others watched longingly as Hackett drew deeply on the smoke. They wanted him to share. They felt the need of some comfort.

'Don't wet it,' warned Hackett as he passed the cigarette to the Scout. Hackett hated getting a cigarette back soaked in another's saliva. The last thing a tall, dark, good looking fella needed was a poxy cold sore. Hackett had the look of a rock star and he knew it. His hair was long and combed to the front, his jeans tight, his pointed boots like the Beatles wore.

At the top of the lane beneath the amber reach of a street lamp the boys watched the outline of people passing by, neighbours mostly, who would hardly approve of anyone standing in a laneway waiting for a woman to take off her clothes. After all they were probably on their way back from church and feeling especially devout in this, the month of the Holy Souls.

'Do you know yer woman?' asked Hackett. 'Have you seen her around?'

Brennan looked away. The Scout drew deeply on the cigarette. He gave a look of imminent disclosure. The Scout was the type who would reveal what he knew. He didn't have agendas. And he did okay with the women. They seemed to fall for his way with the words, his long fair hair, his blue eyes. It didn't seem to matter that he was a little on the heavy side. Puppy fat, his mother called it.

'I've seen her,' said the Scout as he blew out a mouthful of smoke, 'she's a fine thing and she knows it. She knows you're watching her and she turns it on. You'd want to see her. I can't wait to see her in the flesh.'

At the mention of flesh Brennan felt a shudder of discomfort. His mind was building pictures. Often he would lose himself in his imagination and see himself with women, loads of them. In those dreams he was taller, stronger, and better with words, not the meek figure that stood in that lane. Someday soon he would write to Charles Atlas, the body building expert, and get the formula. That way his biceps would swell and his torso develop. Then he'd score with the women.

Suddenly from a nearby back garden came the sound of bolts being pulled and a kitchen door opening. Then coughing, spluttering and the clearing of a throat before the hoarse voice of a man called out.

'Go on, Sandy. Out you go and do your business.'

The boys instantly recognised the gruff sounding voice of old man Gormley. He was one of those men who hated most things in life especially teenagers. If a football landed in Gormley's garden he would slit it with a spade and toss it over the wall. Everyone avoided Gormley. It wasn't just his attitude. It was his look, his physique, his reputation as a brawler; as a young man he had lost an eye in a bare knuckle fight in the docklands. A German sailor was said to have gouged his eye out, yet Gormley fought on fiercely. The sailor, they said, never walked again.

'Who's he talking to?' whispered Brennan.

'It's that mad fucking animal of his,' said the Scout who was terrified of Gormley's dog, a Kerry Blue, who like its owner had a fearsome reputation for aggression.

'If that bowler sniffs us out we're done for,' said Brennan.

'Shut it, will you,' snapped Hackett.

They tried to keep still while Gormley and the dog remained in the garden.

'What's he at?'

'He's waiting for the dog to shit.'

Eventually the silence was broken by the sound of the kitchen door opening again and a loud command to the dog.

'Right, Sandy, in you go, in you go.'

The sound of Gormley's door closing was the signal to relax and resume the vigil in the lane.

'What does she be doing going to bed at ten anyway?' wondered Hackett.

'Maybe she has a bloke up there and they like to get at it early,' said the Scout.

Brennan sighed quietly.

'Yeah,' said Hackett. 'Makes sense. A bird like that must have loads of blokes. Maybe a different one every night.'

Brennan did not take that piece of information easily. His over stimulated imagination produced sweat in volume. His pulse was racing.

'What the hell's keeping her?' he said.

'It's not a date Brennan. It's not as if she's expecting us,' jeered the Scout.

'I bet she knows people are looking at her,' said Hackett.

Brennan was tiring of the chatter. He wanted action. He wanted to cast his eyes on the beauty in the window. From the moment he had heard about this woman he could hardly think of anything else. Now he would see the real thing instead of those magazines that the Scout's brother brought back from the navy.

'Where the hell is she?'

'Why don't you call around and knock on her door, tell her we're all waiting,' said Hackett.

'Fuck off.'

'Fuck off yourself.'

For a moment Brennan felt hatred for Hackett. He hated his build, his physique, his confidence. Then the Scout had a question for Brennan.

'Ever seen a woman in the nip, Brennan?'

'Course I have,' lied Brennan.

'Yeah, your old lady!'

Brennan thought of his mother for a moment, the small wizened woman, skinny as a bamboo. He pictured her in his father's dressing gown, the carpet slippers, the hair net enclosing a myriad of pins. Early mornings she looked the worst as she stood over a spitting frying pan, her teeth upstairs in a jar.

4

'What if she's late?' wondered Hackett. 'How long will we give her?'

'If she doesn't show, I'm not pushed,' lied the Scout.

'Finnegan was saying that sometimes she rubs cream into them,' added Hackett.

'Cream?' croaked Brennan. 'Why would she do that?'

'Maybe yer man likes a bit of cream on them,' said the Scout smirking.

If Brennan had been bigger, stronger, he would have lashed out and floored the others.

Then everything went still. It was like the start of a film in the Drumcondra Grand when everyone went silent. The light went on in the woman's bedroom.

The three of them crossed the laneway and rapidly scrambled up the rough concrete wall at the end of the woman's garden. There wasn't much space near the top of the wall. In his excitement Brennan ripped the knee out of his trousers. He didn't care. He was beyond caring. He was like a climber in sight of the summit.

For what seemed like an age there was no sign of the woman. Shadows, yes, vague outlines moving about in the room. It was like one of those games they had played as kids making shapes and shadows with a flashlight.

'Finnegan was having us on,' said the Scout.

'Shut it,' said Hackett.

'Give her time,' pleaded Brennan.

Then they thought they saw another figure in the room.

'Her fella,' said the Scout.

'Lucky fucker,' said Hackett.

Brennan said nothing.

Then without warning she came to the window. Though fully clothed there was no doubting her assets. A tight fitting top accentuated what she had. The boys sucked in the air deeply. The woman they were looking at was a beauty. Long auburn coloured hair hung loosely to her shoulders. Hands on hips she first glanced towards the lane. Then she shook her head and tossed her hair before looking at herself in the mirror. Several times she twisted and turned before holding up clothes to her body as if picturing herself in various ensembles; a dress, several tops and a blouse.

'Bleeding fashion show,' said someone.

At one stage she pressed her face to glass and instinctively the boys on the wall ducked down.

'She can't see us,' said Hackett. 'Not with the light behind her.'

Then she walked away from the window.

'Ah fuck,' said someone.

'She can't be finished? Is she?' croaked Brennan.

But the waiting went on. They were almost choking with despair and ready to abandon the mission when the woman returned to the window. Sighs of relief came from them all. Then suddenly she whipped off her top.

The boys gasped at the sight before them. They had never seen anything like it. Finnegan was right. They were enormous, far bigger than anything they had imagined. They were like two extraordinary magical orbs of pleasure. All three on the wall were spellbound. They couldn't take their eyes off this woman. This was a special treat, a unique firsthand experience of the secret world of adult women. This was an area of life which up to now had only been revealed to the boys in the centre page spreads of banned magazines. Instead of fantasizing over the full colour images of various bunny girls they were now observing reality in its raw state.

No coherent words came from the boys; grunts of exuberance, sighs of wonder. They were transfixed by the vision at the window. They longed for the next stage in the performance. They hadn't long to wait.

With a flamboyant gesture she reached behind and undid the clasp of her bra. Then slowly, tantalisingly, she allowed her bra to slide down the front of her body exposing her nakedness to the mirror.

At this stage the audience on the wall were breathing deeply, their eyes refusing to blink. They secretly hoped that the woman would turn again towards the window for a full frontal picture of blissful lust. But instead she began a type of dance, not overtly erotic, more a gentle swaying of sorts and as she moved she caressed her breasts with her fingers.

By this stage those on the wall were on fire. Brennan was like someone with the early symptoms of flu. His head felt feverish and his eyes were streaming. He wouldn't have been surprised if he heard himself moan.

Then without warning the performance came to an end. At first the boys didn't speak. They were waiting for the encore and hoping that the show would resume. But no one appeared at the window.

'Where's she gone?' whispered Brennan.

'Maybe she's gone to the fridge to get the cream,' said Hackett.

If you asked them later how long they had clung to the wall they wouldn't have been able to say. Time was not the issue. Their minds had been taken over by a force they didn't fully understand. Their arms ached. Their hands were frozen. The cold and the damp made them shiver.

Suddenly they were distracted by another development. It was the sound of a motorbike which came to a stop at the end of the lane. At first the boys ignored it. But when its headlight began to probe the darkness they began to wonder. Like a searchlight from a war movie the beam of light probed the shadows. The boys kept their heads low. They didn't speak. Then the idling of the engine changed. It clicked into gear. The revs built slowly and

7

the heavy machine began to move slowly down the laneway towards them.

The Scout was the first to speak.

'It's the fucking law.'

'What'll we do?' pleaded Brennan.

'Don't know about you,' said Hackett, 'but I'm out of here. If we're caught we're done for.'

It was then the choreography challenged them. Panic took over. Hackett began to haul himself upwards. So did the Scout. It was each man for himself. It was a battle of arms and legs as each of them attempted to climb upwards out of danger.

The Scout, despite his puppy fat, had always been the most agile of climbers. Nimbly, he succeeded in making his way onto a nearby garage roof before sliding down into the dense foliage of another garden. Hackett did well too. He had made it to the top of the wall. All he needed was a final push. In the confusion and the darkness he couldn't see clearly. He used any prop that he could. The one that was closest was Brennan's shoulder. Brennan couldn't take the weight; his aching fingers couldn't take the pressure. He lost his grip on the wall and was powerless to stop himself falling. The deepest of fears gripped him. He couldn't see where he was tumbling. Head over heels he fell until he ended up in a matted clump of brambles. But worse, he had fallen into Gormley's back garden.

Outside in the lane the motorbike came to a stop. The cop dismounted and scaled the wall. He carried a torch which he shone into the gardens.

'Come on,' the cop shouted. 'Out you come! You can't hide from me!'

Suddenly the woman at the window appeared again. She pulled up the sash window and stuck out her head.

'So that's your game is it?' she blared at the cop. 'Instead of enforcing the law you'd prefer to be a peeper. Well you stay there because I'm coming down. I'll have your guts for garters.'

8

The cop tried to protest, but she didn't listen. She slammed the window and disappeared.

Brennan tried to use this diversion to untangle himself from the bushes. He managed to ease himself into a standing position. As he stretched forward a sprig of thorns sprung forward and tore at his face. He wanted to curse and swear but he was gripped by another crisis.

From behind his back a hand reached forward. It covered his mouth and gripped him tightly. Then a voice.

'I've got you, you little cur.'

There was no mistaking the sandpaper growl of old man Gormley.

'So what am I going to do with you? Do I bring you around to that sanctimonious old fellow of yours and tell him what you've been at? Do I? Is that what I should do?'

Brennan couldn't speak. Gormley's rough tobacco stained hand gagged his mouth. The stink of nicotene was noxious. It was at times like this that Brennan wished he was as big as the others. If only he could lash out at Gormley and floor the bastard. Then the woman's voice was heard again. She had opened her back door and stomped down her garden. She confronted the cop on the wall.

'Well,' she said loudly. 'Well what have you to say for yourself now?'

At the sound of her voice Gormley held Brennan even tighter. He turned Brennan round and glared into his face. The message was clear. If Brennan tried to alert the woman or the cop the punishment would be fatal.

Brennan tried to pull his face back from Gormley's. He hated the closeness of this wretched man, his one glass eye, the stink of tobacco and beer. But Gormley held him close.

Across the wall the initial brashness of the woman had subsided. She didn't seem as aggressive. In fact her tone was so low that Brennan couldn't make out what she was saying. The cop and herself seemed to have hit an intimate level. At one stage Brennan was sure there were some chuckles of laughter. Then strangely it all went quiet.

Brennan watched as Gormley's good eye moved about in its socket. The man was perplexed. His moving eye seemed to be searching for a reason for the silence. But suddenly the silence was broken. The engine of the motorbike spluttered into life. The throttle turned, the pistons responded, the sound began to fade as the motorbike moved down the lane.

Gormley seemed as surprised as Brennan. But that didn't lessen his angst.

'Well me bucko, what am I to do with you? I think it's time you and me paid that old fellow of yours a visit. What will he say when he hears that his so called angelic son was watching a woman taking off her clothes?'

'Please Mr Gormley, please,' pleaded Brennan who would have done anything rather than have his father, a daily churchgoer, a bastion of the community, learn about the woman at the window.

'He'd kill me Mr Gormley, he would.'

'No, I think it's best that you face the music. I can't wait to see the face of your old man when he hears that his pride and joy was watching a woman take her bra off.'

It may have been sheer terror which prompted a thought in Brennan's head. Maybe it was survival. But whatever the reason Brennan's logical mind was hit by a puzzle. How could old man Gormley know about the woman at the window and her bra? How could he have seen anything? After all didn't he go back indoors with his dog? Or did he?

'Well,' said Gormley, 'it's time you and me took a walk around to your house.'

Brennan took several deep breaths seeking composure.

'Right,' he said, 'and when we've done that we can come around and see Mrs Gormley.'

'You trying to be smart?' snarled Gormley who by this stage had released his grip on Brennan.

'No,' said Brennan, 'I'm not trying to be smart. It's just that I know that you were watching as well.'

'You cheeky bastard!'

'Lay a finger on me Mr Gormley and it will all come out.'

'You little gur!'

'I have witnesses and they'll swear they saw you.'

Gormley knew he was cornered. His face contorted in confusion. Then without comment he frogmarched Brennan to the end wall of the garden and threw him out the back gate into the lane.

Brennan couldn't believe he was free. He stood for several moments pondering it all. He felt good about himself. He had outwitted the notorious Gormley and lived to tell the tale. And what a tale it was. But there was more.

From overhead the light from the woman's bedroom came on again. The woman came to the window. Again she pulled the sash window upwards and leaned out onto the window sill. She looked in Gormley's direction.

'Out for more air Mr Gormley? Did you not get enough earlier on?'

Brennan didn't wait to hear if Gormley responded. He had heard and seen enough. He began walking up the muddy laneway towards the street light. His body ached. All his limbs were sore. Lacerations from the thorn bushes covered his hands and face. His clothes were in shreds. But he didn't really care. Yes, he would have to explain the gashed knees, the ripped clothes, the cuts and bruises on his body. But all that paled in comparison to what might have happened if the truth had come out.

Brennan pictured his small balding old man standing in the hall with the veins in his neck throbbing as the riot act was read. And behind as always, his mother calling down from heaven all the angels and saints pleading for forgiveness. His mother, the tiny woman who never seemed to shut up; a gasbag full of wind.

When he reached the street he turned the corner and headed for home. As he walked he lit the butt of a cigarette then stopped and leaned against the gable wall of a house. The deep drags of the smoke at first made him dizzy. Then he thought about what had happened. Never in his sixteen years on the planet had he experienced such a night. He had seen it all.

As he looked down on his dishevelled appearance he began thinking of how he would explain how he looked. He could say he was trying to free a cat up a tree and he fell on the thorns underneath. That was a good one. Or, that some unfortunate old lady had locked herself out of her house and he had to climb in an upstairs window. His father would appreciate any act of charity. The old lady story seemed best. Humans were always a better bet than animals.

Stubbing out the cigarette he began walking home. Despite his aches he was elated. In some ways he was even looking forward to telling the story to his parents, to see how his act of Christian charity might move them almost to tears.

Brennan never got an opportunity to tell his story. As he passed the side entrance to Hanlon's house a beam of light hit him abruptly. He stood rigid and blind. A flush of terror coursed through him. Then he heard the revving sound of the motorbike. The cop had been waiting all the time.

The weeks that followed were among the most awful in Brennan's short life. His every movement was watched. He left home each morning at the same time, cycled to school and returned at four on the dot. He was not permitted to speak to anyone. It was like a prison regime. Not much worse than what the cop had threatened on the night of the *window* incident.

'You'll want to keep a close eye on him Mr Brennan, because if it happens again it'll be Mountjoy prison and we don't want that do we?' said the cop in mock authority that evening.

'Don't worry,' said old man Brennan, 'we'll be keeping a close watch on him.'

And that's what they did. Every evening when he came home from school it was up the stairs to his bedroom for study. Apart from meal times he hardly saw the rest of the family. That for Brennan was no bad thing. He hated his sister Maura, a dogged bitch who championed the cause of telling tales and stirring trouble. Her one regret in life was not being the first to have the story of the woman at the window. That would have given her the most devious of joys.

Sitting in silence around the kitchen table suited Brennan. There were no complaints from his mother, no tedious enquiries from his father.

He didn't have to listen to his fussy old man and watch his bushy eyebrows dance up and down. Nor did he have to witness the spectacle of the few strands of hair being dragged across a bare scalp. Best of all was the speechless mother. The small wiry creature never seemed to rest. He couldn't imagine what his old man had seen in this flesh covered skeleton who talked like a machine and looked like a bird.

The only respite in Brennan's monotonous existence was night time. As soon as he knew the house was still he would go to his bedroom window and gaze at the houses across the lane. He couldn't see the special window. Instead he would stare at a similar one and relive the entire experience in his imagination.

He thought of her standing there in front of the mirror brushing her hair and admiring herself. Some nights he imagined that he was one of the fellows in the room watching from the bed waiting for her to be ready for him. He even saw himself walking to the window and holding her close then turning her around to allow those two enormous pleasure points press against him.

Then as he led her from the window he would pause, turn, and wave to Hackett and the Scout on the wall below before turning off the lights and leaving them with their frustrations.

All these imaginings and journeys in his mind left him unsettled. He couldn't get her out of his mind. He wondered how long this woman would haunt him. He didn't want it to go on forever. Yet every night before he slept he actively brought her into his mind. She was like a drug, something he needed to consume. As he thought of her the frustrations built and he released them in the only way he knew how. Then he slept.

In his dreams he was the new muscular Brennan, the one with the expanded chest, the steely torso. He was also taller, maybe not as tall as the others, but tall enough to pull the birds.

That was the only thing that mattered.

CHAPTER TWO

In the days which followed the episode in the lane the Scout and Hackett had difficulty sleeping. This was partly to do with what they had seen that night, but of equal importance was the fear they felt that the truth might emerge. They, like Brennan, could be joined in the crime. They were convinced that Brennan's old man would prise the details from his son. They believed that Brennan was weak; under pressure he would probably cave in.

Brennan had the reputation of always walking away from a fight. But he never saw that as weakness. He preferred the word diplomacy. His facility with langauage usually got him out of trouble, like the time he convinced the animal gang that he had a terminal illness and wouldn't be able to fight.He wasn't like the stocky Scout who always stood his ground. Nor was he like Hackett who used his height to his advantage.

As the days went by the boys changed their view. Maybe Brennan had some inner strength they hadn't recognised.

'Maybe we were wrong about him.'

'Yeah, maybe he has guts after all.'

Once they felt they were safe the boys developed an enormous appetite for information. They wanted to know the full story; about the cop, the woman and what happened Brennan after he fell into Gormley's garden. They knew something had happened. Why else was Brennan out of circulation?

On several mornings they watched as Brennan headed off for school, his mother standing on the step craning her neck outwards, watching with her beady eye the safe dispatch of her son from the street without consorting with others. It was not motherly love that took her out onto the step each morning. It was part of the regime of maintaining a wall of silence.

15

On one occasion Hackett saw Maura, Brennan's sister, and tried to engage her in conversation. Hackett was sure that his charm would work. He would butter her up, tell her that she looked like a film star. Then he would casually bring up the question of Brennan. Maybe he was sick? Or maybe he was swotting. Or maybe, who knows.

Hackett got his answer. It wasn't verbal. It was a look. She almost spat in Hackett's direction. Once a bitch always a bitch.

So, despite their best efforts the boys discovered nothing about the episode in the lane. All they knew was that Brennan was a captive, a prisoner, who as time wore on proved to be loyal to his friends. Hackett and the Scout took back all they had previously said about the frail unsporting Brennan. Instead they saw in their friend a man with a rod of iron as a spine.

Around the same time Hackett had been having problems of his own. It began with a letter to his parents from the school, a fee paying college run by the Jesuits.

The college authorities said they were concerned about Peter. They wondered about his on-going throat problem and the negative effect it might have on his academic prospects. They wished to know if there was anything they could do. Perhaps extra tutorials or study at the weekends? Their interest, as always, was for the boy. Oh, and in a post script to the letter the principal wrote that it was comforting to note that the consultant treating Peter was a past pupil of the college with an excellent academic record.

Old man Hackett read the letter several times. He sat down. He stood up. He lit several cigarettes. Then he showed the letter to his wife. She was equally mystified. But that wasn't strange. The world was largely a mystery to Mrs Hackett, a large country woman who thought the passing of each day was a miracle. Later when Mr Hackett reached his office he telephoned the school. He asked to speak with the principal.

'It's about your letter, Father,' he said deferentially. At the other end of the line Mr Hackett heard a slight clearing of the throat.

'I'm glad you rang Mr Hackett. How is Peter?'

'He's em. . . he's not too bad at the moment.'

'I'm very pleased to hear that. It must have been terrible for him. That sort of illness can be very debilitating. Is he still on the liquids or can he take solids yet?'

Mr Hackett scratched his head. He had no idea where this conversation was going.

'Oh he's eating all right at the moment,' said Mr Hackett, being sure to carefully word his reply. Being a clerk in the legal department of the city rates office he was well aware of the importance of the correct phrasing of words.

'It's always a good sign when they are back on the solids. Has he lost much weight?'

'To be honest Father. . . '

'I know it's difficult to judge when you see him every day. I'd say I'd notice, maybe even get a shock. I mean, I haven't seen him in what? A month? Yes, at least a month.'

A month, thought Mr Hackett. The little fecker has been out of school for a month!

'Anyway, I just thought I'd ring,' said Mr Hackett as he wiped the sweat from his forehead.

'And I'm glad you did. Tell me, when do you expect he'll be back with us in the college?'

'I'd say. . . I'd say, maybe tomorrow.'

When he put down the phone Mr Hackett rose from his desk and walked to the window of his office in Castle Street. He leaned against the wall and looked down on the cobbled street below. He lit a Capstan Full Strength and drew in the smoke deeply. A piece of tobacco stuck to his lip. He peeled it away with his fingers. He was in such a state that he could see little point in going back to work to shuffle through the pile of paper which lay on his desk.

17

Mr Hackett couldn't take pressure. Few people knew this. Outwardly he looked fit and well. He was tall and lean with a full head of dark hair. His appearance was almost distinguished though the suits he wore were faded. In truth many of his clothes had been passed on to him by his more wealthy and successful brothers. Yet he had a certain old fashioned decorum like that of a courtly waiter trying to do his best in an establishment that had seen better days.

He lit another cigarette. Nothing he had heard from the priest made sense. The pit of his stomach rumbled. He belched several times. This is what always happened. It was like a dormant volcano waiting for something to provoke unrest. Finally he decided that he was too ill, that a half day had suddenly become necessary to ease his condition.

Hackett had spent the day playing cards on the banks of the Royal Canal in the shadow of Mountjoy Prison. This was a favourite haunt of his where he was sure to find kindred spirits who believed that all work and no play was a pain in the ass.

Poker was his favourite game and for over four hours that day luck was on his side. He had won over two pounds, enough to sustain him over the next week in trips to the cinema far away from the exploits of Caesar and his unending Gallic Wars.

As he walked along the banks of the canal he thought of his friend Brennan. He wondered how long the curfew would last. On the odd occasion Brennan had joined him on the canal bank, but Brennan never relaxed. Instead of enjoying the freedom Brennan would constantly wonder what was happening in school - eleven thirty history, twelve fifteen religion. And then as evening approached the dread about going home and the constant worry that his parents had discovered his mitching. Maybe a teacher, a parent or a spiteful pupil might have seen him. Then there was the problem of forging a note for the school to excuse his absence. That was something Brennan hated. Bad enough to verbally deceive, but to put it in writing! Hackett had no such worries about letters or sick notes. All his sick note problems had been solved a year earlier. It had happened in the most innocent way while Hackett was away on a sports outing with the school.

Hackett's school had decided to participate in a rugby tournament. Hackett hated all field sports but because it meant free time from school he decided to get involved. Anything was preferable to study.

On the day in question, a bleak December afternoon, the wind was biting and the cold severe. There was also rain. The pitch was like a cutup battlefield. The uneven surface was puckered with puddles. Mud was everywhere. In this slurry the forwards battled like old warhorses. On the wing Hackett had little to do. He moved up and down the pitch with the play. He was frozen. He was sodden.

But midway through the second half things took a different turn. The opposition, which had fallen behind, seemed to rally and find inspiration. Their play became more spirited and expansive. They started to move the ball about the field.

Hackett wasn't sure he liked this change. It meant that there was always the danger of having to tackle. The score too became a factor. The opposition had worn down Hackett's team and there were only two points between them. Hackett's games master reflected the concern in language more appropriate to alleyways and betting shops.

'Bring down the feckers!' he roared several times.

Close to the end of the match when desperation was setting in the opposition launched a major offensive. It seemed that they were abandoning all tactics of caution. Winning at all costs was what they wanted.

In a final burst the ball came out towards the wing. First it was taken by a centre, then a forward moved it further on. Slowly, grindingly, the ball advanced towards Hackett's line. The opposition seemed to have the momentum. In a winning scrum an agile and muscular player got the ball. He began to advance. He had a steady and physical confidence about him. He was an athlete. Hackett saw him coming and inwardly prayed that he'd change direction. But the player continued. Hackett's games master watched in horror.

'Get him Hackett! Get him!'

The player seemed to speed up his pace. All Hackett could see was this mass of human muscle coming his way. Then another roar from the touch-line.

'Get him Hackett! Bring the fecker down!'

When Hackett signed up to play rugby this was not in the script. Now he was the only one between this player and the line. If Hackett let him pass the game was over and the honour of the school in shreds.

'Hackett! Hackett! Get the . . .'

The final profanity from the touch-line did not register with Hackett. Everything went blank. The sound too. He was conveyed to another place and the next thing he remembered was waking up in the casualty department of the Mater Hospital.

'Nothing broken, just mild concussion,' the Doctor said.

Hackett looked about. The overhead lights blinded him slightly.

'How do you feel, Peter?'

Hackett turned his head to the side. The games master was sitting on a chair beside him. Around him were gathered many of the team still muddied from battle. Hackett tried a slight smile of humility before delivering the killer line.

'Did we win?' he asked.

The games master looked about at the others. He nodded at them all then turned to the hero in the bed.

'Yes, Peter, we won. Thanks to your tackle we won.'

Hackett milked his heroism as much as he could. After a week he was back in school. He basked in the glory of it all. But, not long after, he was out sick again. This time it was his stomach. Some of the teachers in the staff room reckoned that Hackett was never the same after that tackle. And they were right. He was plagued by illness. If it wasn't the stomach it was his chest. Then his back would act up. Whatever the reason for the descent of young Peter Hackett into illness, the once brave tackler became a sickly and delicate boy. He became prone to every bug and infection. The college authorities were concerned. They even began to feel guilty believing that it was the incident on the playing field that had started it all. They pitied the Hackett family and all the money they had spent. Doctors and medics didn't come cheap and Hackett had seen many.

Hackett was left lying on a trolley in casualty for hours. It was part of the process of observation. The hospital wanted to ensure that there were no relapses or after effects. So, apart from the odd visit from a nurse, Hackett was left on his own. At one stage he needed to go to the bathroom. He called for a nurse. He called again. He changed his mind, not about needing to relieve himself, but having a nurse attend him. He didn't want just anyone arriving with a glass jar and sticking it between his legs. With his luck it could be one of those rough looking matronly types. She might even look under the sheets.

Pulling back the curtain on the cubicle Hackett went searching for the bathroom. One corridor looked the same as another. Cream and green paint everywhere.

After he had relieved himself and washed his hands using heavily disinfected soap, he headed back for casualty, turning one way, then another, trying to remember the route. The sameness of the decor baffled him, as a result he missed an opening and found himself standing in an office area, a central administration section, surrounded by telephones and typewriters. There was no one else in the place. The temptation to investigate was over-whelming. Innocently he opened a press, rooted on a shelf and came across reams of hospital stationery. He looked at one, then

21

another. The titles of the various consultants impressed him. Some had half the alphabet after their names; doctor this, professor that. It was all too tempting to ignore. That's when Hackett's mind became alive with endless possibilities, and so he filled a large envelope with a selection of headed notepaper from the most eminent of medical prac-titioners.

After leaving the canal bank that day Hackett ambled home. He was pleased with his winnings at poker and was mentally selecting the films he might see during the following week. He turned from Drumcondra Road into his own narrow street of red-bricked houses.

One of the first houses he passed was Fay's where the loud strumming of a bass guitar vibrated onto the street. Fay was the fourth member of the gang who, for reasons of his own, was not present the night they watched the woman at the window. Hackett thought of calling on Fay but decided to walk on. He was afraid of meeting Fay's old man and having to endure endless hours of complex conversation. Old man Fay was regarded by the neighbours as eccentric. The boys called him a nut.

Approaching Brennan's house he quickened his pace. He didn't want to face any of the Brennan family, particularly Maura. She was one of those people who would prise the truth from a convict.

Across the street the Scout's messenger bike was tied to the railings. He wondered how his friend rode that monster every day. It was a big heavy machine with no gears and a saddle as hard as a brick. Still, the Scout got paid to ride it. That was his job, delivering telegrams around the city.

As he came close to his own house he saw the curtains move. Someone was looking out. He thought it looked like the shape of his father. But what was he doing home at this hour. Was he sick, or what?

He knocked on the door and it immediately opened. Passing his father on the step he thought his old man had a flushed look. His father followed him into the kitchen.

'How was school?' he asked.

'Fine.'

'No problems?'

Hackett wanted to turn and study the old man's demeanour to get some idea of what was going on. But instead he kept his focus on the bread he was spreading with butter.

'No problems,' he replied casually.

'Have you homework?'

'Yeah.'

'What?'

'Oh, the usual.'

'And what's usual this weather?'

'History, Latin, that sort of thing.'

'And how is the throat?'

Hackett swallowed the bread he was chewing. His throat was fine, but he didn't answer.

'How is the throat?' he was asked again.

'Fine,' he replied.

'Then . . .' his old man said, moving forward menacingly, 'then why have you been out of school for a month?'

Hackett knew the game was up but it was never a good policy to admit defeat immediately.

'A month, what do you mean?'

'Don't mess me about, I've spoken with the principal.'

Sometimes it was best to put your hands up and use an alternative tactic. That's what Hackett tried. He went for the sympathy vote.

'I hate it Dad, I really do. You don't know what it's like. You don't know what I've to suffer there. I've tried hard but I can't take it. I can't take it anymore.'

He looked up at his old man with a broken look and frowned. He even tried to bring on a tear. The old man stood back. Hackett felt he was getting somewhere. The old man seemed perplexed, confused and maybe even sympathetic. But that was far from reality.

'I don't give a shite whether you hate it or not,' the old man bellowed. 'Not a shite. You're supposed to be there. If you don't go what chance will you have in life? Of getting a job? Getting anything? What do you want? To end up a telegram boy like your mate across the street, the Scout or whatever the hell you call him.'

'But Dad I don't want to be there. I hate going. I'm sick of it.'

'I don't care what you think,' the old man said his face getting redder. 'I couldn't give two fiddlers what you think. You're going to school and that's it.'

Hackett had never seen his old man this animated and upset. It wasn't just his annoyance; it was his inability to deal with the situation. He began flailing his hands about and darting in and out of the kitchen. Normally this placid clerk from the Rates Office took life in his stride. He believed in the quiet life, a regular routine. He liked day to follow day in an ordered sequence knowing exactly what he would be doing at every hour of the day. Order also suited his stomach.

Hackett decided on one last appeal.

'If you want me to go back, I'll go,' he whispered.

The old man relaxed a little, but Hackett wasn't finished.

'The only problem is that I'll be expelled when they find out what happened.'

Mr Hackett allowed himself a little smile.

'But they're not going to find out, are they? Who's going to tell them?'

Advantage Mr Hackett.

'The school think you're sick and I never made them any the wiser. And you, me bucko, won't open your mouth either. You'll go on as if you have been sick. Isn't that right? Isn't it?'

Mr Hackett waited for his son to reply.

'If that's what you want,' he said.

Then the interrogation began as to how Hackett had spent the last month. Naturally he couldn't admit to card games on the canal bank or afternoon visits to the cinema. He decided to try and rescue some respect.

'Most days I went to the National Library.'

'To do what?'

'Research into history and general study.'

This seemed to impress his father. The old man relaxed a little, lit a cigarette. Hackett caught the wisps of smoke, the first burn of the Virginia tobacco. If only, if only.

'And tell me,' his old man continued in a more conversational air, 'how did you arrange those letters from the consultant?'

Hackett would have liked to share and boast about how he had amassed such a selection of headed notepaper, but sense won out.

'I found a letter.'

'Just one?'

'Just one.'

'You're sure, you've no more?'

'No more. Honest.'

Hackett thought he detected a sense of disappointment in his old man's reaction. Maybe the old chancer would have liked a sick note himself.

His old man lit another cigarette.

'I wouldn't mind,' he said, 'but you've got the brains. All we want is the best for you, that's all. In years to come you'll thank me, you will. Peter, you could be anything you wanted to be.'

Hackett knew that his old man was expecting great things from his only son. He wanted Peter to be more successful than

25

him, to be more than an ordinary clerk in the Rates Office. His old man wanted to feel proud and vindicated, to prove that his genes were capable of producing the best academically.

Hackett could picture his old man standing there in Granny Hackett's on Christmas morning declaring to the family that Peter was doing medicine or law, or anything impressive for that matter. Hackett's father craved that special moment when his self-esteem would soar. Of all the Hacketts, his was the branch of the family that had not done well. All the others were set up in business or had letters after their names. Hackett's father desperately wanted his son to have a brass plate outside his door. He wanted him to live in a fine suburb instead of a small red-bricked house in Lower Drumcondra.

Money was another reason that old man Hackett wanted Peter to succeed. His wages as a clerk were so meagre that Mr Hackett could never have afforded to send his son to a fee paying school. The money came from Granny. She had taken a shine to her grandson. She thought she detected some promise in her offspring and backed her hunch with cash. Old man Hackett was never allowed forget where the school fees came from and his constant worry was that Granny might see her investment as a waste. The source of the fees was something that Hackett was reminded of regularly.

'You know your grandmother would be very disappointed Peter, if she heard about this,' said Mr Hackett wearily.

Peter nodded his head.

'It would break her heart. It could kill her.'

As far as Hackett was concerned the demise of Granny might be no bad thing. While he liked the old bird in a detached sort of way he found it hard to warm to the woman dressed in black. For as long as he could remember she had sat in her wing-backed chair in a musty room full of doilies and drapes. Permanently dark, the place was crammed with old furniture. It was like one of those auction houses on the quays where other people's junk was sold off as antique. Lot number four a burnished print, artist unknown.

Granny Hackett's room was a tabernacle of a hundred thousand memories. In the midst of all this, the old woman held court, the pink-red rouge on her cheeks a reminder to those present that, despite what they thought, a pulse was just about beating in the human frame before them.

Hackett remembered going to his Granny's every Sunday morning with his father. He recalled how his father sat in front of the old lady listening to her every word, a man who became a boy every time he entered that room.

He looked up at his father standing before him, his jacket off, the worsted cloth of his trousers shining. He felt pity for this man who had endured the tedium of being subservient to the coldness of Granny Hackett for years. The woman took no pleasure in her son. Instead his presence was a reminder that one of her sons had ended up as a humble clerk whose only claim to notoriety was sending out a million rate demands in twenty years.

Before he left the kitchen to read his *Evening Herald* by a slackened fire old man Hackett made a final plea.

'Peter please, for God's sake please make an effort. It's only a few years and then it'll be behind you. Promise me you'll do your best. Please.'

'I will Da, honest, I will.'

'Promise?'

'I promise.'

When he left the room Hackett felt a pang of guilt, not a dark cloud or dense shadow, but enough of a tinge to reassure the boy that he was human. He went upstairs to his room and lay on the bed. He looked up at the ceiling at the shadow cast by the hanging bulb and the shade. Some of his winnings fell from his pocket. The sound of the coins on the bed made him think of money. There must be better ways to make a fortune than going to school.

The words of his father filtered into his head, words induced by fear of that old woman living on her tree-lined avenue in the prosperous part of the area. The people who lived there ate meat most days of the week. These were the senior civil servants, the business people, the bankers, people who had disposable income, went to the opera, had foreign holidays, walked on fitted carpets and ordered their groceries by phone and paid at the end of the month.

Though Granny Hackett lived among them she was not part of them. She had cut herself adrift when her husband died in a boating accident. Her only interest, as far as the family were concerned, was the vigil in her room, her family and her cats. But Granny had another more clandestine interest. Every day she scoured the racing pages of the newspaper and, having made a selection, laid her bets down by telephone. Sometimes when the weather was mild a car would call and take her to the track. She liked the Curragh but her favourite was the Phoenix Park where, several times a year, she had lunch with a well known trainer. For his father's sake Hackett decided to return to school. He would do the exam and see how it went.

He rose from the bed and went to the window. Daylight was ebbing away and the street lights were on. For a moment he watched the heavy smut rising from the chimney pots on the roofs beyond. He hated this time of year. The misery of cold and damp, the taste of coal in your mouth as you walked the streets in the evening. He let out a large sigh. God, how he wished things could be different, like that night in the lane. That wonderful erotic night in the lane.

Now there was nothing to look forward to.

Nothing.

Except poxy school in the morning.

CHAPTER THREE

Vincent Fay was the fourth member of the gang. He was taller and leaner than the other three with a full head of curly fair hair which flowed down to his shoulders. Sometimes he wore a headband. He was in some way the street's ambassador for flower power, though most of the residents thought otherwise. Most believed that the young lad was a lost cause, though they didn't blame him entirely. Everyone thought that Fay's old man Harry was responsible; a man who by common consent, was not playing with a full deck.

'Not the full shilling,' they'd say, but not disparagingly.

Fay's old man was the eccentric on the street. Other less polite descriptions were also in circulation, but there was no badness in the man just a general lacking when it came to convention. Unlike the other men on the street he never wore a hat or a cap. Instead he wore a beret which he pulled to the front in a peak. In winter he wore a long black double-breasted coat which trailed almost to his ankles. And almost always, no matter what the climate, a long flowing red scarf was draped around his neck. Facially too he was different. Over time he had cultivated a bushy moustache which at times was waxed at each end. He had the look of a French philosopher.

Despite his eccentricities old man Fay was a pleasant man, a talkative man but not in any way a gossip. It was simply that the man never knew when to stop. He spoke about things the other people on the street didn't understand. He talked of cubists and minimalists and the influence of impressionists. He was passionately interested in everything French, particularly their culture and their wine.

Harry Fay was a unique curiosity, not just a local talking point, but a man who added colour to the community. And, while

29

most avoided him on the street, almost all enjoyed having the man around. He was something to marvel at. What exactly Harry did was a mystery to most. Some thought he was a lecturer, others an artist. A few believed he wrote a column in one of the snobby magazines. All would have been amazed to learn that Harry was a porter in the Municipal Gallery of Modern Art in Parnell Square.

Harry lived three doors down from the Brennans with his only son Vincent. It was assumed that the son had been called after Saint Vincent de Paul, but that was wide of the mark. Harry's son was called after the other Vincent, the one called Van Gogh, a hero of Harry's not only because of his masterpieces, but also his life.

Vincent was not unlike his old man. He shared his relaxed attitude to the world. He didn't get too flustered. Life arrived and was consumed as it came. This attitude was also evident in the house where domesticity was regarded as some sort of disease. Neither of the Fays concerned themselves with housework. The place was a shambles. The only sense of order appeared on the walls where almost every surface was covered in posters and paintings.

Vincent Fay had two principal interests, music and literature. When not listening to Bob Dylan or the Rolling Stones he was deeply immersed and captivated by the classic Russian writers. The Scout regularly described Fay's choice of reading as books as thick as telephone directories and equally boring.

Fay spent most of his free time in his shed at the end of his garden. This was his haven. The boys were convinced that Fay's attachment to the place was largely motivated by his need to get away from his old man. This was not strictly true. The younger Fay was really a dreamer with an amazing capacity to live contentedly in his own world. His shed afforded him a sense of calmness and peace. He could play his music on his record player or strum his electric guitar. If he tired of music he could curl up on the old sofa and devour another chapter of a book by an author whose name the Scout wouldn't have been able to pronounce.

The exterior of the shed was like many of the makeshift outhouses which appeared in people's gardens. It was roughly constructed with concrete walls and a corrugated iron roof. A small window let in the light.

The inside, however, was different than the others. Instead of oil cans and garden implements, Fay's shed was like a den. Apart from the sofa and the record player there was a table, some chairs and a bookcase. And, for warmth and comfort, an old paraffin heater was lit in winter. It was here that the boys regularly gathered to smoke, play cards and discuss the great happenings of their not uneventful lives.

And so it was to the shed that Hackett adjourned after the discovery of his throat problem. But first he walked across the street and called on the Scout whose mother, Mrs O'Neill, opened the door and brought him inside. Hackett liked Mrs O'Neill, a big jolly hearted woman with a head of blonde hair. She had that welcoming capacity that never seemed flustered. Everyone who knocked on her door was made welcome. The Scout's mother was a towering woman who could sing at the drop of a hat. Unlike the other mothers, Mrs O'Neill had a job. She worked as a supervisor in the packing department of Lemon's, the local sweet factory.

Hackett sat in O'Neill's front room waiting for the Scout. It was a room like so many on the street, the china cabinet in the corner, the mirror over the mantelpiece, the three ducks flying upwards across the patterned wallpaper. Hackett stood and walked over to the china cabinet. On top were family photographs, the wedding of the Scout's parents and one of his elder brother Fergus in Royal Navy uniform.

Hackett remembered not alone when Fergus made his way to Belfast to enlist, but also when he came home with his change of accent and navy issue Senior Service cigarettes. Fergus would talk of the exotic, the streets of Singapore and Hong Kong, the nights of drinking and pub crawls. And of course women. Loads of women. The boys would crowd around to hear of his exploits. In rapt attention they would listen, never once disputing the truth that came from the sailor. They never forgot the story of how a week's supply of condoms was used in one night.

The Scout's father was also absent from home. He, because of shortage of work in Dublin, had emigrated to England to find a job in construction. That's the way it had been for years. It was either work abroad or welfare and Tom O'Neill's pride wouldn't allow him depend on the dole.

Hackett knew that the Scout missed his father. It became obvious as holiday time drew near. The Scout would talk of his old man coming home and the presents he might bring. Trips would be planned. Excursions made. But as the fortnight drew to a close the Scout's upbeat demeanour would fade, as he began to dread the few days that were left before he would wave goodbye to the M.V. Leinster as she sailed away from Dublin Port on her way to Liverpool. For weeks afterwards the Scout talked about the fun he had with his father and repeat his wish that, one day soon, his father might return to stay with them forever.

As Hackett moved from the china cabinet the Scout entered the room. As always he was dressed to kill. He winked at Hackett.

'Are we heading for the shed, or what?' he asked.

'Where else?' said Hackett.

Glancing again at the photograph of Fergus, Hackett wondered how the Scout's brother was getting on.

'Having a ball. He sent photographs. You'd want to see them. And the women . . .'

Hackett wondered to himself whether you ever got women out of your head. Though he wouldn't have admitted it, he had been thinking a lot about the woman at the window. Like

Brennan he had imagined himself in a number of erotic situations and in one particularly sinful mental excursion he had been applying the cream with a brush.

'The old man will be home soon,' said the Scout as he glanced at the photograph of his father, 'home for Christmas and all.'

They left the Scout's house, walked across the street and knocked on Fay's door. As they stood waiting old man Brennan walked by carrying a large Clery's shopping bag. Old man Brennan worked as a sales assistant in Clery's menswear department. Another bag of discounted stuff thought Hackett.

'Evening, Mr Brennan,' said the Scout.

When old man Brennan walked by without returning the greeting Hackett attacked his friend.

'What do you want to be talking to that old git for?'

'Because we're meant to know nothing about that night or what happened, right? So act normal.'

Hackett nodded.

They knocked on the door again. From inside they could hear boring classical music. Old man Fay must be listening to the wireless. He was forever listening to that dreary church music, the sort they played on Good Friday. It was the sort of music that would put years on you - dreary music that reminded you of the dead and the dying, the sort that made you imagine coffins on gun-carriages, the dead march and the narrator on the wireless describing the scene in funereal tones. Hackett could almost recite the forlorn voice of the commentary on the wireless, *'And now the final journey for this great man, this brave man, the lone trumpeter sounding the plaintive notes of the last post.'*

They knocked again, this time louder. The music hushed slightly. Then the curtains moved on the window. The door opened and Mr Fay appeared in a long multi-coloured dressing gown with a glass in his hand. Mr Fay drank wine, loads of it.

Mr Fay looked at them as if he had never met them before.

'Yes?' he said in a nasal sounding voice.

33

'Is Vincent in?' asked the Scout.

'In?'

'In the house. Is he in or what?'

'Non,' replied old man Fay in an accent which sounded French.

'So he's not in?' said the Scout again.

'Correct. He is not in,' said old Harry Fay parting his moustache under his nose.

They waited for the door to close but it didn't. Old man Fay held it ajar as if expecting more conversation. The boys were perplexed. They were sure he was pissed. Then the French sounding voice spoke again.

'He is not in the house. He is in his apartment.'

'Apartment?' said Hackett.

The Scout began to snigger. 'You mean the shed?' he said.

'Correct. Entrez s'il vous plait.'

Mr Fay invited them inside with an elaborate hand gesture and a slight bow. As they were walking through the hall he addressed them again.

'There is something I would like to show you, something I would like to discuss with you. . . seek your youthful perspective on.'

Oh shit thought Hackett, he *is* pissed.

'In here if you please.'

They were led into the front room. The source of the music was a large walnut cabinet in the corner. More like a piece of furniture than a Phillips wireless with stations all over the world- Budapest, Moscow, Zurich.

Mr Fay approached the wireless reverently as one would a relic, an icon or some special object. Slowly he turned down the volume then twirled around and gestured to a poster which was hanging above the mantelpiece.

'Now gentlemen, cast your eyes on that creation and give me your thoughts. Don't think about it too much. I want an instantaneous reaction. I want you to give me your unabridged, uncensored thoughts. What do you think? You first, Peter?'

Peter, thought Hackett, that's me. He looked up at the spectacle on the wall. He didn't know what to say. All he could think of was a plate of fried eggs.

'Well let's have you Peter. Come on.'

'It's very colourful. I like the yellow.'

'Yes, but what does it say to you?'

'Say to me?'

'Yes, say to you. What does the painting say to you?'

Hackett wanted to tell the truth, that the painting was like something you'd see on the footpath outside a public house on a Sunday morning. But he didn't.

'I think. . . it says to me. . . hunger.'

'Hunger?'

'Yeah, hunger. All the yellow makes me think of the sun ripening the crops.'

'Very interesting. Very astute. Not exactly what the artist had in mind.'

Then he turned to the Scout.

'Now Mick, what about you? What does the painting say to you?'

'I'm not sure Mr Fay.'

'What does it say to your soul?'

'Would it have anything to do with sickness?'

Old man Fay was perplexed, 'I'm not sure I understand,' he said.

'You know sickness, when people are not feeling too good. When they throw up.'

'You're not talking of vomit, are you?'

Old man Fay stood back. He raised his glass and took a large swig. Then he looked at the Scout with an air of serious disappointment.

'I think it's time I gave you both a detailed analysis of what the artist had in mind.'

This was the worst possible outcome. The boys knew that once the old man began there would be no stopping him. A certain rapture seemed to take hold once he began talking of art. The Scout asked if he could be excused as he needed to go to the toilet. The request was refused.

Hardly had old man Fay begun when a knock came to the hall door. Hackett made to answer but old Harry held him back and went himself instead. From the loud banter in the hallway it became obvious that the caller was Darby Maguire the local agent for the Mater Hospital Pools. Darby, who had retired, supplemented his income by collecting the weekly contributions. Sixpence every week. He was also a drinking buddy of Harry's. Indeed from the colour of his nose it was clear that Darby was a drinking buddy of many. He needed little persuasion to step inside.

'Ah lads, I hope I'm not disturbing you, or anything.'

'We were just going Mr Maguire,' replied the Scout as both he and Hackett darted from the room.

The boys passed through the kitchen which was a mess. The place was littered with discarded cartons and tins. The sink was overflowing with crockery. Neither of the Fays had any interest in housekeeping. That, according to Harry, was women's work, but unfortunately for Harry and his son, there had been no woman living in the house for years. The whereabouts of Mrs Fay was a mystery. All young Vincent would say was that his mother had left and never returned. No one was ever told the full story. The neighbours believed that the woman, to preserve what was left of her sanity, took the first one way ticket that had become available.

Outside in the garden a wall of sound hit them. Fay was playing his favourite record 'Satisfaction' by the Rolling Stones. Fay loved that sound. Nothing compared to the raw energy and pumping rhythm of that song.

Closer to the shed it became obvious that the sound from the record player was being supplemented by the rough strumming of Fay's bass guitar.

They opened the door and looked in. Fay was standing on a tea-chest roaring the lyrics of the song while madly assaulting the four strings of his guitar. He seemed in a trance. His shirt was opened down to his waist and his hair was ringing with sweat.

Across the garden wall Mrs Hickey was hanging out her bloomers on the washing line. She spoke through a mouthful of clothes pegs.

'Now yiz know what I've to put up with,' she said, 'between him and his oulfella I'm near driven demented.'

When the song came to an end the boys applauded. Fay was not at all fazed to discover an audience. He simply got down from his tea-chest and dried off his hair with a towel.

'Are you coming in or what?' he said quietly. It was hard to credit that this mild spoken lad was the same individual that had been assaulting his guitar.

'So what's the story?' asked Fay.

'Nothing much, except. . .' said Hackett, 'except that I was caught with me notes from the doctor.'

'It was only a matter of time,' said Fay.

'Anyway, I've more or less decided to go back and do the exam.'

'You might as well.'

They lit cigarettes and Fay put a match to the paraffin heater. The oily smell spread its own sense of comfort and warmth. They watched the blue flames dancing over the wick.

'Anyone seen Brennan?' asked Fay.

'Seen him all right, but haven't spoken to him.'

'They have him like a prisoner. Won't let him out except to go to school and then the oulwan is watching him like a hawk.'

'She's an ould cow,' said Hackett.

'She's a religious nut,' added the Scout.

37

'So is his old man,' said Fay.

'And he didn't say anything about you pair being with him in the lane that night?'

'Mustn't have,' said Hackett.

'And I'd say they tried hard to get him to squeal,' said Fay.

'Maybe you're right.'

'You know I'm right Hackett,' said Fay. 'You know well that they would have put all sorts of pressure on him.'

'Yeah, well,' answered Hackett.

'Is that all you can say? You owe him a big favour Hackett. You'll have to do something.'

'Like what?'

'I don't know, but something will have to be done. We'll have to come up with a plan. We'll have to get him off the hook. You're the schemer Hackett. You come up with something.'

For almost an hour they tossed about various ideas. They knew that it would have to be a good idea to soften Mr and Mrs Brennan. Fay suggested that they chip in and buy flowers and send them with a lush letter of apology from Brennan himself. The Scout suggested that he could get a telegram sent from the GPO. The problem was what to put in the telegram.

Initially Hackett said nothing. But as the others spoke his ideas started to take shape. He thought he had it. This was the best idea ever, an idea he felt confident would crack the resolve of the Brennans.

They only problem would be the cost.

CHAPTER FOUR

Some days after the boys had met in the shed there was a knock on Brennan's front door. Upstairs in his room studying Brennan ignored the sound. Besides, he knew it wouldn't be for him. No one ever called now. Curiosity, however, caused him to take his eyes off his copybook. He heard the voice of Maura, his sister, in the hall.

'I'll get it,' she said.

Bitch, thought Brennan. Always the same, always wanting to know everything, even who was at the front door.

Maura opened the door.

'Child, are your parents at home?' the caller enquired.

Maura was thrown by the civility and the appearance of the man who stood before her.

'Would you like to step in?' Maura asked deferentially.

The softer tones of Maura made Brennan wonder what sort of caller could produce such a quiet and respectful response. Probably the insurance man, he thought.

Maura ushered the caller into the front room inviting him to sit while she went to find her parents. Mrs Brennan was in the kitchen, both her hands buried in a baking bowl as she worked some egg yokes into white flour. She nearly had a fit when she heard who had called. She whipped off her apron and ran the tap over the sticky goo that clung to her fingers.

'Don't just stand there,' she snarled at Maura. 'Get your father!'

Old man Brennan was out the back filling the coal bucket and having a smoke.

'Who did you say?' he bawled at Maura. 'Who?'

Old man Brennan threw the cigarette away and stroked his bald head nervously before rushing to the kitchen to wash the coal off his hands. What, he asked himself, can this geezer want?

Mrs Brennan entered her own front room like a stranger. She stole a glance at herself in the mirror.

'I hope there's nothing wrong,' she said to the stranger.

'Not at all Mrs Brennan, I'm pleased to say anything but.'

Mrs Brennan sat demurely on her rarely used sofa. She adjusted her skirt for modesty. She smiled shyly. The stranger responded. Then the door burst open and in came old man Brennan. He seemed out of breath.

'Mr Brennan,' the visitor said as he stood.

'That's me.'

Mr Brennan licked his lips, coughed nervously and fingered his pockets for the consoling presence of his cigarettes. He could do with one now but not in the presence of the visitor. Mrs Brennan looked over at her husband.

'There's nothing wrong John,' she said in relief.

Mr Brennan wanted to issue a mild profanity by way of expressing thanks, but thought better of it when he glanced over at the man sitting in the fireside armchair.

Both the Brennans had a high regard for the Franciscan order. Mr Brennan often heard people say that the Franciscans were God's own men, people who really knew what the vow of poverty meant, men who lived simple lives with little or no truck with matters of the flesh. These were the men who dressed frugally, wore sandals without socks even in winter and were reputed to carry no money on their person. They were, in every human sense, the image of God on earth. And that's why the Brennans were in awe of the man who sat among them.

Brother Dominic was a small wiry man with a bushy beard not unlike the tangled mass of horse hair that's used to stuff a mattress. He had the look of a saint, one of those who liked nothing better than rising at four in the morning to chant and pray in his tiny cell. And then, after all that prayer and penance, spent his day working among the poor and feeding the famished.

'You'll have some tea, Brother?' asked Mr Brennan before going to the door and disturbing Maura who had her ear to the keyhole.

'Put the kettle on, Maura,' said Mr Brennan, adding an exaggerated 'please' for the benefit of the holy man in the front room.

When Mr Brennan resumed his seat on the sofa beside his wife he began thinking of his next move. In truth, he had been thrown by the sight of the cleric from the moment he had entered the room. He decided to bite the bullet, hesitantly.

'And what,' he stuttered, 'what can we do for you Brother?' Mr Brennan was normally very good with clerics. Indeed some of them were among his better customers in Clery's men's department. Many asked for him by name. They were impressed with the time he took looking after their needs. Suit fitting was one of his specialities. He took immense care in jotting down the detail. He was a dab hand with the measuring tape and was particularly sensitive when it came to the delicate area of the inner leg. Never once did he ask a man of the cloth on which side his private parts hung. He usually guessed. No one ever complained he got it wrong.

'I'm here,' the Brother began sitting forward on the armchair, 'I'm here on a very sensitive matter concerning your son Francis.'

Brother Dominic paused. Like a preacher he was giving his audience time to reflect on a serious point.

The same thought echoed in each of the Brennans' heads, the window incident.' The policeman had told Mr Brennan to forget it ever happened, to rest easy, to put it out of his mind. But now it was back. Now a man of God was sitting in his front room and all the depravity was about to be spilled out on the floral carpet. If this Brother knew, then the whole street must know. They would be disgraced. They'd have to sell up and move on.

41

'Will I go on?' the Brother enquired.
Mrs Brennan looked over at her husband. There were tears in her eyes. For once she couldn't find words. The speaking machine was empty. Mr Brennan coughed nervously.

'I suppose you'd better,' he sighed.

'As I said, it's a very sensitive issue concerning Francis.'
Brother Dominic emphasised *Francis* in such a manner as if drawing attention not to the name, but the depraved act of watching a woman undress.

Mr Brennan could not hold back.

'Look, Brother, we tried our best with him, myself and his mother, we did,' said Mr Brennan.

Mrs Brennan nodded like one of those figures on top of a collection box when a coin is dropped in.

'He has our hearts near broke,' Mr Brennan continued, 'near broke they are, our hearts. God in Heaven, why should all of this have come down on us? Us, who have been God fearing all our lives?'

Mr Brennan took a soiled handkerchief from his pocket and wiped the sweat from his brow. Mrs Brennan sighed loudly.

Brother Dominic raised his hand seeking silence.

'Please, please,' he said, 'please, maybe it was the way I put it. Maybe I put it wrong?'

'No, Brother, it isn't your fault,' Mr Brennan sighed. If only I could light up a fag he thought.

'Please,' said the Brother again, 'please let me speak for a moment. I have come here this evening to thank you, to thank you as parents but especially Francis.'

'I don't follow,' said Mr Brennan.
The Brother joined his hands as if he was about to pray.

'Look,' began the Brother, 'look, I said it was a sensitive matter and it is. It concerns a matter of confidentiality concerning your son.'

Mr Brennan drew his hand across his balding head.

'Let me go on,' the Brother insisted. 'What I am about to tell you is something I am sure you weren't aware of and that in itself is a further tribute to the boy. Yesterday at the friary I received a visitor. He brought an envelope with him, an envelope that contained the princely sum of ten pounds. This was a donation to the poor of Dublin. . . a donation which came from a boy. . . a boy who happens to live here. That boy is your son.'

Mrs Brennan started to bite her nails.

The Brother continued.

'Apparently your son has been saving his pocket money every week over the last year to contribute to the poor of Dublin. I have been told that the boy himself didn't want it known. In conscience I believed I should come and see you before accepting it, because ten pounds is a lot of money. I wanted to make sure that we were not depriving you, his own family, of money you may need yourselves.'

Mrs Brennan cried. Mr Brennan could not remember the last time he had seen natural moisture on his wife's face. He tried to hold back his emotion, telling himself he always knew that his son was a good boy, a decent lad. Mr Brennan raised his hand. This time *he* would speak.

'Brother, I'm so delighted that it was to yourselves he gave the money, so delighted that I'll add a fiver meself.'

'There's no need, Mr Brennan.'

'There is, Brother, there is,' protested Mr Brennan, who was by now having deep pangs of guilt about how he had misread his own son. 'Call it conscience money,' said Mr Brennan reaching into his pocket.

'And I'll give some too,' Mrs Brennan croaked. She too was overcome by the entire experience. She wanted to participate in the great spirit of generosity which had overtaken her family. The bird-like woman almost took to the air. When the excitement and sense of relief abated Brother Dominic brought up the other reason for his pastoral visitation.

'Tell me,' he said with the air of a confessor who wishes to probe deeper, 'tell me, what do you think of the young lad's vocational intentions? Are you happy he wants to be a Franciscan?'

If Mr Brennan had the same powers of expression as his artistic neighbour Harry Fay, he would have described his state of mind as utterly confused. He was weak, his head swimming in whirlpools of angelic piety, but deep down he felt this wave of immense gratitude for the deliverance of his son. Mrs Brennan was beyond feeling. It was as if a shaft of light shone down from Heaven.

'A priest,' she whispered, 'a priest,' she went on repeating.

'Father Francis Brennan,' Brother Dominic intoned.

The potential priest was surprised by a knock on his bedroom door and his rather sheepish old man appearing before him. Normally the door would be opened with a jerk without any deference to manners or privacy.

'Francis,' his father began.

Brennan had never remembered being called anything by the family other than Frank. Was his oulfella sick in the head or what?

'Francis,' the old man continued, 'come down and meet Brother Dominic.'

'But I haven't finished me studies.'

'Never mind the studies. Come on down. There's a good lad.' Brennan wondered whether the old man had been at the cooking sherry. Who was this softly spoken man with the manners of an undertaker's assistant?

'Come on Francis, let's not keep Brother Dominic waiting.'

Brennan followed his old man down the stairs and into the front room. Brother Dominic stood as Brennan entered.

'I'm delighted to meet you Francis, absolutely delighted. Will you sit down and we'll have a little chat.'

Mrs Brennan stood and offered her seat to her son. In all his years Brennan had never witnessed such behaviour from his parents. It was one thing to observe his father behave as courtly as an usher, but to see his mother offer her seat to an underling was beyond all comprehension. Equally baffling was the way his parents left the room. They retreated backwards as one would do with royalty. The whole thing was bizarre.

Brennan's first inclination when he saw the cleric was suspicion, an inner feeling that his old man had organised it all. He knew it would be just like his father to get one of his religious cronies to help in the process of converting Brennan back from his heathen ways of peering at naked women.

Brennan sat down. He decided to play his cards as cutely as he played poker with the boys. Say nothing, he told himself. Just listen.

Then Brother Dominic spoke. 'I just want to express my profound gratitude to you for your most generous gift to the poor.'

Brennan's mouth hung open.

Brother Dominic continued.

'I know it must have been a struggle for you to save all that money, but as the Lord says, if you do it for the poor you do it for me. And, as regards your calling for the priesthood, all I want you to do for the moment is pray, pray to Saint Francis and if a vocation is your true calling you'll receive your answer in due course. I'm proud of you Francis. Your mother and father are proud of you. You're a good lad. May God and Saint Francis protect you.'

Then the good Brother left the room and went into the kitchen where the parents of the fledgling priest were waiting.

'A lovely lad,' said Brother Dominic, 'he'll make a lovely priest.'

When Brennan went back upstairs to study Brother Dominic took tea and cake with the Brennans in their front room. Brother

45

Dominic stayed talking with them quite late and during this time consumed almost an entire circular fruit cake. He complimented Mrs Brennan's baking so much that she insisted he take the remaining wedge of cake back to the friary to consume in his frugal cell. Later she remarked to her husband, 'They do be starving those monks, they do.'

When Brother Dominic made his way down the street to catch the bus he passed a young man who looked familiar. He remarked to himself that the young man bore a striking resemblance to the visitor he had received at the friary.

Hackett watched the Franciscan turn the corner at the end of the dimly lit street. The plan must have worked. The man of the cloth had done his bidding. Surely Brennan would be freed at last. He'd better be. The whole business had cost Hackett dearly. All his winnings from poker on the canal bank went into the collection. So also did a lump of his savings. But the others hadn't been found wanting either. The Scout donated two pounds which he 'borrowed' from behind the Statue of Prague on the kitchen dresser and Fay contributed the entire contents of the gas meter under the stairs, a resource he regularly tapped into.

Hackett walked home feeling good about himself, confident that another of his schemes had worked. He loved the scheming, the mental gymnastics required to come up with ideas which delivered results. If only school was the same.

When he closed his eyes that night Hackett felt a real swell of satisfaction. They had paid Brennan back in full. Now they were even.

The boys would be back together again.

CHAPTER FIVE

The only woman at the men's retreat was Mrs Hanlon, a small frail creature who played the organ. She sat at the rear of the church on the balcony in front of an enormous keyboard and a myriad of cylindrical pipes that rose up towards Heaven.

She played with gusto. Rarely had she to refer to her music sheets as she pressed down the keys, pulled out knobs and tapped her tiny feet on a vast array of wooden pedals. Her fingers raced along the keyboard like someone possessed, infused and transfixed by the power of her sound. It seemed as if pure music ran through her veins, that every sinew of her being existed for the single purpose of praising creation. Music, she said, should let the soul fly freely upwards to touch the wings of angels. Undoubtedly, one of her favourites was *Soul of my Saviour* which she chose that night to open the men's retreat a week after Brennan's curfew was lifted.

The men's retreat was an important fixture in the annual calendar of Roman Catholic devotional activity. It was an opportunity for renewal of the faith, a time when individual members could take stock of their own spiritual balance sheet. Above all, it was seen as a time for repentance, an opportunity for cleansing, when the individual conscience could be examined and steps taken to change the habits of evil.

The men had mixed views as to its significance. Yes there were some who genuinely subscribed to the concept of recharging their Catholic batteries. There were others who went because it was something to do mid-week. But there were many who found it easier to be there rather than suffer the nagging voices at home, voices which would not cease until they joined the rest of the menfolk of the parish beneath the pulpit of the visiting preacher.

47

As Mrs Hanlon began the second verse she glanced in her mirror to monitor the activity below. The church was packed. The only empty seats were near the front. As expected, she saw the priest ascend the steps to the pulpit. He timed his appearance precisely. The stage management was excellent. Mrs Hanlon smiled broadly. The priest reached the microphone just in time to add his weighty voice to the second chorus.

> 'Soul of my Saviour sanctify my breast,
> Body of Christ be thou my saving guest.'

Before the priest arrived Mrs Hanlon's playing had attracted little vocal support. Catholics in Ireland were not great at church singing, particularly the male of the species. But when the priest added his own voice, the congregation grudgingly made an effort. Even those who didn't actually sing opened their mouths to pretend. And as the singing continued the priest encouraged them.

'All together men. All together. Let's hear you.'

They tried. God help them they tried. As the volume rose, Mrs Hanlon pulled on the knobs opening up yet another pipe of sound until the noise was deafening. Still the priest wasn't happy. He increased his own pitch and began to sway with the music. He called again for another effort.

'Come on men. Come on. It doesn't matter if you haven't a note in your head. This is not a singing contest. The Almighty is with us to listen, not judge.'

Towards the back of the church in a cluster were the neighbours. Harry Fay sat beside Darby Maguire, the pools collector. Harry was the exception to the rule when it came to the singing. He had no inhibitions when it came to any performance; from the opening bar he blared out the words. Darby was far more reticent preferring instead to mime. Old man Brennan tried hard. He revelled in any religious service, and was particularly

48

devout on the night of the retreat as he recalled the pleasure of his audience with Brother Dominic.

Mr Hackett was the least earnest of all. He hated all this church singing. He tried to disguise his failure to sing with bouts of sneezing and coughing. For a long time he held a handkerchief to his mouth.

Behind the men, the boys sat in a row. They could sense the awkwardness of their elders. They loved the notion of the adults being bullied into singing.

Eventually the hymn came to an end. Splutters of coughing erupted. They all sat down. Behind the boys was old man Gormley, the one who had caught Brennan in the garden. As Brennan sat he recognised Gormley. Inwardly he swore. He had almost erased the glass-eyed bastard from his brain. Now he was back and Brennan could feel his heart begin to pound.

When they all settled into their seats, the priest began. Everyone craned their necks to see where the voice of God was coming from. Some checked their watches wondering how long the whole thing would last. Would they have time for a pint on the way home?

The priest began by introducing himself. He told them all how happy he was to be back amongst them, back in Drumcondra on the Northside of Dublin. He cracked a joke, a rather innocent one-liner, like something you'd read on the inside of a Christmas cracker. The men all laughed, some rather forcefully, others in relief that the visiting preacher seemed a decent sort. Harry Fay turned to Darby and nodded. Then the sermon began.

'Tonight, my dear men, I'm going to talk to you about the sins of the flesh.'

Immediately the coughing and shuffling began. Men did not like this sort of talk, at least not in this environment, coming from a celibate man on an altar. It was all right to crack a smutty or risqué joke in Fagan's public house or the Cat and Cage, but not

49

here, especially in front of their children. After a pause to allow his opening to sink in, the priest went on.

'Maybe we don't concentrate enough on the role of Adam in the whole affair. Maybe it suits us not to, after all, aren't we like Adam ourselves? Aren't we? Aren't we?'

The congregation were not at all convinced of the comparison. Some looked at the ground. Quite a few sought refuge in another bout of coughing. There was worse to come.

'Today, my dear men, we live in a society that seems to be besotted by that three lettered word 'sex'.'

For emphasis he spelt out the word – S. E. X. - and as each letter left his mouth he paused for a beat.

Fay nudged Hackett. They were really enjoying the discomfort in the church. The Scout couldn't stop giggling.

'And why,' the priest went on, 'why are we besotted with that word? Why is it that everywhere we look nowadays there are images of profanity, images of temptation? Why? I'll tell you why. The images are there because we as a society seem to respond to those images. We seem to like what we see. Why else would those images be on television, in the cinema, in the magazines and newspapers we read? They are there because we pay heed to them. Let me ask you a question.'

Around the congregation there seemed to be a collective inward drawing of breath. They were absolutely terrified that the question could be asked of them all individually. What if each had to stand up in front if everyone? This priest was capable of anything.

'Think hard before you answer. Look into your hearts before you answer. How many of you are buying English newspapers on a Sunday? How many of you walk out the door of this church on the Sabbath and spend your money on foreign newspapers, publications which are full of every imaginable form of titillation? How many of you part with your hard earned money to look at scantily clad women every Sunday? Well, how many?'

Fay was thoroughly enjoying himself. Unlike the rest of the congregation he sat up straight taking everything in. All the heads about him were bowed. There was absolute silence. Even the coughing had stopped. The men were in a state of absolute mortification. You could almost hear the wick of the beeswax candle burning on the altar.

The question was asked again.

'Well?' the priest said, 'well, how many of you fall into that trap every Sunday and give into temptation?'

The only sound was the wheezing of breath. Not a word came from the congregation.

'I know by your silence men that most of you don't succumb to temptation because in your hearts you know it is wrong. It's wrong to bring filth into any Catholic home particularly on the Lord's Day. But the fact is, my dear men, that there are some among us who spend their money to look at these evil images. And do you know where those images lead us? They lead us into the darkness of the sin of Adam. Yes, the sin of Adam. Not Eve this time. Adam. We are back with Adam again in that dreadful place. Where are we men? We are back in the darkness of despair. Where are we men? I'll tell you where we are. We are back in that garden. Yes, back in that garden.'

Brennan felt the spotlight of hell had picked him out. He could feel the burning heat of the lamps of evil. He could see himself at the Oscar ceremonies of the damned, winning the best actor award for the most explicit porn film. As he was presented with the gold statue of a naked woman, her boobs stuck out and then she melted in the heat. All around him they cried out and screamed. The noise was horrific. He was among his own, a collection of the most vile.

The tone of the priest became graver.

'How many of us, my dear men, have been in that garden? How many? How many of us go into that garden of temptation regularly to lust after evil? How many of us lose the path of

51

decency in the overgrowth of temptation? Think about it my dear men. Think about that garden.'

The priest paused and lifted a glass of water to his lips. When Brennan saw the water all he could think of was fire. Fire and water. He thought of flames, images from the Catechism, the wailing of the wretched. He felt hot and weak, his forehead lathered in sweat. It was like a fever or flu. Next, he would surely faint.

The priest put down the glass and wiped his lips with a starched white handkerchief. He drew breath.

'We see these evil images all around us and, sad to say, they are not confined to foreign newspapers. Alas no. You may have heard or read reports about a certain exhibition which recently opened in our capital city. An exhibition which professes to be art. Art, if you don't mind. The so-called experts tell us it is art. Well I'm going to tell you one thing, those so-called experts are wrong. It is not art. This exhibition is nothing other than pornographic filth, images of painted naked women. That's not art my dear men, it's pornographic filth.'

Well Harry Fay had heard enough. He didn't mind the talk about the English newspapers, in fact he was quite enjoying it, but when the man of the cloth started talking about something close to the heart of the porter from the Municipal Gallery he could not remain seated.

Harry stood up. The word quickly spread that a distraction had revealed itself. Heads turned to see the small arty looking man with the long coat and the busy moustache. They wondered was he mad? Was he drunk? Who was he anyway? Harry stepped out into the aisle. He faced the priest. The men couldn't believe what was happening. Surely he was not going to take on the priest? But he was.

'And tell me father,' he asked in a deep voice, 'tell me if you don't mind, were you ever in the Sistine Chapel in Rome?'

In his twenty seven years giving sermons the priest had never had an interruption. Did the man not know his place? Was he drunk? Best to ignore him.

The priest decided to continue, but Harry spoke again.

'Have you Father? Have you ever been in the Sistine Chapel?'

The priest glared at Harry. This sort of behaviour was intolerable. Where were the stewards?

Harry took several steps forward.

'Because Father, if you ever were in the Sistine Chapel in Rome and happened to look up at the ceiling you'd see that it is covered by what is generally regarded by everyone as art. The art of Michelangelo, no less a man. And what art did he create? Nudes. Yes nudes. Nudes of every description. And who paid him to paint the nudes? The Pope, yes the Holy Father himself. Well if it's good enough for him, it's good enough for me. So, there you are, nudes is art.'

From the back of the church two stewards rushed forward. They had to get the lunatic out of the church.

The priest tried to continue but No one was listening. They were all caught up in the extraordinary antics of Harry. It was an amazing display. Never had any of them seen a priest being contradicted like this before. It was unheard of. Maybe Harry would be excommunicated. Maybe the Pope himself would send Harry a letter telling him to hand back his Baptismal Certificate.

One of the stewards grabbed Harry by the arm.

'Right you,' he said.

'Take your hands off me or I'll have you charged with assault,' threatened Harry.

'Like a good man, come on.'

'Take your hands off me.'

'Come on, we don't want any trouble.'

'And there won't be if you take your hands off me.'

The congregation were loving it. Everyone was secretly rooting for Harry. He might be a nut case, but he had stopped the sermon. And you never know, Harry could have a point. After all wasn't he a painter or an art critic, or something?

The main steward then joined the group. He was an imperious type with a pointed chin. Everyone recognised the small spindly figure of Mr Monroe - the walking saint of the parish, the chair of all the religious committees, the daily mass goer, the non-drinker, non-smoker, the one who was rumoured to have left the marriage bed after the birth of his seventh child. Marriage was for procreation; anything else was lust.

'Get out of here,' Monroe hissed at Harry, 'get him out of here,' he ordered the stewards.

'Take your hands off me. I've every right to be here. Take your hands off me.'

'Get the lunatic out of here,' whispered Monroe to the stewards.

'I heard that,' shouted Harry, 'I might be a lunatic but at least I'm not a religious lunatic.'

Then the priest intervened. He thought humour might work.

'I see we've an art critic with us tonight,' he said as a wide smile falsely took over his face.

There were no laughs.

Harry shouted back.

'Well at least I know what I'm talking about.'

That, for Monroe was the final straw. He pushed at Harry, then thumped him in the pit of his stomach. Harry at first fell back, then panting for breath he stood and, eyeing Monroe,he began to move forward just as Darby Maguire stood up.

'There's no call for violence Monroe,' said Darby.

'You stay out of this.'

'Not while a friend of mine is being assaulted in the house of God. Call yourself a Catholic?'

At this stage the younger Fay had seen enough. His old man may have had a few loose slates on top, but he was still his old man and blood was thicker than water. Vincent Fay jumped from his seat and rushed at the scrapping in the aisle. He singled out Monroe and rushed directly at the senior steward flooring him with a blow. The others scattered, shaken and surprised by the appearance of Fay. One steward looked at the other. Monroe growled at them madly. Humiliation was more hurtful than pain.

The priest pleaded from the altar. Gone was the air of superiority. Humility had taken over.

'Please men, please, stop this insult to Almighty God. Please men, stop.'

No one wanted to stop it. They wanted it to go on. They wanted more. They were so grateful to Harry for stopping the sermon of guilt. They almost cheered when Monroe hit the deck. Another steward joined the group. Fay fended him off with a blow to his solar plexus. By now Darby had joined the joust, not to take part in the fighting, but to try and separate and bring order.

'Will yiz stop it, for God's sake,' shouted Darby.

Monroe was now standing again and clinging to a pew for support.

'Get out of here,' he spat.

Harry broke away from the tussle and headed for the back door but, seeing that his way was blocked by another steward, raced down the centre aisle towards the pulpit.

'Get him!' shouted Monroe.

The scuffle had now turned into a chase.

Both Harry and Vincent ran towards the side door. The stewards raced after them.

By now the entire congregation was on its feet. Everyone wanted to see.

The Fays made it to the side door but it was locked. There was no other option but to head up the main aisle again, and face Monroe. Vincent led the way. His father followed. Monroe by this stage was standing in front of the main door gripping a window pole he had taken from a side altar. As the Fays came closer

Monroe waved the pole. The man looked deranged. His face was aflame with anger. The veins stood proud on his shrivelled neck. Froth had congealed on the corners of his mouth.

Vincent Fay moved onward. Monroe began waving the pole. Then Darby Maguire stepped forward.

'Stop this nonsense,' said Darby. 'Stop it, you fool.'

Monroe had not alone been physically assaulted, he had been publicly humiliated. And now this cheap, whiskey drinking pools collector had challenged him in front of the entire retreat. Monroe needed revenge. He lunged at Fay with the pole. The younger Fay caught the pole, but as he did he was grabbed from behind by the stewards.

And then from the body of the congregation a man pushed his way forward.

'Make way,' he demanded, 'make way.'

Old man Gormley the one-eyed boxer came forward. He faced the stewards.

'Let him go or I'll break your bloody neck.'

By the tone of his voice and the way he looked, the stewards and Monroe knew he meant it. They, like everyone else, were not quite sure which eye was which. But it didn't matter. They got the message. The stewards looked to Monroe and the chief steward looked to the priest. The sermon about gardens had come to an end.

'Let them go Mr Monroe,' the priest said quietly, 'let them go.'

Monroe stood aside and the Fays walked slowly to the door. As he made his way Harry acknowledged the smiles of those he passed and, to one older gent he knew by sight, he offered a bow. In an effort to regain some control the priest decided that a hymn might ease the tension. He invited Mrs Hanlon to work her magic and the wizened old lady, who had been totally engrossed in the antics of Harry, obliged. This time she played *Hail Glorious Saint Patrick*. Even she found it hard to raise her performance to her usual standard. It was mellow and subdued. Her flights on the keyboard were reserved. She even missed several notes because, as she explained later to a senior figure in the sodality, her mind was elsewhere as she kept one eye glued to the mirror in case there was a further disturbance below.

When the singing ended it was a changed man that spoke into the microphone. The garden sermon was abandoned. Instead they were all invited to kneel and join in the five sorrowful decades of the rosary. When it came to *The Agony in the Garden* there were more than a few titters from the assembled.

CHAPTER SIX

The pubs in Drumcondra had rarely seen such a swell in trade on a mid-week night in November. It seemed that all those who had been at the men's retreat had a pressing need to discuss and relive what they had witnessed earlier. Even old man Brennan, who was not a regular in any public house, turned up.

Many hoped that Harry Fay might be in the men-only bar in Fagan's. They wanted, perhaps for the first time in their lives, to listen to Harry's side of the story. What had made him stand in the centre aisle and confront the priest? What was going through his head?

None of them had an opportunity to engage the art expert. Harry had headed home directly. Almost the entire male population of Drumcondra were sipping pints and marvelling at Harry's courage while the porter from the Municipal Gallery was at home drinking Bovril, munching cream crackers and cheese listening to Bach's Brandenburg Concerto.

At the rear of Harry's house the boys gathered in the shed. They sat around the low table smoking cigarettes in the candlelight. The flickering light cast odd shaped shadows on the walls. The smoke from their cigarettes diffused the light even further. It had that graveyard feel like the Hammer productions they watched in the Drumcondra Grand.

Individually they may have felt a little uncomfortable, but as a group they felt secure. They wanted to be there to show solidarity with Fay and explain that, no matter how much they might have wanted to lend their physical support in the fracas, they could hardly have taken part in front of their fathers. The Scout, whose father was in England, assured Fay that he would have jumped in had he been needed. Fay didn't seem to care one way or the other.

'I'll tell you this lads,' he announced, 'I won't be going back to that place. They can keep their religion as far as I'm concerned.'

'But do you not believe in God?' asked Hackett.

'You can believe in God and still not go to church,' answered Fay. Brennan, whose entire formative years had been totally immersed in Catholic teaching, was not so sure.

'What about keep holy the Sabbath day and all that stuff?' said Brennan.

'What about it? You can keep it holy if you want to and still not go,' said Fay lighting another cigarette.

That seemed logical to the Scout who was grateful for any reason not to go to mass.

'Fay's right,' said the Scout, 'most of them go just to be seen anyway.'

'Sure even Gormley goes, the dirty old man,' added Hackett.

'Yeah, but if Gormley's a dirty old man what does that make us?' wondered Brennan whose conscience was still persecuting him. He was also suffering from the after effects of the vivid imaginings he had experienced during the sermon about the garden, fire and water, and Hell.

Hackett had the answer for Brennan.

'If Gormley's a dirty old man, we're dirty *young* men.'

Their laughter broke the solemnity of the discussion. But not for long. Brennan was still having problems

'So where does sin come into all this?' he asked.

'It's all shite,' said Fay, 'all mumbo jumbo.'

'So it's not a sin for us to watch the woman at the window?' asked the Scout.

'It's a sin if you think it's a sin,' answered Fay. 'We didn't ask her to strip did we?'

'That's right,' said Hackett who didn't think too deeply about sins of any description.

'Anyway,' said Fay, 'it's all me arse if you ask me.'

'You don't believe in sins,' asked Brennan, drawing deeply on a fag and trying to look cool.

'I believe murder is a sin, robbing a bank is a sin, but I don't believe looking at some bird stripping off is a sin. What harm is in it? Who do you injure? No one.'

Brennan wanted to agree. He wanted to feel that the Church was wrong, that all their teaching about impure thoughts and actions were misguided. He wanted to freely indulge his imagination with all sorts of fantasies without any pang of guilt. He wanted to be free of the shame.

'Look,' said Fay, 'it's all about brainwashing. They want us to believe that we're wrong. That's their game. And not only that, they tell us that if we don't believe we're done for, unless of course you go to confession. It's all a con. It's about power. They say that we can't get into Heaven unless we talk to them. Where does it say in the Bible that you have to confess to a priest before you can get a ticket for Heaven? That's of course if you believe in Heaven.'

Fay knew he was drawing his audience into uncharted and controversial territory. They may have gone along with him about sin, but to question Heaven, to say that the only place you go after death was a hole in the ground, that was something the other three didn't want to contemplate.

'Are you saying now that you don't believe in Heaven?' asked Brennan who seemed genuinely shocked.

'I didn't say one way or another,' said Fay stretching forward to light a butt from the candle.

'Yeah but what do you reckon?'

'Yeah, tell us,' said the Scout.

'Can anyone prove it,' said Fay sitting back, 'can anyone here prove it?'

They were stung. They looked at each other in the flickering candlelight waiting for someone to speak. Fay was enjoying the moment. He had that lofty imperious look.

'Well?' he repeated, 'can anyone prove it?'

Brennan, who had always been attentive to doctrinal studies and always scored highly in tests on religious knowledge, was not prepared for a question. Surely after so many years study he could answer such a fundamental question about his own faith? He did believe in Heaven. What was the point of life if there wasn't something at the end? Why all the penance and the suffering? It didn't make sense otherwise.

'For God's sake Fay, even the Protestants believe in Heaven,' blurted Brennan showing his frustration.

'And how do they know?'

'Are you telling me that all those ministers and priests, all those bishops and archbishops are wrong?'

'All I'm asking is for someone to prove it.'

'And what about the Bible?' said Brennan.

'What about it? Who's to say that the four guys who wrote it didn't make it all up?'

'Ah, come on Fay,' said Hackett who thought the argument was becoming absurd.

The Scout was not only out of his depth, but getting extremely bored.

'Can we talk about something else?' he pleaded.

Fay dismissed the plea with another line of questions. 'You're a Catholic Scout, right?' he asked.

'Right,' answered the Scout hesitantly unsure where the question was leading.

'Well, if you are, then you believe all that stuff they teach you, right?'

'Eh . . .' the Scout was clearly unsure.

'Well, prove it?' demanded Fay.

The Scout thought for a moment and remembered a quote from the Catechism.

'I can't prove it,' he said, 'because it's a mystery and we're not supposed to understand mysteries.'

They were all impressed with the Scout. He was impressed himself. Hackett nodded. Brennan sat back. They all believed that was the end of the argument, after all everyone knew there were mysteries in religion.

There was long pause. It seemed that the argument had run its course. But it hadn't.

'Mystery or no mystery it still proves nothing,' said Fay.

The Scout who had heard enough, stood up.

'If yiz don't stop this shite talk I'm going home,' he threatened.

'What about poker?' suggested Hackett.

And so it was that the gambling session overtook the theological discussion in the shed. In the dim light of the candle they strained their eyes to check as each hand was dealt and revealed. But after an hour they tired of cards and decided to head home.

They left the shed and passed in through Fay's house on their way to the street. The kitchen was as before with its clutter and unwashed crockery in the sink. The usual sounds blared from the front room. Harry was at it again.

'A symphony,' said Fay to the others.

'More like a bleeding funeral,' said Hackett.

Fay opened the hall door and they drifted on to the street.

It was almost closing time and the male population of Drumcondra were still holding up the counters of all the local pubs. There was one exception, old man Finnegan, father of the chemist's messenger boy, the one who had spread the story of the woman at the window. Old man Finnegan, who happened to be a barman on the Dublin to Cork train and must have been its best customer, was staggering up the street. His son, Rob, was with him. This was something Rob had to do every night, something he hated, not just the task itself, but the ignominy of having to go down to Fagan's and cajole his father into leaving and head for the terminus of home. As Hackett was about to go into his house he spotted father and son on the footpath across the street. Hackett walked over.

'All right Rob?' said Hackett.

Rob shook his head and sighed.

'And why wouldn't he be?' stuttered old man Finnegan.

'There you are Mr Finnegan.'

'Here I am is right, but if I'd any fecking sense I wouldn't be.'

'And where would you be?'

'I'd be in England like yer man the Scout's father,' said old man Finnegan as he leaned one hand against the red-bricked surround of a neighbour's portal.

'Come on Da,' pleaded Rob.

'Come on where?'

'Ma will be waiting.'

'Oh she'll be waiting all right.'

Rob looked at Hackett in mortification. No matter how many times he had walked this path it never got easier. Indeed as he got older his sensitivity to the looks of others became more acute. When he was younger it didn't seem to matter, but now, now as he was hitting seventeen the shame of it all was crushing. And yet he bore it stoutly. He did it for peace. He did it for his mother.

It was generally agreed that working for the chemist was the plum job if you were a messenger boy. Unlike the grocer's messenger boy who often had to pedal a basket full of potatoes up a steep hill, Rob Finnegan rarely had more than a handful of tablets to deliver. Among all the cycling jobs, Rob's was the prestige post. But he would argue that while the job may have been less strenuous physically, it was far more important than all the others. You could last for days, weeks without food, but medicine was a life saver.

Hackett loved the stories Rob told about his job. He knew what every oulwan and oulfella in the area was suffering from. He knew about sedatives and cough mixtures, laxatives and

63

inhalers. He knew all about disease. He claimed he knew as much as the doctor. Often he would diagnose his friends.

'It's only a cold,' he'd say, 'there's no flu going at the moment.'

And he'd be right. The boys thought that Rob could have done with a tonic himself. The boy who delivered to the sick had an undernourished look about him.

'I think I'll go back down to Fagan's for one more,' said old man Finnegan as he tried to pull away from Rob.

'Da, please.'

'Just the one.'

'Da, your dinner's in the oven.'

'A burnt offering, a dried up burnt offering.'

Rob tried to urge his father on. He caught him under the arm but the old man resisted and pulled away and, as he staggered forward, he fell against a car.

'Da, please come home, please.'

'Please me arse.'

Hackett reached down to help.

'I'm all right. I'm all right.'

'I know you're all right Mr Finnegan. I saw what happened, you tripped. Anyone can trip. Anyone.'

'You're right, that's what happened.'

'Anyone can trip.'

'You're right. He's right.'

Hackett's diplomatic skills were working.

'Come on Mr Finnegan, your leg could be bruised.'

'It could. It could.'

'I'm going up your direction. Do you mind if I walk with you?' said Hackett giving Rob a wink.

And so, another night in the saga of old man Finnegan and his son Rob came to an end.

When Fay closed over his door he walked into the kitchen. One of these days he knew he would have to tackle the mess, but not that night because that night was special. One he wished to recall in detail. The night his old man had taken on the might of the Catholic Church. Fay wanted to savour it all, to allow each detail energise his rebellious nature as he lay in his bed looking out his window at a leaden sky swollen with the murky rain of November, not a star to be seen, not a hint of moonlight, only the bleakness and darkness of a mid-week night in the month of the Holy Souls.

CHAPTER SEVEN

Life for the boys over the next few months was largely uneventful. That's not to say that they hadn't had their moments, they had. In comparison to November there was little to get too excited about.

Mr O'Neill, the Scout's father, came home at Christmas. As usual he was laden with presents. The house sang out in celebration. Fergus got time off from the Royal Navy and the entire family, reunited for the first time in years, rejoiced.

Christmas was a hectic time for the O'Neills. The Scout had to work right up to six o'clock on Christmas Eve delivering telegrams all over the city while his mother was rushed off her feet dispatching *Season's Greetings Selections* of Lemon's sweets to shops all over the country.

Though exhausted by the time the day came, Mrs O'Neill delighted in the occasion. They all did. It was so seldom the family were together.

Mrs O'Neill was thrilled with the gifts she was given. Perfume and make-up mostly. The rest of the family insisted that she try out all her presents, and the large framed woman with the dyed blond hair, who by that stage was a little tipsy on sherry, obliged. By the time she had opened every jar and tube of cosmetics her face had become a multi-coloured canvas and she smelt like a poodle parlour.

But all good things come to an end. The departure of the M.V. Leinster from the North Wall in Dublin with thousands on board marked the end of the festive season for so many. The Scout hated his father leaving. It seemed that he was only getting to know the man again when he had to leave. So he coped as he always did, telling himself over and over that Easter would come around soon.

Since the appearance of Brother Dominic into the lives of the Brennans the atmosphere in their house changed radically. Decorum and civility became the norm. Frank became Francis as both parents saw in their son qualities which were almost divine. He was, as Mrs Brennan regularly said, a gift from God. There was never a word about the window incident. It was as if it never had happened. The regular visits from Brother Dominic brought a new spirituality into their lives.

At first Brennan viewed the visits with deep suspicion. He feared that each visit might include some forensic examination of his vocational intentions. Yes, there were some spiritual conversations between the cleric and the boy in the front room, but the old monk had a sense that a vocation was not an absolute certainty. Yet Brennan kept up the pretence. Things were too good at home to do otherwise.

But whatever Brother Dominic felt, he said little to Brennan's parents. Indeed, when asked about the vocation, he would take upon himself that mysterious air of pious reflection and declare solemnly that things were moving along nicely. He too had a lot to lose. He enjoyed immensely coming to the Brennans and filling himself with the assortment of delicacies that were set before him. He'd even put on some weight. His fondness for tuck made listening to the Brennans bearable. He wondered to himself how such a bird-like woman had so much energy to launch so many words. The woman never ceased. He found himself thinking that his vow of celibacy was no bad thing.

Brennan studied hard over the next few months. He wanted to do well. He didn't want to end up like his old man measuring the inside legs of withered oulfellas. He wanted more. And study seemed the solution.

As the months moved by and study consumed his thoughts he became less consumed by the woman at the window. His visions of her faded. Not altogether, though. Sometimes late at night as the curtain of sleep was closing over he would see her standing at the window looking out at him. He took pleasure in those thoughts and felt guilty less and less. Maybe he, like the rest of them, was growing up.

Some months after the retreat the Fays had an unexpected caller. Old Harry answered the door. A priest was standing on the step. He told Harry that he hadn't called to add fuel to the fire. He was there in a spirit of Christianity. He wanted conciliation, not confrontation. Harry welcomed him in and Vincent served tea in a cracked cup he had retrieved from the sink.

The priest explained that he was new to the parish and had been away when the incident at the retreat happened. He had only heard the detail on his return.

The Fays listened as the priest went on. Rambling stuff mostly about unfortunate misunderstandings, loving one's neighbour, that sort of thing. The priest sensed, very shortly after sitting among them, that he wasn't making any headway. The Fays seemed to have little interest in what he was saying. It appeared as if they were going through the motions, affording the visitor the courtesy of an audience. Indeed at one stage he thought that both father and son were asleep. The priest coughed lightly. Both the Fays sat up.

'Fay,' the priest began, 'the name Fay, is that French?'

'French,' repeated Harry, 'what gave you that idea?'

'Oh, just something that somebody said.'

'Something about me was it?' asked Harry.

'Can't have been that important,' said the priest as he looked about the place. Never in all the years he had been involved in pastoral visitations had he sat in such a house. The walls were covered in the strangest posters and paintings. He was particularly intrigued by the one above the fireplace.

'I see,' he began, 'I see you have a fine collection of contemporary art.'

Harry looked intently at the guest.

'You like art?' he asked.

'I do indeed.'

Harry immediatly sprang from his seat.

'You're aware of course that it was the subject of art that gave rise to the incident in the church,' said Harry.

'So I'm told,' answered the priest.

'And do you have any interest in the subject yourself?'

'Well actually . . .' and before the priest could continue Harry began waving his hands at the posters that covered his walls.

'And are there any here that you are particulary attracted to? What about that one there?' said Harry pointing to the one Hackett and the Scout had likened to two fried eggs, 'what does that say to you?'

The priest looked up at the painting.

'Say to me?' he said.

'Yes yes, go on, go on,' pleaded Harry.

'To me it conveys the meaning of life. . .'

'Go on, go on,' said Harry.

'The circles of life, yes the circles of life.'

It was as if the priest had lit a fuse. Harry began his routine of explaining every poster on every wall, the detail, the brush strokes, the light. The priest was invited to give his own interpretation, but hardly had he issued a word when the porter from the Municipal gallery was off again on another tangent. Not alone did Harry know the paintings, he knew the artists as if they were friends.

In the midst of Harry's performance a bottle of port was produced.

'Some goblets if you please,' ordered Harry as Vincent was dispatched to the kitchen to fish two heavily stained glasses from the sink. The priest was encouraged to drink, to salute the artists on the wall, indeed to praise all creation which he did with relish sensing he was making progress in the quest of reconciliation. And still Harry went on. It seemed as if the tempo of his performance was rising and, as it did, the contents of another bottle went down. The priest began to get some sense of what had happened at the men's retreat, but not for long because his faculties of deduction were leaving him. Indeed the man was almost in a coma. Then the lights went out.

The Fays waited until after dark before Vincent escorted the pastoral visitor home. He never called again.

Since Hackett's medical problems had been discovered he came to seriously regret having promised his father that he would go back to school and study. No matter how he tried he couldn't settle back into the school regime. He found it impossible to study. The teachers were sympathetic. They put his lethargy down to all his medical problems, the amount of medication he must have consumed.

On many occasions Hackett had been sorely tempted to fall victim to another illness. The epidemiologist hadn't been consulted. Neither had the cardiovascular man, nor indeed the many others whose letterheads were still hidden at the bottom of Hackett's wardrobe. But he withstood the temptation. Despite the drudgery of school and study he did not succumb to even the mildest flu right up to exam time in June.

Each evening after school Hackett would wearily climb the stairs to his room and force himself to open his books. He would stare at them for ages, make notes, underline passages. He tried hard to drive the facts into his brain. But nothing worked.

The fact that Brennan and Fay were swotting hard didn't help matters. It made them worse. Hackett didn't care so much about

Brennan, but the news that Fay was swotting was a surprise. Fay, he thought, didn't care. But Fay did. Not because he liked study, he didn't. He saw getting the exam as part of a process of moving on in the world, maybe eventually going to university to study music or literature; books that were, as the Scout described, as thick as telephone books and equally boring.

Hackett had no ambition other than to make money; all this study business was a nuisance, a colossal waste of time. All that Latin and Irish, those complex geometrical theorems, the boring antics of the long dead historical figures had no relevance to the real world. And yet he went through the motions every night, a seemingly endless process of boredom, whose only compensation was the satisfaction it gave Mr Hackett.

The Hackett couple were convinced that they were witnessing the turning of a new leaf in the book of life of their son. Mrs Hackett didn't need a lot of convincing. She had always believed that her son was a model pupil and hadn't been surprised when her husband told her that the letter from the school had been a mistake. Mr Hackett thought it prudent to keep his son's medical history to himself. He dreaded the likelihood of his wife blurting the whole thing out after a couple of sherries at Christmas in Granny Hackett's. That was all he needed; so father and son kept the delicate matter a secret.

Christmas in Granny Hackett's was a family ritual. It was also an ordeal. All the family were there. Every year was the same. Each of Mr Hackett's brothers had done well and they liked everyone to know. Their wives were even worse.

'Show Granny your new dress, Sandra.'

'Turn around Philomena, not that way, the other.'

'Andrew, show Granny your new suit.'

Hackett hated these gatherings. Every year it seemed to draw attention to the material differences within the family, how his own father had failed to make it, while the others had excelled.

71

Hackett watched as his mother and father tried to mingle, how they would try to belong, cracking jokes, adding comments that no one cared to listen to. What would a clerk in the Rates Office know anyway?

In earlier years his mother tried hard to become part of this family, but they merely tolerated this overweight woman from the country with her frumpy woolly dresses, probably bought off-the-peg at a sale. In later years his mother would develop a headache, a cramp, a mysterious pain in a part of the anatomy unmentionable to males, and his father would make the appropriate apologies. All understood.

Hackett particularly hated his cousins, their accents, the way they would howl in forced laughter at the most banal of jokes or comments. They were like characters from an English public school comic strip. Billy Bunter types with affected manners and tone. To Hackett they were snobs and jerks full to the brim with shit.

And every year in the midst of it all Granny Hackett would sit sipping vintage port from a long stemmed glass. The finest of Findlater's port couldn't add any colour to the death-mask pallor of her face. Yet they all told her how wonderful she looked.

The previous Christmas, after his medical problems, Hackett felt obliged to go with his father. His mother refused to go. It was as it always was, that ritual of falseness with air-kissing and fake hugs. Everyone loved everyone and yet everyone wanted to be out of that place at the first opportunity.

Hackett watched his father refill Granny Hackett's glass. She beckoned him to come closer. He lowered his head and put his ear to her mouth. Hackett saw her lips move. Mr Hackett nodded earnestly, then stood and faced his son.

'Granny wants to know how you're doing in school, Peter.'

'Well?' the woman in black said.

Hackett looked around. A hush spread. The snobs and jerks wanted to know how the Northside kid was doing. Hackett felt sure that they all suspected that Granny Hackett paid his school fees. And now the benefactor wanted to know how her charge was doing.

'Well Peter?' she said, raising her voice a little to emphasise her insistence.

Hackett stepped forward. He looked around at the expectant faces, children and adults who longed for bad news.

'Go on, Peter, don't keep us in suspense.'

'I won a gold medal for an essay on Homer.'

Hackett didn't know anything about Homer other than he wrote some long-winded story about some bloke that went wandering. He had seen Fay reading it in the shed.

Hackett looked around. He knew that behind every smile in the room there was envy.

'A gold medal Peter?'

'Pure gold Gran.'

He thought he saw the flicker of a smile on the old woman's face. She looked around.

'Good boy,' she said. 'Did you all hear that? I'm telling you, you can't beat the Jesuits.'

Mr Hackett's older brother Bob began to extol the achievements of his own son, young Bob, a pimply faced fifteen year old who, at the mention of his name, glowed.

'Yes we know, Bob. You told us earlier,' said the old lady in a dismissive tone, and Hackett surprised himself for a moment by thinking well of the old lady.

Then it was time to go. More handshakes, more empty gestures of affection, more seasonal guff and more comments about keeping in touch.

Hackett and his old man headed for home, passing the freshly waxed motorcars in the driveway especially buffed up for the benefit of the car-less Hacketts from Drumcondra. If Hackett had had a nail in his pocket he would have punctured the tyres.

The two of them walked along Griffith Avenue and turned to head down Drumcondra Road. They walked slowly. They were heading for their own place, their own small house where there would be no standing on ceremony. They would relax, enjoy the dinner and wait for a neighbour to call, share a drink, sing a song, and allow the evening age into night-time.

As they turned the corner into their street his father stopped for a moment.

'Did you really win a gold medal?' he asked. Hackett smiled, but didn't say.

'Don't tell me, I don't want to know.'
As he pushed the key in the door his old man spoke once more.

'That gold medal,' he said, 'best bloody Christmas present I ever got.'

Hackett looked over at his old man and smiled, and for the first time in years felt real affection for the man, maybe even love.

CHAPTER EIGHT

You could always depend on the weather in June. May could be unpredictable, but June was always a scorcher bringing floral patterned dresses onto the streets of Dublin. This climatic certainty had nothing to do with hot air currents drifting up from Southern Europe or the balmy effects of Gulf Stream waters. The reasons were much more basic. June was the month when thousands of students sat at their desks pouring over taxing questions in stuffy halls, while outside the tanning rays of sunshine brought joy to the lives of the free.

In lower Drumcondra June was also the time for house decoration. All along the street the acrid smell of burning paint hung in the air as hall doors and windows were carefully prepared for redecoration.

Neighbour watched neighbour in restrained anxiety waiting for the final colour to be revealed. No one wanted to be outdone, to have their colour stolen, to see it appear on another's door. This preoccupation with individual expression usually resulted in an array of colours which would be the envy of any circus.

Some on the street took the painting very seriously. Old man Brennan always went back to the bare wood. He was a great fan of the blow torch and scraper. As in life, he didn't believe in shortcuts. He enjoyed the pain of endless preparation, knowing that to toil and suffer was part of man's destiny.

Old Harry Fay was different. He had no truck with blow torches or putty knives. He was a man who believed in the instant makeover. Colour was to be enjoyed not endured, and while old man Brennan was only at the priming stage Harry would have his door fully painted and the brushes back in their jars of turpentine.

Hackett's old man hated all this painting business. It was just one more intrusion into his practised pattern of doing nothing. Only after every door on the street would be done would old man Hackett slap on a coat. His colour was green, always was, and would continue to be as long as there was something left in the rusted can he kept under the stairs.

While the painting frenzy went on another equally intense activity was taking place in the bedrooms of three of the boys. Brennan was cramming like never before, staying up late, consuming books and notes at a ferocious rate. The only time he was seen was at mealtime. He wanted so much to do well.

Up the street Fay was also working. His pace may have been different, yet he was doing enough to get through. He still retained his detached demeanour and went about life in his usual dreamlike way. His hair grew longer. Mrs Hickey next door was heard say that she was living beside a cross between John the Baptist and Rasputin.

Hackett, however, was near despair. Since the gold medal revelation at Christmas time he had been going through Hell. At the time he blurted out the fabricated story it seemed like a good idea. Even his old man thought so. But what he hadn't reckoned on was the subsequent pressure that would come. Apparently all his relations were watching - Uncle and Cousin Bob in particular. They were still smarting from being outdone on Christmas morning. Regularly they would ask Granny Hackett and she in turn would pass the message on.

'How is Peter doing? We're expecting great things from him in the exam,' she would say to old man Hackett every time he was summoned to the dark room.

And old man Hackett would ask his son who as always replied, very well. To Hackett it was a sort of detached process of lying. He didn't take it too seriously. Not until he was summoned to the dark room himself. The old lady, perhaps because she wanted to know how her investment in his education was going, decided to take a special interest in the boy. She asked that he call and see her.

'I hear you're doing really well, Peter.'

'Yes, Gran.'

'I'm so pleased.'

Granny Hackett smiled a little and before Hackett left for home, she called him over.

'I'm so pleased,' she said again as she pressed a pound note into his hand.

Before he left that first meeting she asked that he call again. A week later he obliged, and did the same the following week and the week after, lured by the cash the old bird parted with. And every week she would ask the same question.

'How are you doing, Peter?'

Hackett couldn't help himself.

'Another gold medal, Gran.'

'Another one? Which subject?'

'Latin, Gran.'

'God bless the Jesuits.'

Week after week Hackett excelled in every subject on the curriculum. Medals of all sorts were conferred on the boy. Every time he would tell another lie he would tell himself, *no more*. And yet, once in that room sitting before her, he just couldn't help himself. It wasn't just the money. He seemed to enjoy the adulation and the news that his academic achievements were creating havoc in the family. Apparently that pimply faced jerk of a cousin Bob was almost at the point of a breakdown.

But all of his achievements came at a price. As time moved on and the exam became a stark reality, the same imagination which had dreamed up self-brilliance was now visualising disaster. He was now seeing mockery and derision, an assembled family in *that* dark room doubled up and creased with laughter. He could see the pimply one standing next to Granny Hackett as she stuffed his pockets with five pound notes. Like one of Granny Hackett's cats, young Bob would be purring as his self-esteem and ego were stroked. The bastard, thought Hackett, the plummy accented Southside git.

As the date drew nearer his panic became palpable. He told himself to stop thinking about his cousin. He had to make room in his mind for study and fill his memory with the facts. And there they lay on the table before him. All the notes, the notes about notes, the facts and the details. No matter how he tried he couldn't settle down. Study was like a foreign radio station on his old man's Pye radio, somewhere you could never connect with. Every night was the same. Up he'd go to the room full of determination and sit. But always the same thing happened. His mind would drift. He'd be in orbit encircling a disconnected collection of ramblings.

At one stage he thought the only solution was to opt out. He could fall prey again to another illness. This time it would be real. He would talk to Finnegan, the chemist's messenger boy, and ask him to concoct something, a powder or liquid, to make him ill. Nothing too drastic, just something that might produce spots or a fever. Spots would be best. People might think they were contagious.

He rummaged in every part of his brain for a way out but the only believable solution he found was death. For a fleeting moment he was in the church with the mourners listening to his eulogy, a tribute to a boy whose brain had exploded with knowledge.

Finally, he decided that he had no choice, he would do the bloody exam. But he would do it in a different way. He would go into the exam hall prepared. This didn't mean study. He would cheat. He would need to secrete on his person all the necessary facts. That's what he would do. He would pass the bloody thing. Pass it with flying colours. No more of this study nonsense.

Then, having made his decision, he relaxed.

CHAPTER NINE

The weathermen got it wrong. They had predicted a cloudy day with a belt of rain moving across the country. They had talked of frequent showers, blustery conditions and the odd thunderstorm. None of that happened. The sun was up early, like the thousands of students ready for the first day of the June exams.

There was one element they got right. At the end of the forecast they mentioned a deep depression settling in the east of the country.

Hackett was deeply troubled. He had seriously under-estimated the amount of work involved in cheating. The sheer volume of note-taking was enormous. He had spent the previous night preparing his arsenal of facts and figures. He was almost blind from transcribing all the information in tiny block letters onto scraps of paper. The writing was so minute he could hardly read it.

At six o'clock he began the process of secreting all the information. The tiny scraps of paper were rolled up and hidden in the refills of ball-point pens. The caps of fountain pens were also ideal hiding places. Pins were used to attach information behind the lapels of his jacket. Dates were written on his arm. Paper was stuffed down his socks, his trousers, his shoes. All his pockets were full with pens, rulers and other junk which might hold precious data. He even borrowed his mother's inhaler which he crammed with information. When the job was complete, he was exhausted. He tried to relax. He told himself over and over that everything was under control, but deep down the nagging abrading of his confidence went on. The image of his pimply faced cousin haunted him.

Before he went down to breakfast he tried to compose himself. He had never been this uptight before. Despite his scheming, he'd never been prone to even the mildest twinge of nerves. But the scheming was different. The schemes were of his own making. He was in control. The exam was foreign territory. For once he had no control over the outcome. If he failed he was finished. He would be exposed to all as a conman, and this is what worried him most.

His parents turned to greet him as he entered the kitchen. They were beaming. His mother, who had already been to mass, was standing over the gas rings cracking eggs into a pan.

'I've made a nice fry for you,' she said.

'Most important meal of the day,' said his father who rarely had more than a gulp of tea and a couple of mouthfuls of toast.

'You'll need all your energy today, Peter,' said his mother as she dropped a rasher into the molten fat. The fresh bacon hissed and the grease spat. Then she added several thick slices of black pudding and as the pig's blood began to fry a sizzling steam rose up that clouded the back window. On any other day Hackett would have woolfed the contents of the pan, but that day was different. He didn't want any breakfast. What he wanted most were several cigarettes smoked one after the other. The thought of pork and a runny egg was revolting.

'And how do you feel?' his mother asked.

'Fine.'

'And why wouldn't he be fine?' said his old man, 'and all the hours, days, weeks he's spent up in that room studying. Why wouldn't he be fine?'

Oh God, thought Hackett, why don't they shut up?

Then his father fished out an envelope from his pocket and passed it over.

'Go on, open it.'

It looked like a greeting card. He opened it. It *was* a card, a good-luck card from the woman in black, Granny Hackett. He could just about decipher the spidery scrawl.

'What does it say?' his old man asked.

'Well?' added his mother.

Hackett looked at the note again - *We're expecting great things from you Peter*, it read.

Instead of reading it out he handed the card over to his father who read out each word slowly like a child, for he was a child whenever he was under the influence of his mother.

'Isn't that lovely,' said his mother as she placed an enormous fry before Hackett. Rashers, sausages, black pudding and, in the centre, two runny fried eggs. She stood beside him. He sensed her expectation.

'Thanks, Ma.'

'Isn't she great?' asked Mister Hackett, 'down to Mackey's first thing this morning to get the grub for the scholar.'

Scholar, thought Hackett. If only they knew. There he was sitting before them the picture of innocence; every spare inch of space on his person was crammed with the condensed version of the Educational Company's complete European History from the French Revolution to the First World War. Scholar? More like a waste paper basket. He could hardly move without the sound of creasing paper.

He looked down at the eggs floating in a film of grease. All he could think of were those appalling images that hung on Harry Fay's wall; the images that had prompted the Scout to describe them as sickness and Harry to recoil shouting vomit.'

'Go on and eat them before they get cold.'

They were like two prison guards watching the condemned man take his last meal. They wanted him to consume the lot. He could feel their pride beaming at him. They were expecting great things. He was their only son, the one who was going to show the world that the Hacketts from lower Drumcondra were of the finest stock, the purest pedigree.

The two runny eggs looked up at him like cartoon eyes as the grease surrounding them began to congeal.

'Ah, Peter,' his mother said. 'You have to eat.'

'Your mother is right son.'

Hackett promised himself that he would never eat eggs again. His father lit up a cigarette and the smoke drifted across the table. Oh God, thought Hackett, what he wouldn't do for a fag. He pierced one of the yokes with his knife. The yellow goo oozed and spread across the oily solution. If I eat this, thought Hackett, I'll puke. For an instant he thought puking might not be a bad idea. A sudden bout of food poisoning might do the trick. But first he'd have to eat it all. Then he had an idea.

'I've had terrible diarrhoea,' he said in a sheepish tone.

'Are you not well love?' his mother asked in alarm.

'Don't tell me you're sick again?' his father blurted, emphasising the word 'sick' with such force that both father and son knew exactly what was meant.

'I'm just terrified that if I eat anything I might be running to the toilet all day and miss part of the exam.'

Old man Hackett didn't hesitate.

'Take it away, Nora. Take it away.'

His mother whipped the plate away.

'Would you like some hot milk or anything?' she asked.

'No, I think it's best if I eat nothing,' he said, rising from the table and soaking up all the sympathy in the room.

They walked him to the hall door. They wished him luck, his father patting him on the back, his mother planting a rubbery kiss on his reluctant cheek. They stood for a while watching as he walked down the street. He didn't turn back.

At the corner he met Fay and Brennan. Both of them were composed. Brennan's level headed state of mind had been brought about by his quiet confidence in the amount of work he had done. Fay was Fay. He could have been on a trip to the cinema or a browse in a second-hand book shop for all the difference it made.

'Well, the big day,' said Brennan.

'Yeah, the big day,' sneered Hackett as he walked on.

'Going to be a bleeding scorcher,' said Fay as he flicked away a butt into the gutter.

They walked along Drumcomdra Road without much conversation. Hackett kept his head down. Inwardly he was going over the location of his various pieces of information. At the bridge they parted.

The weathermen got it wrong again. As the day wore on, the sun got stronger, the heat more intense. It was like any June that anyone could remember, typical exam weather. As thousands sat on wooden desks, others wrapped egg and onion sandwiches in greaseproof paper and headed for the beaches, to laze in the sand dunes or swim in the cooling waters of the Irish Sea.

CHAPTER TEN

In Hackett's school the exam was held in the old concert hall, a drab building which had seen better days. It was here that the plays and school concerts were performed in front of an enthusiastic audience of parents and pupils. The parents came to be proud of their young protégés. The pupils came mostly to laugh and hoot and crease themselves with hilarity as their peers made exhibitions of themselves.

Hackett so wished he was back there now. The plays were a welcome diversion from the boring monotony of daily school life. He remembered the outstanding moments; the time when a boy dressed as a sailor lost his footing and ended up in the audience, the butler who closed a set door too firmly and literally brought the house down. And of course his own debut.

He had been extremely reluctant to join the cast until he discovered that all the participants were excused homework for the duration of the rehearsals. But this information came late to Hackett so by the time he signed up virtually all the parts were gone. However there was one part left which Father Morris thought would be ideal. With extreme reluctance Hackett accepted what was offered and took to the stage as a servant girl, a timid creature who seemed to get every instruction wrong.

On opening night Hackett made every effort to disguise himself. The make-up was put on in layers. He shaved his legs. He wore a wig. He spoke in an accent like Harry Fay. He even walked with a limp. But as soon as he appeared on stage the cat-calls rang out and the whistles blared. The audience loved it. They had never seen such a servant girl in their lives. By the final performance nobody knew him as Hackett. Everyone called him Maud.

Naturally his first experience on stage made him reluctant to take to the boards again. Father Morris persisted and prevailed. There were, however, conditions. He would never play the part of a woman, he would insist on nothing other than manly roles.

The part he was eventually offered seemed ideal. There would be little or no speaking lines, no feminine aspect to the character, and he wouldn't be on stage for long. Though it may have seemed a small part, Father Morris impressed upon Hackett the vital significance of the role in the unfolding of the drama. Hackett would play the part of a soldier in the Easter Passion play. Not just any soldier. Hackett was given the task of lashing the actor who played Christ.

Over the course of the rehearsals Hackett developed a particular eagerness to play the part. Father Morris put this enthusiasm down to a deep desire to kill forever the memory of Maud.

On the opening night the audience said his performance was stunning. The review in the school magazine singled him out. It said that the boy who played the Centurion seemed to totally immerse himself in the part, that never had such a minor role in a school production been played with such conviction.

The star of the show, the one who played Christ, was a boy called Adam Fogarty, a leading light in the Temperance Society, the Legion of Mary and the Boy's Sodality. He also happened to be a prefect in Hackett's class who, on more than one occasion, used his lofty authority to report the Roman soldier for the most minor indiscretions. Fogarty was that sort of boy who infuriated the others. He would answer every question, question every answer and have an opinion on everything whether it involved him or not.

During rehearsals Fogarty played the star. Will I stand here, Father Morris? Or will I stand there? All through the reading of the lines Hackett and the others had to stand and listen to the boy playing Christ who thought he was God.

Even during the rehearsals of Hackett's lashing scene, Fogarty had an opinion. He didn't want Hackett to stand between him and the audience. Everyone, for the sake of the drama, should see the star's face.

When opening night came, Hackett took up his position and stood above the cowering Christ. Fogarty looked up at him wearing a tormented expression. Hackett drew breath. Menacingly he raised the instrument of torture above his head. He looked at Fogarty. The star blinked and sighed as if accepting the inevitable. But what he was given was not written in the script.

Those that were there that night believed they were watching the real thing. One lash, then another. They came with ferocity. The torturer didn't falter. He seemed to rally to the cheers of the mob. On and on he went lashing the figure on the ground. The star was doing well. He was showing real emotion and pain. It was as if the blows were real. The audience felt that they had been transported back two thousand years to that fateful Good Friday. Never had Father Morris seen such realism. Hackett was a find.

And through it all the one who played Christ bore it all stoically. By the end of the week he too performed as if it were the real thing. Some in the cast were convinced that the cries they had heard were real. They were.

Fogarty never again offered to play Christ. Indeed his acting career ended when the curtains closed on the final night. He took his decision, not because of the pain, but the cheers that came from the audience. The loudest of all were for Hackett.

He was brought back to reality by the announcement that the exam was about to begin. Hackett looked around. He spotted Fogarty three rows in front. The angelic one would be well prepared. He wouldn't have to root in pockets, search in his shoe, rummage in a sock. He would have it all in his head.

At ten on the dot, the exam papers were handed out. The papers were placed face downwards on each desk until everyone had a copy. Then they were told to begin. The moment of truth had arrived.

The exam technique advised that you should read the questions slowly, then read them again to fully understand. Only then should you begin. It was psychologically important to have a good start. Building confidence early was important. But all this technique presupposed that you had studied the subject and had some idea of what you were being asked.

When he turned the exam paper over, Hackett's eyes raced down the questions. As much as he'd practised his exercises in composure, he found it hard to relax. The heat didn't help either. Many of the boys had their jackets draped over the back of their chairs. Hackett didn't have this option. He needed the jacket close for access to all his information. He read the questions again. He wanted to see something that was so familiar that he could start immediately without having to refer to his notes.

There were six questions in two hours. Two hours, one hundred and twenty minutes, twenty minutes per question. He looked up at the clock. Already five minutes gone.

Before reading the questions again he looked around. To his left he could see that Madden had already begun scratching his fountain pen across the ruled paper. Hanly too, who was sitting in front, had also started. It had to be Hanly. No one else wrote in that contortionist fashion, his head down on his right hand while he wrote almost backwards. And Brady, who by general agreement, was destined for failure, was also making progress.

Hackett wanted to begin. Time was ticking by. What he wanted to see was something about Napoleon. He was a great fan of the Frenchman. He hadn't studied him much but he'd seen the film, the advance on Moscow, the drifts of snow, the slow progress of the march through the Russian winter. This was a story he could tell. Napoleon wasn't mentioned. Instead he was invited to describe the social conditions in France before the revolution. That required background reading.

Ten past ten. Now down to eighteen minutes per question. Madden was now on his second page. What had he seen that was so bloody easy?

Out of all the questions he could only find four that he had some vague notion about, ones where his supply of information might help. He reckoned that if he even got these partly right it might be enough to pass. He did some rough figures. A pass was forty per cent. So, if he only did four of the questions he'd need *what* in each question? He did the sums. For an instant he thought he was doing the maths exam. This was ridiculous, mad. Everyone around was writing furiously. Fogarty was now even stretching, a signal to all that he was producing in volume.

He decided to start. The supervisor at the top of the hall had a newspaper spread out in front of him. That was a good sign. The other one was walking about. Hackett knew this not because he could see him, but because his shoes creaked.

The question he picked concerned the First World War. He remembered a poem he had read once by W.B. Yeats about an Irish airman that was killed in the war. It wasn't the quality of the poetry that attracted him, it was the dogfights over France, the action in the air, the daring courage of the pilots. He decided to mention the poem. He thought that was a novel idea. It would show the examiner that the student had a well-rounded education. He tried to remember the lines, but they wouldn't come. Instead he wrote in general terms about war and how so many were inspired to write about the horror of death and destruction. Deep down he knew this was wide of the mark, but at least he'd begun.

He was about half way down the first page when he decided that it would be a good idea to mention those that were involved in the war. He knew about England and France. But who were the others? He was sure he had that information somewhere. He trawled his mind for the location. Eventually he decided that the note was either pinned to the inside of his lapel or in the pouch of his mother's inhaler.

He checked the location of the supervisors. The man at the top was still engrossed in his newspaper. The creaking shoe was the other side of the hall. He took out the inhaler. He unscrewed the top. Inside he could see the notes which had been rolled up tightly. What he hadn't bargained on was the paper unfolding in the pouch. The carefully prepared data was stuck.

Next he tried folding back the lapel of his jacket. The writing was so tiny he couldn't make out the words. He looked about. He was safe. He tore the note from his lapel and slid it under the paper. Instead of the First World War it was all about the Famine.

It was now ten thirty. Only ninety minutes left. All about him the students were writing furiously, sticking up their hands, requesting more paper. He hated them all. He wanted to shout out, to curse them all, to tell them what he thought, how he couldn't give a fiddler's about the deeds and antics of the long-dead.

As the frustration was building he gripped a biro. He held it so tightly the plastic barrel snapped in his fingers. The noise, in the stillness of the room, was sharp.

Everyone turned to look. The man with the paper stopped reading. The creaking shoe became louder. Hackett's face flushed red. He looked down at the two halves of the shattered plastic in his hands. The ink was all over his fingers. He reached into his pocket for a handkerchief, but he couldn't take anything out. His pockets were stuffed full of facts.

Then he remembered the Famine notes. They were still on his desk. If he was caught, he was destroyed, disgraced. The creaking shoe was close. Instinctively he covered the notes with his sleeve. The eyes of all the others were on him. Madden, Hanly and, most hateful of all, Fogarty, the one who'd played Christ. Perhaps Fogarty was hoping that this was Hackett's last supper.

The creaking shoe stood over him. Hackett, for the first time in years, felt like crying. He held up the two halves of the biro. He knew if he was instructed to stand and go to the toilet to wash his hands he was finished. The notes would be exposed on the desk. And so would he. He looked up at the supervisor in despair. The look in his eyes seemed to beg.

The man looked at the ink all over Hackett's hands. He shook his head and sighed. Then slowly he reached into his pocket, took out some paper and passed it to Hackett. With a look of eternal gratitude, Hackett took the paper.

The rest were told to get on with the exam as the creaking shoe walked away.

A strange calm descended on Hackett. He was so relieved by not being found out as a cheat that nothing else seemed to matter. He forgot about his notes, dismissed any notion of cheating. He would carry on with the questions.

As the time ebbed by he filled several pages. He knew that most of it was rubbish. When he came to the final question he literally had no idea whatsoever. It was so vague and foreign to him that he couldn't even spoof. There were still twenty minutes to go. He thought of handing up the paper and leaving. But that would send out the wrong signal. The others, particularly Fogarty, would know he had failed. Instead he had an idea. There could still be an outside chance of salvation.

He began writing a letter to the examiner. It was more of a plea than an exercise in correspondence. He explained in detail how he had tried to answer the questions. He acknowledged that his efforts were bad. But in his defence he offered an excuse.

In a detailed list, he set down all his medical history. He knew the terminology well. He listed all his consultants. Some he mentioned by name. He explained that because he had been dogged by ill health, study and attendance at school had been patchy. He apologised for his lack of knowledge and the impertinence of writing such a letter.

And then the bell went.

The history exam was over.

Hackett heard himself say, thanks be to God, not Christ, who by that time had filled seventeen pages of foolscap paper in his copperplate hand writing.

CHAPTER ELEVEN

Fay suggested that they should celebrate once the exam was over. A Friday night when old Harry would be away visiting his sister in Tramore would be the ideal opportunity. The house would be free and the boys could enjoy themselves uninterrupted by the restraining influence of adults.

'So, what are you thinking of having?' asked the Scout.

'Just a small select gathering,' answered Fay.

'In the shed?'

'Where else?'

'What's the plan?' asked Brennan warily.

'I was thinking of having some music, some refreshments and some birds.'

'Birds, what birds?' asked Brennan who liked very much what he was hearing.

'I haven't decided what birds yet. I was thinking of some from Lemon's.'

'What?' said the Scout, who was immediately alarmed at the prospect of birds from Lemon's sweet factory being invited and the word filtering back to his mother who worked there.

'What if my oulwan finds out?'

'She won't find out. Anyway I haven't made up me mind. I might invite some from the Holy Faith in Glasnevin.'

'Ah no,' said Hackett, 'they're all so prim and proper.'

'Are you going to have many?' asked Brennan.

'No, I said a small select gathering and that's what it'll be. There'll be the four of us. Maybe Finnegan. And five women. That's all.'

'Sounds all right to me,' said Hackett nodding.

Everyone agreed that a gathering with a woman each was just the job. They would leave the choice of woman to Fay. He had a way with the women. They seemed to like his looks and the way he talked about poetry and music.

As the night of the gathering drew near the boys'curiosity grew. Brennan was particularly anxious, not just about the identity of the girls but the prospect of being with a woman at all. Any woman.

'Fay didn't say who the birds were?' he asked casually.

'What does it matter? Birds is birds.'

'Just wondered.'

'What happens,' asked the Scout, 'when you get off with one of them? Can we use the house as well?'

'What do you mean?' said Brennan.

'Are you thick or what? You're hardly going to do it in the shed in front of the rest. That's why we need to know the story about the house, the bedrooms, the sofa, anywhere you can be on your own with the lucky lady.'

'There won't be a problem, sure the place couldn't be in a worse mess than it's in,' added Hackett.

'I hope he picks nice women,' said the Scout, as he licked his lips at the prospect.

'Once they go all the way, I don't give a shit,' said Hackett.

'Yeah!' nodded the Scout. 'All the way.'

All the way, thought Brennan, *all the way*. His heart was racing. His experience with women was limited, very limited. It wasn't his looks that created the problem. It was his confidence, his ability to relax. The more he tried to be casual the worse it got. Often he would lie in bed at night and rehearse a line of conversation. He would imagine himself in the Rainbow Café sitting opposite a stunning creature looking into her eyes and enthralling her with his spellbinding words. But the reality was very different. Often he'd watch Fay in action and marvel at his friend. But Brennan couldn't talk like Fay. He couldn't lure the women with conversation about the poetic lyrics of a song or the soulful delivery of the singer.

Brennan's strength was silence. He liked nothing more than a slow lurch on the dance floor where the volume of the music made it impossible to talk. He would let his actions speak. Slowly, yet progressively as the dance went on, he would attempt to hold the woman closer. He would do it slowly, moving his hands cautiously, hoping for no sign of rejection.

But the problems began when the music stopped. Once he had talked about the band, the music, the crowd, he was stuck. All his practised routine evaporated. And so, because of his inability to open his mouth and have words flow, his strike rate with women was low. He hoped that all this might change at Fay's gathering, that something magical might happen and finally he might get his first chance to go *all the way*.

The Scout's success rate was better. He got on well with women. He could talk to them, tell them jokes. His natural outgoing personality helped. It was said that he was much like his mother who had raised him in an atmosphere of love and kindness. The fact that Mrs O'Neill had to do it on her own, with her husband in England, never affected her attitude to her son. She remained good humoured and her warm-hearted nature was clearly evident in the demeanour and attitude of her son.

The Scout had another advantage. He had a job, he had money. He could buy new clothes, the latest fashion and gear. He was also very generous.

Like all the others Hackett loved women and most of them loved him. They didn't seem to mind his spoofing about his wealth, his prospects, his scheming. As for his looks, he told himself that he was the spit of George in the Beatles, and there was some truth to that. His hair was long and dark and he wore it down to his collar, except in school, when he brushed it behind his ears.

Though their looks and personalities differed, they were all besotted by girls. They continually talked about them. To listen to them a stranger would be convinced that these young men had an intimate knowledge of the various positions and acrobatics in the Karma Sutra manual of sex.

Fay had instructed them all to be in the shed by eight. They were bursting with anticipation. For several days they had been barred from the place. Fay had decided that the place was off-limits. The boys had no idea what was going on.

Fay wanted time to create an atmosphere, to change the décor and turn the place into a party setting. Fay had his own ideas. The last thing he needed was design by committee. He didn't want any interference and that's why he created an embargo.

At ten to eight Hackett crossed the road to call for the Scout. The Scout was ready. Then they called for Brennan.

Maura, Brennan's sister, opened the door. She shrugged and left them on the step. There was no invitation to enter, to sit in the front room and wait. That inner sanctum was reserved for the insurance man and the monk.

Brennan rushed down the stairs. He didn't want any of the household to see. Even the mildest glance could raise suspicion. The last thing he needed was endless questions about his appearance. He, like the pair on the step, had been in the bathroom for almost an hour. The teeth had been washed several times, the hair anointed with various lotions and every part of his anatomy scrubbed in lathers of Lux. All of them were spanking clean. Freshly shaved faces stank with the smell of Old Spice. Blackheads had been squeezed. Pimples had been treated all week with Clearasil.

As they moved away from Brennan's, Rob Finnegan, the Chemist's messenger boy, joined them. He too, had spent an age before the sink. Finnegan had the added advantage of getting his cosmetics at cost. He smelt like a florist.

They knew themselves that the hygiene and the stink was awesome. None of them could remember seeing the others so clean. Yet all of them tried to act casual. They also wanted to hide their anxiety and expectation. They lit cigarettes and they bantered.

'God, Brennan, will you look at your collar,' said Hackett.

'What's wrong with it?' answered Brennan.

'It's manky,' said Hackett.

'Destroyed,' added the Scout.

'What's wrong with it? Tell me.'

'It's crawling,' said the Scout.

'Lads please, what are yiz talking about?'

'Dandruff. Covered in dandruff,' laughed Hackett.

Brennan whipped off his jacket. The collar was clean.

'Well, shag you,' he said, 'shag yiz all!'

After calming Brennan down, they moved towards Fay's door. There was an increasing giddiness in their behaviour. They were now jousting with each other, pushing and jabbing, playfully sparring. They couldn't stay still. They were like small children in a queue.

Hackett knocked on the door. No response. He knocked again.

'What's going on?' wondered Brennan.

'Maybe he's writing another poem,' said Hackett.

'Knock again, Hackett.'

'Just like his oulfella,' said Hackett banging the door yet again.

'Come on Fay, open up,' sighed the Scout.

'Knock again.'

A mild tension began to build. Surely this wasn't one of Fay's practical jokes?

Their preoccupation was broken by the appearance of Darby Maguire, the pools' collector, who was making his way home from Fagan's public house. He had all the signs of having sat at the bar for some time. His eyes were slightly blurred and his normally reddened nose was glowing even brighter in the centre of his seventy year old face.

'There yiz are,' he said.

The boys turned round. Darby! That was all they needed.

'What's the smell?' asked Darby.

'What smell?'

'Do yiz not get it? Perfume or something. One of yiz must be wearing perfume.'

'It's ointment,' said Finnegan.

Darby looked at the chemist's messenger boy. He went to speak, then hesitated. He recognised Finnegan, knew that the young lad knew a thing or two about medicine.

'Ointment? Queerest smelling ointment I ever smelt. Did you knock on the door?'

'No answer,' said Hackett.

'There must be an answer. Knock again.'

'There mustn't be anyone in,' insisted Brennan.

'He has to be in.'

'He's not. He's gone to visit his sister in Tramore,' explained Hackett.

'Sure he hardly ever goes out. Knock again.'

They all knew the danger of having Darby spoil everything. What if Darby insisted on going inside and all the women were there?

'There's no one in, Mr Maguire.'

'There has to be. He's always in on a Friday, knows I do be calling.'

'What do you need to see him about, Mr Maguire?'

'The pools, the sixpence for the pools.'

Finnegan reached into his pocket. He would willingly pay to get rid of Darby.

'Here's sixpence,' said Finnegan.

'Ah no son, if Harry's not in he'd have left it for me. Anyway where are yiz all off to?'

97

'We're going nowhere.'

'Well yiz are dressed to kill. Is it a party you're off to?'

'No, no party.'

'Well, you could have fooled me.'

The door suddenly opened and Fay appeared wearing his old man's multi-coloured dressing gown. Before Darby could speak, Fay handed him sixpence and turned to the others.

'Come in boys, the prayer meeting is about to begin. Would you like to join us Mr Maguire? We start with a longer version of the rosary, fifteen decades in all. I can get you a cushion to kneel on if you like.'

'You can't be serious?' said Darby.

'Fifteen decades,' said Fay earnestly.

'No,' said Darby. 'I'll leave you to it. I have another appointment down the road.'

The boys watched as Darby tottered down the road. Then they went inside.

The party was about to begin.

CHAPTER TWELVE

Fay led them inside to the small front room where half a dozen wine glasses were laid out on a low sized table. He pointed to the table.

'An aperitif?' he announced, making an elaborate hand gesture and a bow.

Most of them had no idea what an aperitif was.

Fay filled five glasses with a sparkling white wine and passed everyone a drink. Fay raised his glass.

'To an evening of special delights,' he proposed.

'Where did you get the booze?' said Hackett.

'Compliments of Harry's stock and there's plenty more. Drink up lads. Drink up.'

They all drank. It was a light Bavarian wine, slightly sweet, not unpleasant.

'This isn't bad at all,' said the Scout as he downed the contents in a gulp.

'You're meant to sip it,' said Fay.

'Well fill us another and I'll sip that,' said the Scout to hoots of laughter from the others.

While the drink was a novelty and a distraction, all of their minds were thinking of other things.

'And what about the other guests?' said Hackett.

'Patience Hackett, patience.'

'Yeah, but where are they?'

'They're on their way.'

'Which way?' said Brennan in a slight panic. He was terrified of a tribe of women walking down the street heading for Fay's. What if his sister saw them?

'Are they coming down the street or what?'

'No Brennan, they're coming down the lane.'

99

They all relaxed. Fay recharged their glasses, then produced several more bottles from his old man's stock.

'Is this strong stuff?' asked Brennan.

'It's rocket fuel,' said Fay.

Bravado drove them on. One glass followed another. Then Fay changed colours. He introduced them all to a Bordeaux red. This wasn't as easy to drink, yet they did their best and several glasses went down.

'And tell us Fay,' said the Scout. 'What happens when the birds arrive?'

'That's up to you.'

'But what's the plan?'

'The plan is that they arrive and then it's every man for himself.'

'Do we know them?' asked the Scout.

'You might.'

'Do they know us?' wondered Brennan.

'They might.'

'Ah come on Fay,' said Hackett. 'Do they know us or what?'

'All right, I think they might know you.'

'All of us?' asked Brennan.

'Brennan's worried. Look at him, he's worried.'

'Fuck off, Rob.'

'Fuck off yourself.'

'Cool it lads,' said Hackett.

'Are the natives getting restless?' asked Fay. 'Maybe I should play some music.'

'Ah no,' said the Scout, 'not your old man's funeral music.'

'Fay, when are we going to the shed?'

'Yeah Fay, let's go to the shed.'

'One more glass and then we'll go. Don't be too anxious lads.'

In the forty minutes they'd spent in Fay's front room they consumed almost a bottle of wine each. While all of them had dabbled with drink before, this was their first really concentrated session. The alcohol affected them in different ways. Fay became more eloquent. The Scout quietened down. Hackett and Rob became giddy, while Brennan found that he was becoming less anxious about the visit to the shed.

Finally Fay announced that the first stage in the evening was over. It was time to go to the shed.

They passed through the kitchen, out the back door and into the garden. Fay led the way. They all looked around for any tell-tale signs. Then Fay went into the shed alone. He wanted to make some last minute preparations.

They stood in the garden like children.

'This is crazy,' said the Scout. 'He's a nutcase.'

'Give him time,' said Brennan.

Then the sound of *A Whiter Shade of Pale* by Procol Harum was heard. They loved that song. It reminded them of dancing close and holding women. They knew all the words. They couldn't resist singing out. They wallowed in the sense of belonging that came when singing a song together. It was like an anthem.

As the song played, a glow of light began to build in the shed. Fay was lighting candles.

Then the door opened. Fay stood on the step and called them forward. The singing filtered away. The serious business was at hand.

In the shrine-like atmosphere of several dozen candles they tried to take in the scene. Fay had transformed the place. Gone was the junk. He had painted the walls, covered the floor in carpet. And everywhere suspended from the rafters were lace curtains which seemed to partition the space. They looked at the place in awe.

At the other end, near the door to the back lane, a number of mattresses had been laid. Above them large plumes of pampas grass hung from the roof. Fern-like shrubs filled several pots in the corners and everywhere they looked candles of differing colours glowed.To complete the setting Fay had incense burning in a bowl.

'What do you think?' asked Fay.

'It's like eh. . .' began the Scout.

'It's like. I tell you what it's like. It's. . .'

'It's like one of those tents in the desert. You know the ones, where yer man the Arab has his way with birds.'

'A harem?'

'Yeah, a harem.'

'All we need now is the birds.'

Fay changed the record. This time he played *You've lost that Loving Feeling,* another song which brought back memories. He turned up the volume. They all sang out. Then he produced more wine and filled another five glasses.

'Drink up lads,' said Fay, 'welcome to the den of a thousand promises.'

Then without warning several knocks came from the door to the lane. They all stopped singing. They turned the record player down. Fay whipped off the multi-coloured dressing gown to reveal a see-through cheesecloth shirt that hung over his jeans. He walked towards the other door. He looked at the boys and smiled. They were too nervous to smile back.

Fay opened the door and five young women waltzed in. They were giggling and laughing and pushing each other forward. None of them wanted to be first. They could hardly talk with the laughter.

The one thing they had in common was their look. All of them wore mini skirts, tiny pieces that hardly covered their underwear. Their hair was mostly long and straight. Some had fringes that almost covered their eyes. They certainly looked more than their average age of sixteen.

They were giddy and excited as they crammed into the shed.

'Ah would you look at the place.'

'Fay, what have you done?'

'It's what he's going to do.'

They roared in convulsive laughter. Once one started, the others caved in. Then they'd try and be serious, but the merest giggle set them off. They were in knots.

'Where did you get all the curtains, Fay?'

'Must have robbed the basement in Guiney's.'

Fay went to the table and filled more glasses with wine. He signalled to the Scout to help and both of them carried the glasses to the women at the door. The laughter seemed to subside.

Hackett, Rob and Brennan watched as the Scout went into action straight away, telling his jokes, using his charm.

Fay too had started. Even at this early stage he had taken the hand of Babs and led her over to the record player to look at his collection. He turned up the volume and then began dancing. Brennan looked at Babs closely, her tiny mini-skirt, the way she hung on to Fay, how she wrapped her arms around him. Fay must have known her before now. No one could be as fast as that. Not even Fay. Then Fay stopped dancing for a moment.

'Are yiz dancing or what? Introduce yourselves to our guests.'

And the 'guests' exploded with laughter. Guests to a shed!

The Scout started lurching with Susie beside the pampas grass in the corner. She seemed to like the Scout and every so often would throw her head back in fits of laughter.

Hackett filled himself another glass of wine. Brennan did the same. He was beginning to hate the taste of the stuff but the sense of courage it gave him won out. His nervousness was diluting.

Then Hackett did something strange. He took the bottle of wine and approached the three girls in the corner. This was Hackett in operational mood. Hackett was cute. He was acting the gentleman. He offered them more wine and passed a packet of cigarettes around which he lit with a Ronson lighter he had picked up in Granny Hackett's. When it hadn't been reported as missing by Uncle Bob at Christmas time, Hackett kept it.

Next to move was Rob. Brennan had been hoping that the chemist's messenger boy would stay close, but Rob couldn't wait. Seeing the progress of the others made him anxious. He didn't want to be left out, so he took the hand of a girl the other side of Hackett and began dancing with her.

There was only one woman left. Brennan was beginning to panic.

Fay changed the record. This time he played *Something's Gotten Hold of my Heart* by Gene Pitney. The girls screamed. Fay turned the volume up and the girls went on screaming. Brennan knew that he would have to act. If he didn't do something the remaining girl would think he was odd. He lit a cigarette. He took another swig of wine. Then Fay caught his eye and nodded at the woman. Brennan held up the cigarette. He would dance as soon as he was finished.

Hackett was still with the other two at the door. He wanted to dance with one of them, but she wouldn't leave her friend. Hackett looked down at Brennan.

'Bring down another bottle of wine, Brennan.'

That was exactly what Brennan wanted. Any excuse to move. An instruction to act. He took a bottle by the neck and, as casually as he could, strolled down towards Hackett.

'This is Brennan,' said Hackett. 'That's Jean. That's Fiona.'

'Howya.'

'Hello.'

'How's it going?'

'Brennan's old man is a pilot,' said Hackett. 'Gets loads of duty free, that sort of thing. Brennan has seen the world.'

Hackett led Jean towards a corner. They started to dance, to move and sway slowly together. Brennan still had the bottle in his hand. He offered Fiona another drink, but she hadn't touched the last refill. He caught her eye. She smiled. She looked at the bottle, so did Brennan. He put the bottle down and took her arm. She put her hand on Brennan's shoulder and they danced.

Fiona wanted to hear about the world, about all the places that Brennan had been. Brennan wanted to say nothing. Why did Hackett have to spoof and say that his old man was a pilot? The drapery assistant at twenty thousand feet; bushy eyebrows pouring over the radar.

Over Fiona's shoulder, Brennan watched Hackett in action. He was wrapped around Jean. They were hardly moving at all. Hackett was massaging the small of her back, trying hard to pull her closer.

Rob wasn't doing that well. His partner, Cathy, kept resisting his advances. Every time Rob pulled her close she would throw her head back and take another pull of her cigarette.

The Scout, who had started so well, seemed to be running out of steam. All his jokes must have been used up. Susie didn't seem interested physically. At each advance, when the Scout would move his head closer, she would pull back her head and flick her hair with her hand.

Brennan saw all this rejection as a lesson. He didn't want Fiona to say, no. He didn't want to make a move and have her pull back. He knew it might be fatal to be pushy. Besides, he was enjoying the closeness and intimacy of it all, the touch of her skin, the smell of her perfume. He wanted very much to draw her close, but he didn't want to risk it.

At one stage Fay looked over. He winked at Brennan and this signal of approval meant everything.

The music came to an end. None of the boys wanted to risk leaving their partners. They waited for more music. Fay was too busy to change records. By now he and Babs were lying on the mattress. Fay was whispering in her ear, playing with the strands of her hair. She seemed to like his tactile approach, the way he was so gentle. Fay was a master. Brennan felt sure Fay's next move would be a poem.

Then to everyone's relief the record player clicked into action. Gene Pitney got another play. The boys didn't care. They would have willingly listened to any of Harry's old funeral music rather than silence.

Brennan knew that he would have to come up with a plan. In a few minutes Gene Pitney would finish singing and Brennan would be challenged to talk. He was sorry he hadn't had more to drink. Before dancing he had felt the sap of confidence rise as the wine went down. Now he felt he could do with a boost. When the singing stopped he spoke.

'Would you like another drink?'

'I haven't touched the last one.'

He was about to give up when he was inspired with a thought.

'That's probably stale. What about a fresh one?'

Fiona thought, then nodded.

Brennan led her down to the other end of the shed to the small table which held the wine. He poured two glasses and passed one to Fiona. Then he raised his own and she clinked it. In that instant Brennan felt so mature. He took a swallow of the fruity liquid. In truth, he didn't like it much and it showed.

'You don't like it, do you?' she said.

He reddened a little though she, in the dim light, couldn't see.

'It's all right,' he said unconvincingly.

'Would you prefer something else?' she asked.

'There isn't anything else.'

'I've got something in me bag.'

'What?'

'A special, a Carlsberg Special.'

Brennan said yes. The fact that she was offering him a drink said something. It meant she must like him. Why else would she offer? She didn't have to.

Brennan took a gulp of the Carlsberg. The gas seemed to shoot up his nose. He spluttered and sneezed. He was terrified that the front of his jacket might be covered in snot. She passed him a tissue.

'Tell us about the world, Brennan,' she said.

'The world?' said Brennan.

'Yes, the world. The world that you've seen every part of.'

Shag Hackett, thought Brennan. Just when everything was going okay. Just when he thought he was getting somewhere. Shag Hackett.

Brennan had a decision to make. Would he spoof or be honest? He knew what Hackett would do, but he wasn't Hackett.

'Well,' she teased, 'what about the world?'

'The world,' he said with a sigh.

He looked at her closely. He felt that his next remark would be the decider. If he spoofed and was caught he was finished.

'Hackett was spoofing,' he said.

'You haven't seen the world then?'

'No.'

'Neither have I,' and she smiled.

He was so relieved. He sighed loudly. He sat down, then stood immediately and asked her would she like to sit. They both sat. He sighed again. He looked over at her and she smiled. He felt like holding her hand, but didn't. That might be too great a move. It was all right to touch while dancing, but not while sitting together.

'Why are you so uptight, Brennan?'

He could feel his whole neck and face glow. He didn't know what to say.

'Well, why?'

'Uptight?'

'Yeah, uptight.'

'Do I look uptight?'

'To me, yes.'

He had watched Fay and Hackett, marvelled at how confident they were, often wished that he had their composure. Instead he was a bag of nerves and now a woman had noticed.

'Are you nervous or what?'

107

'Nervous of what?'

'I don't know. Girls?'

If he said yes he feared she was gone. Maybe she was looking for the confident type and all this talk was an excuse to walk away. What was he to say?

'I don't know,' he said.

'You don't know what?'

'I just don't know.'

He felt he was a child again at home, a child caught without an excuse for doing wrong. It was always easier to say you didn't know. If you knew, there had to be reasons and explanations; if you didn't, you couldn't be blamed.

But Brennan *did* know. He knew that he was nervous of women. He was intrigued by them, besotted by them, but in his heart he had no confidence to deal with them as equals. He felt threatened by them. He felt they had the capacity to expose him.

All his thoughts about going *all the way* were a thing of the past. Even if Fiona wanted to, would let him, he was sure that no amount of drink or stimulation would give him the courage to go the distance. He felt that familiar sense of despair, that pervasive sense of self-doubt that continually stalked him. He wanted the night to end and be allowed to go back to looking at women from afar.

He thought of the woman at the window. He thought of the dirty magazines and the cheap thrills they gave him. And with each thought he felt the shame of it all and the impotence to do anything about it.

He was now confronted with reality. A wound had been opened and its exposure was hurting deeply. The more he thought about it, the more embarrassed he became. He wanted to tell her that his silence was not meant as an insult. He liked the girl. He would have loved to have been able to relax with her.

'Tell us why you don't know,' she asked. Her tone was sympathetic. She seemed really interested.

He rubbed his face in his hands. He was deeply uncomfortable and it showed.

'Is it that bad?' she asked.

He began regretting that he had ever asked her to sit down. It seemed like a good idea, but now he was trapped with nothing to say.

'It's very stuffy in here,' she said. 'How about some air?'

With unspeakable relief Brennan stood and followed Fiona out to the garden, his mind racing as he walked.

CHAPTER THIRTEEN

Brennan had never been invited anywhere by a woman but as he followed Fiona outside he felt a sense of achievement. As he left the shed he looked back at the others. He wanted them to see him leave, to have them believe that Brennan had clicked, that he was on his way to a space of intimacy with Fiona, that he was going to go *all the way*.

It was a warm night. The skies were clear and already a sprinkling of stars had appeared in the sky. Fiona walked across the garden. Brennan followed, but as he walked he felt unsteady on his feet. The sudden blast of air was having an effect.

He walked slowly towards her.

'You're the silent one all right,' she said, taking out a packet of cigarettes and offering him one. They both lit up and sat down on a couple of tea-chests that Fay had cleared from the shed. As Brennan smoked he was careful not to inhale too deeply, he didn't want his head to spin.

'What did you think of in there?' Fiona asked, nodding in the direction of the shed.

'It was all right.'

'I didn't like it much,' she said. 'I prefer it here.'

Brennan looked at her intently. She smiled warmly.

Inside the shed the music was blaring. Brennan wondered how they all were getting on. He knew Fay would be doing fine. Hackett too, but the Scout and Rob were probably struggling.

Out of the corner of his eye he could see Fiona looking up at the sky. Then she lowered her head and turned towards him.

'Why did you come here tonight?' she asked, and before he could answer she warned him not to say that he didn't know.

'I came for the party.'

'Yeah, but why?'

'To have a laugh.'

'That all?'

He couldn't tell her that he came to meet a woman and go all the way. He couldn't say that. Nor could he admit the week of anxiety he had been through, how all his waking moments had been preoccupied by sex. At one stage, he had seen himself not just being with one girl but more, deluding himself that he was some modern day Casanova. Or maybe James Bond in the movies. James Bond was never stuck for a line. He had women all over the place in cars, in planes, in beds the size of football fields. Even under water. Shaken but not stirred. Brennan's mind was racing.

As he sat in the garden with Fiona, all these images embarrassed him.

'What's your real name?' she asked. 'I can't keep calling you Brennan.'

The fact that she asked such a question gave him hope. She said, *'keep calling.'*

'Everyone calls me Brennan.'

'Yeah, but what's your real name?'

'Frank. At home I'm Francis.'

'I'll call you Frank. So what do we do now Frank?'

'What do you want to do?'

She smiled, drew her head back and looked at him.

'You know,' she said, 'you'd look a lot better if your hair was shorter.'

He liked her talking like that.

'All those curly bits at the end don't really suit you.'

'These bits?'

'You don't mind me saying?'

He loved her talking like that. No one except his mother ever spoke about his appearance. And she just seemed to bark. That tiny woman, the width of a brush handle, with a mouth that rarely closed.

111

'So Frank, what will we do?'

'Do you want to go back inside?'

'Not really.'

'So what then?'

'I don't care, but let's do something.'

Brennan was ecstatic. A woman had actually asked him to do something with her. She didn't want to go back to her friends. She wanted to stay in his company. That meant he'd scored with a bird. A woman beside him, a real woman, not some figment, not some imaginary creature. He almost said a prayer in thanksgiving, but rejected that notion in case he might be praying for forgiveness later on.

He started to relax. The furrowed brow smoothed over, the tightness in his face loosened up. He even started to smile.

'What's so funny?' she asked.

'Nothing.'

'Go on, tell me, what's so funny?'

'Nothing.'

'Tell me. I want to know.'

'It's just . . .I don't know . . . I just em . . . It's just nice being here.'

'You're a strange one,' she said and she laughed.

He laughed too. He never remembered laughing real laughs with a girl. Real ones, not put on, or forced. Genuine laughter. He could feel a tenseness fall away from his body. A feeling of relaxation evolving. He had a sense that something had happened, that he had crossed some obstacle; the fear of females, the lack of confidence in their company. He hoped this feeling would last. He knew the talking would still be hard, but maybe that too might ease.

'So tell us about your world, Frank?'

'My world?'

'Yeah your world. What do you do? Where do you go? Have you got a girl?'

'No,' he said, 'no girl.'

She pulled closer to him. She looked into his face. He thought she was going to kiss him.

'You've a bit of an eyelash in the corner of your eye,' she said, looking closer.

He lifted his hand to brush it away.

'Leave it,' she said, 'I'll get it.'

She leaned the palm of her hand on his face as she fished the eyelash away with her fingers. Her wrist was close to his nose. He sniffed the fragrance of her scent. It was delicate and sensuous.

'Got it,' she said as she took her hand away. 'What now?' she asked.

He had no idea what to say.

'Do you know what I'd like?' she said.

'What?'

'I'd like a bag of chips, I'm starving.'

'Me too,' he said.

Then she leaned over and kissed him, it was not long and passionate, but tender and moist. She pulled her head back and stood up. He sat for a moment as if coming to terms with something that was very special.

Then he stood up and together they left the party behind, the throbbing sound from the shed, the condensation running down the window and a mixture of confused emotions in the den of a thousand promises.

CHAPTER FOURTEEN

Inside the shed the music blared. Fay and Hackett were doing well with the girls, Sally and Jean. Fay had progressed from earlier fingering the strands of her hair to deep snogging on the mattress. Hackett was in the corner and beneath the pampas grass the action was earnest.

Susie and Cathy refused to dance any more with the Scout or Rob. Neither would they entertain any amorous advances. They sat together smoking and sipping beer. They were fed up and only stayed because the shed was a safe haven for drinking.

The Scout and Rob sat at the table. Rob had difficulty staying awake and each time he nodded the Scout prodded him in the ribs.

In an effort to create more privacy Fay had blown out most of the candles. Both he and Hackett cursed the fact that the boys had not made it with the women. It was uncomfortable to be entangled in a heavy embrace with an audience looking on. Fay suggested that the boys might like to go into the house but neither of them took the hint. Perhaps they felt that there still was hope with the women.

The Scout couldn't take his eyes off Fay's woman. She lay flat out on the mattress and her tiny miniskirt had worked its way up her body. It was more exciting than some of the magazines his brother brought back from the navy. He wished he was Fay. He wished he was anyone other than the lonely figure sitting there, looking longingly at his friend having his way with a stunner. It wasn't fair. Even Brennan got a bird and, maybe he too was having his way up in Harry's bedroom.

As time drifted by, the Scout gave up all hope that his fortunes would change. He sat there bored. He wished the so-called party was over. He hadn't long to wait.

After drinking more beer, the women in the corner decided that they needed to visit the bathroom. They stood and swayed towards the door, then headed for the house. The Scout watched them pass by.

The Scout nudged Rob. He wanted to get out of the place. He was sure that Rob, given the drink he had consumed, would need help. He had been burping and farting for ages.

Then suddenly the door burst open. It was Susie.

'Cathy is locked in the jacks,' she shrieked.

The Scout was delighted. Fay and Hackett groaned.

'Will someone do something? She's locked in the jacks I said.' Fay sat up. Babs pulled her miniskirt down.

'She's stuck in the jacks, Fay.'

'I heard you.'

'Well, do something. She can't get out.'

'It's that fucking lock again,' said Fay as he rolled off the mattress.

They all followed Fay out to the garden and into the house. They climbed the stairs to the landing. Fay looked at the toilet door.

'Ah no,' he cursed, 'she didn't lock it, did she?'

'And what are you supposed to do with a toilet door? Leave it open? And have anyone who likes barge in?'

'The lock's jammy,' said Fay.

'Well someone should have said, shouldn't they?'

The lock on the toilet door was one of the myriad of jobs that Harry had made a mental note to attend to. But jobs around the house were not something he found pressing. He had far more important issues in life such as art and wine and music. Anyway, why did they need a lock? After all there was just himself and Vincent living there?

The problem with the lock was age. Years of turning the key had worn the teeth down. The internal mechanism had worn away. The key was no longer capable of moving the parts, so they didn't turn it at all.

Fay stood outside the door and spoke to Cathy inside.

'Cathy, try and turn the key gently.'

'What?' she shouted back.

'Turn the key gently.'

'Right.'

They all waited in silence.

'Did you try it?' said Fay.

'Yes.'

'Well try again. Turn it now.'

'I'm turning it now.'

'Gently Cathy, gently.'

'I am being gentle.'

'Well be more gentle.'

'It's no use, Fay.'

'Try again, gently.'

'I can't.'

'Yes you can.'

'I can't stay here all night trying to turn a key.'

'You'll have to.'

'It's no use, Fay.'

'Try again, Cathy.'

'This is fecking ridiculous, Fay. The lock is broken. It won't turn Fay. Do something. Fayyyyyy!'

The Scout was hugely enjoying it all. He was delighted that Cathy was stuck inside.

Then Susie, the other one, joined in.

'What are you going to do Fay? You can't leave her in there all night. What are you going to do?'

'I'm thinking.'

'Well you'd want to think fast because she has the key of my house in her bag.'

Great, thought the Scout. The other bitch is in trouble as well.

'You'll have to break the door down,' said Hackett.

'I can't break it down.'

'Can you not dismantle the lock from out here?'

'How can I dismantle it when the lock's inside? I'm not fucking Houdini.'

'Cursing is not going to solve the problem,' whinged Susie.

Then Hackett's girlfriend joined in.

'It's ridiculous,' she said, 'having a lock on a toilet door that doesn't work. Ridiculous. Can you not do something?'

'I'm trying.'

'Well I don't see much effort.'

Fay was about to say something deeply offensive but he held back. He was in a deep quandary.

'Can you not think of something?' he said to the Scout.

Even if the Scout had the perfect solution, he wouldn't have said a word. He wanted the show to go on. What had he to lose? The party was over. And he hadn't scored.

'I don't know what to do,' said the Scout, 'I'd say she's stuck in there for the night. You won't be able to get a locksmith until tomorrow.'

'She has the key to my hall door.'

Then they thought they heard whimpering sounds from inside.

'What's happening out there?'

'Are you all right, Cathy?' asked Susie.

'No, I'm not all right. Get me out of here. Get me out.'

'We're trying,' shouted Fay.

'You're doing nothing.'

'Get me out of here. Get me out.'

'Ah shut the fuck up,' shouted Fay.

'What did you say?'

'Was it not loud enough for you?'

Then Hackett had an idea.

'If we can't open the lock and we can't break down the door, there's only one other way.'

117

They all looked at Hackett.

'She'll have to go out the window.'

'Brilliant,' said Fay.

'How will she get down?' demanded Susie.

'Down the drainpipe,' answered Fay.

'Hang on a minute,' said Fay as he rushed down the stairs and into the back garden to look up at the toilet window. Hackett went with him.

'If she's any good she could climb down,' said Fay. 'You stay there and I'll go back upstairs and get her to open the window.'

Back on the landing all the women had their faces pressed to the door trying to console their trapped friend.

'Okay, Cathy?'

'Don't worry, Cathy.'

'It'll be okay, Cathy.'

'Don't worry.'

But she was worried. She was demented. She was sobbing, sending out despairing messages that none of them could assuage.

'What's going to happen me?'

Then Fay arrived back on the landing. The others moved away from the door.

'Cathy, can you open the window?'

'What?'

'Open the window.'

'I'll freeze.'

'She will Fay, she's only got a light dress on,' said Susie.

'Open the bloody window.'

'Why?'

'Open the window and look out.'

Fay rushed down the stairs again to where Hackett was standing beneath the window. They both looked up.

'Open it, Cathy. Open it.'

118

Slowly the window was opened. A head appeared and looked down.

'See that drainpipe, Cathy?'

'Which one?'

'The one to your left.'

'What about it?'

'Could you reach over to it?'

'For what?'

'To climb down it?'

Loud profanities came from the window. She screeched at Fay.

'You want to kill me.'

'Try it, Cathy.'

'Are you mad, I'll kill myself.'

Then the girls appeared in the garden beside Fay and Hackett. They looked up at their friend.

'That lunatic,' Cathy cried out, pointing at Fay. 'That lunatic wants me to climb down the drainpipe.'

'I asked you to try it.'

'Well I won't, I won't, I won't.'

Then Susie spoke.

'Cathy, can you drop down my key?'

'What key?'

'They key to my house. It's in your bag.'

'I'm stuck up here and all you can think of is your key. You're some bitch.'

The Scout who was standing in the background almost cheered. The prim and proper girls were now fighting among themselves.

'There's only one solution,' said Hackett. 'Get a ladder. Get a ladder and get her to climb down.'

'Where will we get a ladder?'

'Search me.'

'Would you climb down a ladder, Cathy?' said one of the women.

119

'What?'

'A ladder, would you climb down a ladder?'

'I'm afraid of heights.'

'For fuck's sake,' blurted Fay who was rapidly losing his normally laid-back composure.

Then the shed door burst open and out came Rob Finnegan. He looked up at the window.

'What's she doing up there?' shouted Rob before swaying, then staggering back into the shed.

'Get me out of here!' screamed Cathy. 'Get me out of here!'

The boys huddled together and tried to figure out where they might find a ladder. Mentally, they went through every garden on the street. Who'd have a double extension ladder? There was only one person they knew. Old man Brennan had one, a heavy old timber cumbersome thing. But they couldn't call and ask old crabby Brennan for the ladder. He'd want to know why. He'd want all the details. Brennan would have to get it. But where was Brennan? They searched all over the house. But there was no sign of their friend.

CHAPTER FIFTEEN

There was always a long queue in the chipper after the pubs had closed. The customers stood in an orderly line along the stainless steel cooking vat waiting their turn. Long ray, fresh cod, and burgers; everything covered in a thick coating of batter before being dropped into the fat.

Mr Cassoni wrapped the chips for Brennan.

'Salt and vinegar?' he asked.

'Plenty of salt, no vinegar.'

Brennan and Fiona left the chipper and walked out onto Drumcondra Road. Brennan loved the chips in early summer. The new potatoes were special. They were clean and fresh and had less black eyes.

They walked past the Cat and Cage. Outside a group were arguing about football - something to do with a disallowed goal in Tolka Park the previous weekend.

Passing the teacher training college, Brennan shook up his chips. There was nothing worse than the salt congealing on the top. Outside the college, a group of students were babbling away in country accents. Brennan and Fiona walked on.

They stopped at the cinema. They looked into the glass case outside the cinema to see what was showing. Two colour photos depicted the action of some war movie. Brennan hoped that he might get the opportunity sometime to take Fiona, sit in the back row, allow his hand reach behind her seat and find her shoulder to rest on. If she didn't resist he would be made.

They walked over the bridge past Lemon's sweet factory and down by Fagan's public house towards Botanic Avenue. When they finished the chips Brennan stuffed the empty chip bag into his pocket. Fiona began to link him, holding his arm gently. Brennan felt good about having a woman attached to him. He felt manly and mature. He would have liked to tell her how much he loved having her by his side. He wanted to say romantic things, but he couldn't think of the words. He would have liked to tell her that she was the best thing to happen to him in ages, maybe ever.

They walked along by the high green railings of Griffith Park. Through the bars Brennan could see the dense shrubbery and foliage, the sort of location that his imagination would take him in flights of fancy about sex. But he wasn't thinking about sex. Kissing her, yes, but not going all the way. Anyway, he might be useless when it came to the act.

Fiona lived in a more modern house than Brennan, a semi-detached one with a driveway. A new Corsair was parked outside. She led him past the house and into a small laneway behind a newsagent's shop. She turned to face him.

'Well,' she said.

'Well what?'

She smiled. He looked into her face, her blue eyes, the soft down of her fair hair above her pouted lips.

'Well,' she said again. 'Did you like tonight?'

'Yeah, I did,' he said.

He didn't know what to do now. He was terrified of rejection.

'I suppose I'd better go in,' she said.

This was the moment he had been dreading. How did you ask her for a date? What if she said no? But if he didn't ask, it would all be over and she would be out of his life for good.

'I suppose I'd better go in,' she said again.

'I suppose,' was all he could manage.

'Is that all you can say?'

'No.'

'Then say something. Talk.'

'Okay, okay.'

'I'm listening.'

'I was wondering. . .'

'Wondering what?' she said after a long pause.

Brennan let out a heavy sigh.

'I was just wondering. . .'

'Yes?'

'Would you like to go out sometime?'

'Yes, I would.'

Relief flooded through Brennan. He smiled at her and she smiled back. Then she moved closer and pressed her lips against his. She was a tender kisser. She opened her lips and so did he. He could taste a trace of lipstick. He opened his mouth a little wider and she responded. She stroked his lips with her tongue. She was leading the action. She held him tightly, pressing her body against his. He could feel the arousal growing. He felt sure that she could feel his erection. Then she broke away.

'I'd better go in,' she said.

'Okay.'

'Thanks for the chips and all.'

'That's okay.'

'See you, Frank.'

'Right.'

'Have you forgotten something?'

'What?'

'The date?'

'Where would you like to go?'

'You decide.'

'The pictures?'

'The pictures. Sunday night?'

'Great.'

'What time?'

'Half seven outside the park gate?'

'I'll be there.'

And then she kissed him again, a short one this time, before walking away. He followed and watched her walk up her driveway. At the door she paused and turned to wave. He waved back.

He stood looking at the house for a time watching the lights go on and off. It was like tracing her movements, imagining her moving around the house. He saw a light go on upstairs at the front of the house. That must be her bedroom, he thought, the love of his life, Fiona. He wanted to shout out her name.

When her light went out, he walked on. Then he started to run madly waving his fists in the air. It was as if he had scored the winning goal in the Cup Final. It was unrestrained joy, pure bliss as he had never experienced before. It was better than going all the way, much better. She was brilliant. She was lovely. Not alone good looking, but great to be with. She seemed to understand him already. She was patient when he couldn't find the words. She teased him playfully. Not once did she mock. It was love. It had to be. There was no other word for it. Love, real love. It had to be.

When he stopped running he licked his lips searching for a taste of her. He wanted that taste forever. He stopped on the steps of Mannix Hill and lit a cigarette. As he blew out the smoke he pictured her. He saw the smile on her face. What a feeling this love was. Then he broke into a run again. He bounded up the steps of the hill two at a time.

This was the best night of his life. Frank Brennan had a real woman now. He didn't need to look up at strange windows from dark lanes. He didn't need to sweat over Fergus O'Neill's dirty magazines. All he needed now was to gaze at Fiona. He must get a photograph of her. He would give her a photograph of himself. But he'd wait until he got his hair trimmed, wait until all the curly bits fell onto the floor of Paddy Fallon's barber shop. Yes, he would get his hair cut tomorrow. He wouldn't wait. He would have his new style by Sunday. That way she'd know that her advice was important to him.

The he began to sing. It was that Gene Pitney song, the one that was playing when he asked her to dance – *Something's Gotten Hold Of My Heart*. He must buy the record. Maybe he'd give it to her as a present, a souvenir of their first night. He tried to remember the lines. This was their song and he must know all the words. Gene Pitney was brilliant. He hadn't thought much about the singer up to then, but now he was great. Maybe Gene Pitney might be coming to Dublin. That would be cool. He'd take her to a Gene Pitney concert, maybe get his autograph. A dedication. To Fiona, from Gene.

He ran the full length of Hollybank Road. He was almost home. Then he stopped. Slowly he walked on. The night was warm, the sky well lit by a bright moon and a rich scattering of stars. Tonight he would lie awake and think of Fiona. He was thinking of her now, her tenderness, the way she moved towards him in the garden, the way she kissed him. He could still remember the softness of her lips, a sensation that excited him beyond anything his imagination could create. And her smell, something he had not experienced before, not strong or overpowering like the smell in the bathroom after Maura, but subtle and penetrating like some exotic plant in the glasshouses of the Botanic Gardens.

Tonight he would fall asleep smiling and dream of the woman that had changed his life.

When he turned into his street he knew something was wrong. All the neighbours were standing at their doors pointing and talking. Near the top of the street the reason for the commotion became clear. Outside Fay's door the blue beacon of a fire engine twirled. Beyond it, with its doors open, was an ambulance.

Brennan's first thought was a fire. The candles must have set the curtains ablaze. Or maybe it was a cigarette. Maybe they all were asleep and had been poisoned by fumes.

He walked on slowly, cautiously, full of fear. Then the doors of the ambulance were closed and its siren began to wail. It seemed louder at night-time. He watched as the ambulance drove down the street. Through the back window he saw the outline of figures. Medics working on the maimed? As he came close to Fay's house, Darby Maguire approached him.

'That was some prayer meeting all right,' said the pools' collector with a strong whiff of whiskey on his breath.

'What was that, Mr Maguire?'

'I said that was some prayer meeting and the house full of drunken women. One of them was so bad she locked herself in the toilet and was threatening to kill herself.'

'What was that?' said Fay's neighbour Mrs Hickey.

'A young girl,' said Darby, 'a drunken young girl screaming from Fay's toilet window that she'd kill herself.'

'Mad, they are,' sighed Mrs Hickey.

'Young people today.'

'They're all mad so they are.'

'It's that music they listen to,' pronounced Darby.

'Don't talk to me about music,' said Mrs Hickey. 'You'd want to hear what I've to listen to. If it's not that gibberish the young fellow plays, it's the bloody death march from his father's record player.'

'Was anyone hurt?' asked Brennan.

'No, but it could have been a disaster. They took the girl away in an ambulance.'

'And what about the fire brigade?'

'Your father called them. It was the grace of God that he happened to be putting the milk bottles out when he heard your woman screaming.'

Brennan looked over towards his house. His mother stood on the step. He scanned the crowd for his father. He knew that he would have to show himself to give the old man the impression that Brennan was not at the party. Then he saw him. He walked over slowly.

'Darby Maguire just told me what happened.'

'You were talking to Darby?'

'Yeah, just now. I was on me way home from the chipper,' said Brennan, taking the chip bag from his pocket.

'So where were you tonight?'

'Just meeting some of the lads. We were going over some exam papers.'

'Good man.'

Brennan turned and walked slowly towards his house. All through the conversation with his father Brennan had tried not to talk directly to the old man. He was terrified that the smell of drink might be obvious. As he approached his hall door he thought of Fiona. It was she who had saved him. Were it not for her he would have stayed at the party and now he would be in serious trouble.

He began to hum the tune. Their tune. Tomorrow he would go into town and buy the record.

Tonight, before falling asleep, he would lie in his bed and recall all that happened. He would savour it, every single moment of the most extraordinary night of his life.

CHAPTER SIXTEEN

What had started out as a brilliant idea ended in disaster. Fay blamed Cathy and Cathy blamed Fay.

When they had failed to find Brennan and get the ladder, Hackett came up with the idea of a rope. The idea was that Hackett would climb up the drainpipe, tie the rope around Cathy's waist as a safety harness while she tried to slide down the drainpipe. But, as Hackett began scaling the wall, the girl at the window started to panic. Maybe it was the sight of the noose. Her screaming reached a new level. It was piercing. She kept repeating that she would be killed. And no amount of pleading could calm her.

At eleven o'clock old man Brennan opened his front door. He carefully rolled up a note for the milkman and stuck it in the neck of a bottle. Two bottles, not three.

As he straightened himself he thought he heard a scream. He listened more intently. He heard it again. It was a scream. He closed his door over and walked down the street. It seemed to be coming from Fay's.

'I'll kill meself. I'll kill meself.'

Old man Brennan rushed across the street to Darby Maguire's house. There was no time to lose. Darby had a phone. Nine. Nine. Nine. Old man Brennan told them it sounded like suicide.

Then it was back to the street. Old man Brennan and Darby rushed over to Fay's. They banged on the door loudly. But those inside heard nothing.

Then the flashing blue light of a squad car came into the street. Darby waved it down, told them about the rear entrance and the car took off again.

Meanwhile, in the garden, the sight of the blue light caused more panic. All the girls started to scream. Hackett, who had been half-way up the pipe, dropped to the ground. Fay shouted for calm while the Scout jumped the wall into Hickey's.

In the back lane the squad car came to a halt. The policemen jumped out and scaled the wall. Then they dropped into the garden. No one was to move, no one. Their concern was the girl at the window, the one who was clearly distressed. Everyone in the garden wanted to explain their case, to have their version heard. But the cops didn't want to know.

The smaller of the cops stood below Cathy at the window. He talked to her calmly. Everything would be fine. They'd get her down and set her free. There was no need to jump. She was far too young to do such a thing. By now Cathy's screaming had changed. She was now sobbing deeply in a mournful way.

All the time the radio crackled. The cop turned the volume down. He spoke into the receiver and called for an ambulance and a fire engine to get her down.

He asked Cathy her name, suggested that she move back from the window to try and stay warm. Help was coming and she'd be okay. She seemed to respond, to rely on his word. For the first time since the window opened, she felt she might not die.

On the street the drama was building. The normally quiet and darkened facades were alive with activity. Doors opened one after another and the people poured onto the street. It was like New Year's Eve without the celebration. There was a dark sense of tragedy. The arrival of the ambulance and the fire brigade added to the gloom.

The large red machine came to a halt outside Fay's. The firemen jumped out of their cab and rushed forward. They didn't hesitate. They didn't wait. A well-aimed blow from a heavy lump hammer was all that was needed. The thud was heavy and solid.

129

Fay's newly painted front door gave way, the wood splitting like a wound. The firemen rushed into the house.

The crowd moved forward. They were desperate to see. A nervous babble spread. They were weighing up the outcomes. What if this? What if that? It was just like the news, just like television. Nothing like this had ever happened on the street.

As the news spread the number of onlookers grew. And with each new spectator, the story of the drama became bleaker in the telling.

Finally the ambulance men emerged from the house. The crowd gasped. They craned their necks to see. Where was the stretcher and the dying? But no stretcher emerged. What they saw was the shape of a young woman wrapped in a blanket being led from the house.

The firemen came next. They ambled out of Fay's house and climbed into their cab. The engine fired, the siren sounded and the giant red machine rumbled out of the street.

The crowd hung around for ages. They wanted to know all the details. There was no point in being an eye witness if you hadn't any facts. How could you tell the story tomorrow? How could you share the drama?

Inside the house Fay, Hackett and Rob were telling their story. The girls were present as well. The smaller policeman wrote in his book. He listened to each of their versions.

Between the tears and regrets the picture emerged. It wasn't what it seemed. The girls were particularly remorseful. They dreaded the story travelling home.

Finally the squad car left the street with three of the girls in the back. It seemed that the drama was over. The crowd began to disperse. Their heads held a mix of emotions, a deep relief that no one had been killed, but equally a sense of having been cheated. A spill of blood, no matter how little, always added spice to a story. They would have liked to have been able to say how difficult it was to watch.

When everyone left, Fay surveyed the damage. The freshly painted hall door was banjaxed. It was beyond repair. Upstairs the toilet door didn't need a new lock. It needed a new door. What had been a fine panelled door was reduced to matchwood and splinters. A fireman's axe had done the damage.

In his mind he counted the cost. It wouldn't come cheap. It would all have to be fixed before Harry came home. Where would he get the cash?

It was a chastened Fay who walked down the stairs. A night that had started off with so much promise had ended in disaster. If only this? If only that?

He sat at the bottom of the stairs. What was left of the damaged door creaked in the gentle breeze. Tomorrow he would be busy.

He opened the door under the stairs. Amongst the clutter and the wine bottles was the gas meter. He prayed that its belly was full. Tomorrow he would need to borrow from the Gas Company again.

So much for the night of a thousand promises.

CHAPTER SEVENTEEN

Fay spent the night in a sleeping bag propped against a make-shift door he had erected in the hall. He hadn't really slept. He wasn't overly disturbed by what had taken place. He was more annoyed that the replacement of the doors would interrupt his routine of doing as little as possible. It was, he told himself again and again, a pain in the arse.

As he dozed off he worked out a plan. He would call and see O'Meara the builder who lived down the street. He would plead a case and try to work out a payment plan. Maybe a couple of pounds every week! But Fay held out little hope of getting the builder to agree.

The following morning Fay walked down the street and knocked on the builder's door. O'Meara immediately answered. Fay didn't like the builder. He saw him as a sly type, the sort who would overcharge the vulnerable. And Fay knew he was vulnerable. O'Meara was a small man with a hunted expression on his face. Fay forced a smile.

'Mr O'Meara.'

'Ah, and who have we here?' said O'Meara, in that shrill voice of his that sounded like a bodysnatcher's assistant.

'Mr O'Meara I have a problem,' said Fay.

'Haven't we all son, haven't we all,' said O'Meara in mock sympathy as he rubbed his hands in delight. Fay explained his dilemma and O'Meara jumped at the chance of quoting for the work. He had never been in Fay's house before and this was a golden opportunity to see where the nutcase lived.

An hour later he had surveyed the place. Fay watched as O'Meara did the calculations in his book, scrawling his stub of a pencil across the page and using his fingers to count. It was like watching a child in school.

'Twenty five pounds for the lot,' he said.

'Twenty five pounds?' said Fay in a mixture of dismay and despair. 'Twenty five pounds?' he said again.

'A four panelled door at the front and an inlaid door upstairs.'

'Is that the best you can do?'

'You want it done on a Saturday.'

'I'd say I can get it cheaper than that,' said Fay thinking that a mild threat to take the business elsewhere might work.

'Well if you can do better, off you go,' said O'Meara who began walking towards the door.

'All right,' said Fay.

'That doesn't include the locks or the hinges,' added the builder.

'You're not serious?'

'Oh but I am son, deadly serious.'

'And how much will the locks and hinges be?'

'Hard to say son. Do you want the same type?'

'Exactly the same.'

'Probably hard to get.'

'Okay,' said Fay, 'I'll pay. Whatever they cost, I'll pay.'

Fay decided to abandon his earlier idea of asking for credit. He sensed that O'Meara would say no and maybe abandon the mission. That was too much to risk.

The take from the gas meter was a few shillings short of five pounds. That meant that Fay had to raise another twenty, maybe twenty five. Hackett would have to be consulted.

'What do you want?' said Hackett frostily when Fay called.

'That's some way to greet a friend.'

'You've some neck calling here.'

'Why?'

'Are you stupid or what? Do you not remember last night?'

Hackett had spent the morning and most of the previous night listening to a rant from his old man. Words like disgrace and filth dominated his father's conversation. Hackett had tried to explain it all away. It wasn't a party as such. Apparently the girls from Holy Faith were part of a debating team and Fay invited them round for a game of Monopoly. It was all very innocent. What the boys hadn't realised was that one of the girls had brought drink. The same girl had gone up the stairs to Fay's toilet. She had lifted the lid of the cistern and hidden the bottles of alcohol in the cloudy water. At first nobody noticed. They didn't think it strange that the same girl seemed to be continually in need of the toilet. It was only when she sold Shrewsbury Road for the giveaway sum of ten pounds that they knew that something was wrong.

Hackett told his old man that Fay got extremely annoyed when he discovered that the girls had been drinking. The one who had hidden the bottles took offence. She tore upstairs and locked herself in the toilet. They tried to talk to her, to convince her to flush the drink down the toilet but the girl refused. Instead, she finished the drink that was left. It was then that Fay said he would have to ring her parents. The girl panicked and threatened them all with suicide. That, according to Hackett, was a fact.

Old man Hackett wasn't entirely convinced. He had a real suspicion that the boys had been drinking as well. Hackett eventually admitted to a glass of wine, a sticky red substance he didn't enjoy.

Hackett closed over his door and walked down the street with Fay.

'How much did you say?' said Hackett.

'Twenty five pounds at least.'

'That's a lot of cash.'

'Hackett, I have to get it.'

'How much have you got?'

'About a fiver from the gas meter.'

'And where are you going to get the rest?'

'That's why I'm talking to you. Hackett you're going to have to come up with a plan.'

At around the same time Brennan was sitting in Paddy Fallon's barber shop reading an out of date copy of *Time* magazine. Some article about Fidel Castro. The place was jammed. They sat around the walls reading the sports pages and the racing. The smoke hung like a suspended cloud above them all. Three barbers were in action bent over the heads of their customers, chatting as they clipped.

Brennan hadn't much interest in conversation. He sat gazing into the mirror hoping that the instructions he had given had been listened to. He didn't want the embarrassment of having to complain. Certainly not on a Saturday in front of a room full of customers sitting around the walls.

He watched as the curly bits fell away and a new shape began to show itself. Fiona had been right. Already it was looking better. The new style made him look older, more mature. The entire mass of his hair had been thinned out. He knew that Fiona would be impressed.

He left the barbershop a happy man. He walked onto Drumcondra Road and crossed over to the bus stop. As he stood there waiting he saw Rob, the chemist's messenger boy, descend the hill with another delivery of medicine.

Then a number eleven bus pulled up and Brennan got on. His next destination was the record shop. He wouldn't have to browse. He knew what he had to buy.

Fay made coffee for himself and Hackett in the room that masqueraded as a kitchen. Hackett watched Fay select two cracked cups from the sink. Given the situation he didn't complain. Fay's troubles were bad enough. The place was like a bombsite.

'So what are you going to do?' asked Hackett as he turned the cup round to avoid drinking from the cracked side.

'Do about what?'

'Are you for real? What are you going to do about money?'

'That's your department.'

'My department?'

'Yes, your department. You're the schemer.'

'Now come on, Fay.'

'No. You were part of the problem so you've got to be part of the solution.'

'So all you got from the gas meter was a fiver?'

'That's all.'

'No other money about the house?'

'You joking? Harry hasn't a bean.'

Hackett put down the cracked cup and walked into the hall. The remains of the door hung like a hoarding on a derelict building site. If it wasn't so tragic, it would have been hilarious. Hackett started to laugh. He couldn't help it. He looked at the door. Then he looked at Fay. He tried to stop laughing but it only got worse. He started to splutter through his nose. The whole episode was ridiculous. He pushed the door with his hand. It creaked and groaned as it moved and Hackett nearly collapsed with the laughter.

'I'm glad you think it's so funny,' said Fay who barely got the words out before he too exploded. They rocked with laughter. The tears ran down their cheeks. They were almost sick with it all.

'What would Harry say now?' said Hackett.'If he saw it?'

'I tell you what he'd say,' answered Fay, 'he'd say . . . and wait for it . . . he'd say . . . Entrez si'l vous plait.'

Eventually they settled. They sat in the front room and went through as many fund raising possibilities as they could imagine. The prospect of a collection for the poor was dismissed. So also was a monster raffle. They thought of an auction but couldn't come up with anything that might sell. Finally Hackett summed up the position.

'There's only two ways left,' he said.

'Go on.'

'We either rob something or we pawn something.'

'I'm in enough trouble with the gas meter.'

'Then you pawn something.'

'Like what?'

'Like something that would raise twenty quid.'

Fay stroked his chin, lit another cigarette and entered his dream world. A few moments later he returned.

'There's nothing worth twenty quid here,' he said.

'What about the art?'

'Are you joking? Would you pay twenty quid for any of the stuff here?'

They were stuck. There was no point in even considering the pawn shop unless you had something to sell. Hackett drained his cup. The coffee was cold. Then he had a thought.

'What if we won it?'

'Won it on what?'

'The gee gees. The horses.'

'Are you mad?'

'No, think about it. What if we bet the gas money on a sure thing?'

'It's a mug's game.'

'What choice do we have? Look, Darby Maguire knows all about horses. He wins all the time. He's forever in the bookie's shop. He knows all about tips and form. I'm telling you, Darby is the man. All we have to do is bet the fiver on a horse at four or five to one and we're made. The panic is over.'

Deep in his heart Hackett knew that it was a mad idea. No one really won at horses. If they did, why were the bookies still in business? But what other choice had they? They were in the shit

137

already. What difference does another load of it make? Despite reservations, Hackett was attracted to the excitement of it all. It was something different, a new thrill, a daredevil scheme.

'So what do you think?'

'I don't think we've much of a choice,' said Fay.

An hour later O'Meara's van pulled up outside. The boys went out to look. On top of the van were the new doors. O'Meara was the first to speak.

'Have you the cash son?'

'How much is it altogether?'

'Travelled the town looking for those doors,' began O'Meara.

'So how much?'

'Must have travelled to a dozen places. That right Tom?' he said as he turned towards his assistant.

'That's right,' said the assistant. 'Hard to get any place open on a Saturday.'

'The entire bill,' continued O'Meara, 'comes to twenty nine pounds.'

'Twenty nine pounds?' said Fay.

'And that includes the special discount for a neighbour.'

'A very fair price,' added the assistant.

'So,' said O'Meara, 'do we begin?'

'Sure,' said Fay.

'Yes, but where's the money. We insist on cash up front first.'

'We're going to get it now.'

'That a fact?' said O'Meara.

'Yes,' said Hackett, 'Fay, I mean Vincent here, has to go to the post office to get it.'

'Well we'll wait,' said O'Meara.

'It's just he'll have to go into town because the local post office is closed.'

'And how,' asked O'Meara, 'how do we know that there's enough money in the post office at all?'

'Because,' said Hackett, 'you can look at the book if you like.'

Hackett produced the book and handed it over. He hoped that the builder wouldn't notice that the most recent deposit of thirty pounds hadn't got a rubber stamp beside it. O'Meara took the book and passed it to his assistant.

'Can you make that out?' he asked.

The assistant took the book and peered at it.

'How much is in it?' demanded O'Meara.

'Thirty one pounds four shillings.'

'You sure?'

'Yeah.'

'Really sure?'

'Sure look at it yourself if you don't believe me.'

'Right,' said O'Meara, 'you get the money and we'll start the work and by the time you're back the job will be finished.'

Fay knew that he had been right to call for Hackett. Peter Hackett may have been a lost cause when it came to the academic world, but when it came to scheming and surviving there was none better.

They both left O'Meara and his assistant and walked down towards Drumcondra Road. They didn't talk. They didn't look back. They walked straight on and tried to stay calm. They wanted to shout out and scream their sense of satisfaction.

Hackett was tingling with excitement. The scheme had worked so far. Already the adrenaline was pumping through his body. He was high.

When they reached the corner, they turned and headed in the direction of the bookmaker's. Their pace slowed down. It was as if they began to realise that something strange and foreign, something they knew little or nothing about, yet something they badly needed to exploit, was about to happen.

CHAPTER EIGHTEEN

There was something almost sinister about Kilmartin's Turf Accountant's office on Drumcondra Road. It was a dreary and drab looking place with faded paintwork and darkened windows you couldn't see through. Its exterior had every appearance of a business that didn't care or didn't need to.

The people who frequented this place were not those who walked the parade rings or stood in the stands with binoculars. They didn't have a pass for the members' enclosure or wear trilby hats. These were the ordinary punters who bet their shillings and cheered on their mounts from the high stools of nearby public houses. They didn't have the luxury of a form card. They made do with the racing page in the *Herald*.

When Hackett and Fay reached the place they stood outside for a while. They were reluctant to enter as if this were a strange and foreboding world of adult males.

They watched as a steady stream of people passed in and out. Some of the faces they knew. One was Mr Finnegan, who even at that stage of the day, was twisted. Another was old man Brennan. He was the last person they wanted to meet. Brennan was the sort who would stop and talk with O'Meara the builder and, if he heard that the boys had gone into town to get the money from the post office, old man Brennan would take the same delight as a pantomime character and say 'Oh no they're not!' and the whole scheme would collapse.

Hackett and Fay knew they were in danger. Old man Brennan was heading their way. They had to hide. They'd no choice. The only place to go was Kilmartin's. But as they moved closer to the door an old woman was being helped outside. A man in a shop coat was escorting her towards a car with darkened windows. Hackett looked closely at the woman. The frame, the shape, the outline of the woman, reminded him of someone. But it couldn't be. That woman never left her house, never vacated the sanctuary of her darkened room. Or did she?

Inside the bookie's shop the punters stood around in a preoccupied state. Some scoured the racing pages that hung on the walls. Others listened transfixed as the radio speaker crackled with racing results. There was no emotion in the voice, no sense of sport or excitement. It was matter of fact. It didn't make any difference if you had lost your last bob or won a thousand, the voice was the same impassive droning of fact. Number four first, number eight second, number eleven third, and a photo for fourth. The voice didn't care. You paid your money and you invariably lost.

The temperature inside the place was sweltering. Despite the heat, several of the older men wore their coats. It was a uniform of sorts, a dark coloured gabardine tied with a belt. One of the men examined the runners with a giant magnifying glass. Then he spat on the floor.

The smoke was thick in the place. Everyone seemed to be puffing. The more the tension grew, the more the fumes of tobacco went upwards.

Besides the smoke there were other odours, the strong smell of sweat, the bitter smell of porter and, from the floor, the stench of newspapers as they soaked up the wet from that morning's shower.

The place was crowded. Men pushed and shoved, angled their bodies for a better view of the pages that hung on the walls. Everyone wanted to see the runners. Stronger men made it to the front while the weaker had to crane their necks for a view. All the time that incessant speaker in the corner crackled. Another announcement of despair. Another hope extinguished. Some tore up their betting slips in disgust. Others tried to hide their emotion. Many reached into their pockets and spread the coins they had left along their cupped hands. Would they try again?

Would they try and win back everything that was lost? Or would they drown their sorrows next door?

This was a dark place, a refuge of false hope, a dismal underbelly where there was only ever one winner. And yet they kept coming in. Men in their weekend clothes, men in their working clothes, busmen, coalmen, men in butchers' aprons, men with dogs, men alone with their dreams. They came and they went. Some were new faces. In the main it was the same faces coming back again and again, hoping in vain that something could be salvaged.

The boys found it pitiful. It was hard to remain enthusiastic about their mission. Yet they had to go on. But they couldn't stay any longer in that place.

'That's some fecking place,' said Hackett once they were outside.

'Do you know what it's like?' said Fay. 'It's like the outpatient department in Grangegorman.'

Hackett wondered how Fay could compare the bookie's with the outpatient department of the local mental hospital, but he didn't ask. Maybe Fay had taken old Harry there.

'So what now?' asked Fay.

'We find Darby.'

'Yeah, but where?'

'Where else? Come on.'

Hackett led the way. He headed down the road towards the 'Men Only' bar in Fagan's public house. This was Darby's favourite place. As they pushed the door open the heavy smell of porter hit them. The place was crowded. Two barmen in blue aprons passed out pints of stout across the well-worn timber counter. Hackett pushed his way through the crowd. He looked around, hoping to see Darby. Again he saw many faces he knew.

At the back near the rear entrance there was a crowd gathered around the table. They seemed older that the rest. He carried on and before he could reach them a voice called out. It was Darby on his way back from the toilet.

'What are you doing here? You pair are under age.'
Hackett said nothing. Darby sat down at his table, settled himself and looked again at Hackett.

'I said, what are you pair doing here?'
'Ah leave them, Darby,' said an old boy sitting beside Darby.
'What are you doing here, I said?'
'They're here for a drink,' said Darby's friend and he laughed.
'From what I heard,' said Darby, 'they had enough last night.'
'Sure didn't we all do it, Darby?'
'You might have done,' rebuked Darby.
'Go away with yourself Darby, you were no angel.'
'Well,' said Darby, 'are you looking for someone?'
'We're eh. . . '
'You're what?'
'We're actually eh, looking for you.'
Darby took a large gulp of his drink, licked his lips.
'Me, is it?'
'Yes, Mr Maguire.'
'Well you'd better come over here and sit down.'
Darby and his friend moved around and made space. Hackett and Fay sat.

'Will you have a drink?' said Darby's friend.
'Am I not after telling you that they are under age?'
'Ah get them a drink for God's sake. No one will see them down here.'
'Do you want me to get them drunk?'
'We were all young once Darby. You know he was a terrible man himself.'
'You hold your tongue,' barked Darby.
'Well are you going to introduce us or what?' said Darby's friend.

Darby seemed reluctant at first to introduce the boys as if to do such a thing might confer a certain status on the pair. Darby's friend stretched out his hand and it was then that the introductions were made.

The boys discovered that their new acquaintance was Tom Crosby, an old school pal of Darby and a fellow collector of the pools. Crosby had a weather-beaten look about him. His cheeks had a purple hue and the white of his eyes had yellowed. When he laughed the teeth he had left were heavily stained and below his flared nostrils, his thin moustache was tinged with smoke.

'You collect the pools as well, Mr Crosby?'

'I do son, I've been doing it for years.'

Then there was a pause. Darby was waiting for further information. He didn't want to appear too anxious to hear why they wanted to see him. Finally he could contain himself no longer.

'So why were you looking for me?'

'It's eh, it's eh. It's kind of embarrassing,' said Hackett.

'Go on,' said Darby. 'You can talk freely in front of Mr Crosby.'

'We have a problem,' said Fay.

'Join the club,' said Crosby and he laughed.

Darby shot a look of rebuke at Crosby and the laughing stopped.

'Go on,' said Darby with a serious tone.

'We're looking for your advice.'

Darby sat up. He liked the role of advisor and counsellor, the status and importance of such a position.

'I'm listening.'

Fay found it hard to put the words together, not because of any deficiency in his command of language, but principally because he was sitting beside a friend of his old man and he was about to ask advice on how to deceive his father. Fay looked over at Hackett.

'You tell him,' he said.

'Go on,' said Darby, 'we haven't all day.'

'It's very delicate,' said Hackett. 'Very delicate.'

'It's not women problems, is it?'

At the mention of women, Crosby leaned closer.

'Go on, you can tell Mr Maguire. He'll know how to help.'

'It's not about women,' said Hackett and once he had spoken he could immediately detect a sense of disappointment in Crosby's expression. Hackett continued,

'It's much more serious than women.'

Crosby took a large swallow of porter. Darby added some water to his whiskey and downed the lot in one go.

Hackett was about to continue but Crosby held up his hand.

'Hold on,' he cautioned, 'we'd better get another round first.'

'Good idea,' said Darby as he waved his hand at the floorwalker.

'A pint and a small one,' said Darby.

'And what about the boys?' asked Crosby. 'Get them a couple of glasses of ale.'

Darby relented and agreed that the boys be allowed a glass, but just one. They sat back again. Crosby lit up a Gold Flake cigarette and burst into a splutter of coughing.

'You'd want to give those bloody things up,' said Darby.

'There, you see,' coughed Crosby, 'full of advice he is.'

When the drink arrived and after the empty glasses had been removed, the ashtray emptied and the table wiped down they were ready. It was like a ceremonious preamble to the dispensing of advice.

'Now,' said Darby, 'you were saying.'

Crosby pulled closer. Fay looked over at Hackett and nodded. Hackett hesitated. Crosby took a long drag on his smoke.

'Go on,' ordered Darby.

'We're in trouble, Mr Maguire.'

'Serious trouble,' added Fay.

145

'We need to raise twenty five pounds.'

'Are yiz taking the boat? Are yiz going to England?'

'No, Mr Maguire, but if we don't raise the money we might have to take the boat.'

'And why do you want that sort of money?'

'Tell him,' said Fay, wondering what Hackett would come up with. Hackett took a deep breath and covered his face in a shroud of sorrow. He furrowed his brow, he dropped his head, he swallowed deeply.

'We need the money,' Hackett said in a loud whisper, 'we need the money to send a crippled child to Lourdes.'

Fay looked at his friend in awe. How did he come up with such an idea? The man was a marvel, a total genius.

'Yes,' began Darby, 'but how does sending a child to Lourdes land you in such terrible trouble?'

'Trouble worse than woman,' added Crosby.

'Because, Mr Maguire, we promised. Me and Vincent here promised, promised ages ago, to raise the money and we tried, we really tried. We had a collection box in both our schools and when we opened them today this is all that was inside.'

Hackett placed the bag of shillings from the gas meter on the table. The two old men looked at the bag, looked at the boys and then looked at each other. Darby opened the bag and fingered the shillings.

'All shillings, strange that!' mused Darby.
Crosby lit another Gold Flake. Darby sipped his drink, and as he put it back down on the table wiped his lips with the back of his hand. Then he looked at Hackett.

'Well it's original, I'll give you that.'

'A twelve year old girl who can't walk,' said Hackett, 'and we promised her and her family. We gave our word and that's why we're in so much trouble.'

Darby looked at Crosby. Then Crosby spoke.

146

'And why,' Crosby enquired, 'why, if you don't mind my asking, are you consulting my friend here, Mr Maguire?'

'Because,' said Hackett, 'this five pounds has to become thirty pounds before the day is out and we think that you two men here, with your special experience, are the ones who could do it for us.'

From the expressions on their faces Hackett felt he was doing well. The two old boys were clearly enjoying the deference to their seniority. Too many young people dismissed the wisdom of their elders, dismissed the counsel of experience that comes with age.

'You're our only hope,' said Fay.

'That's right gentlemen. We've come to you because we believe that you are the ones who can help bring that little child to Lourdes.'

'And how,' Darby enquired, 'how may I ask is this five pounds here to become thirty before the day is out, if that's not too complex a question?'

The old men nodded to one and other. That last statement was a true and accurate summary of the situation. They liked the almost legalistic tone of the enquiry.

'There's only one way,' said Hackett, 'we'll have to put the money on a certainty to win in the bookie's.'

'What?' spluttered Darby, 'you want to put the collection box on a horse? You can't do that, can you?'

'We've no choice,' said Hackett. 'Otherwise the poor girl won't go to Lourdes.'

'And what if you lose?'

'Then the child's no worse off than she is now. At least she's some chance with the bookies.'

'I don't know,' said Darby. 'What do you think?'

'Me?' asked Crosby.

'Yes, you. What do you think?'

'It's getting very late.'

'I can read the time. What do you think?'

147

'There were a couple of horses I fancied at Leopardstown.'

'You never said.'

'You never asked.'

'Will we do it?' said Darby.

'It's a good cause,' answered Crosby.

'It is,' said Darby, 'but first we'll organise another drink.'

It was after six o'clock when Hackett and Fay walked up the road towards home. It had been one of the most stressful days of their lives. They had spent almost four hours with the pools collectors. During that time they had watched the old boys in action as they scoured the papers, checked the form, argued about the merits of various horses and jockeys and discussed the ground conditions on every track in the British Isles.

Long before the first bet was laid the tactics were set out. It would not be wise to risk the entire five pounds on the head of one nag. They reasoned that a two pound straight bet to win on an odds-on favourite at Chester should be the first piece of business. Both of them agreed on the horse.

The bet was placed and they sat in the pub to watch the race. At the last minute the horse was withdrawn. At least the money was saved. Then another detailed discussion began as to what should be done. Another horse had to be selected. Reaching an agreement on an alternative was not easy. Darby and Crosby argued loudly. Finally agreement was reached and another bet was placed. But that ran into trouble too.

When they returned to the pub to watch the race they discovered that it wasn't being televised. The old boys were not happy punters. They sat glum faced inwardly accusing the other of making a tactical blunder.

To discover the winner Hackett was sent into the bookie's. They watched his face as he returned. They didn't like his expression.

'It's a photo finish,' Hackett said.

This meant another wait, another period of tense uncertainty. Hackett was again dispatched to the bookie's. This time when he came back, he was beaming. The four year old mare had done the business and the two pound became four. Now they were moving.

Fay was sent out to buy copies of all the newspapers. The table was cleared and the racing pages put down. Never had the customers in Fagan's seen Darby and Crosby so engrossed in racing. Normally these two quiet and reserved men would have placed their bets early in the day and watched the racing from their usual seats near the door. Never would they have been loud or argumentative. That had changed. They were now almost frantic, writing down bets, crossing them off and tearing into Kilmartin's.

After an hour the purse had grown to twelve pounds. Up to that point their tactic had been cautious, speculating the winnings and never risking the seed capital. But time was moving on and there were less and less races to choose from.

By this stage Crosby's blotchy skin was heavily flushed and he was into his second packet of Gold Flake. His clothes were covered in ash. Darby's nose was glowing. He was drinking whiskey as if prohibition were looming.

They decided to continue their single bet strategy. A horse at the Curragh was selected and Hackett was sent with the bet. Throughout the pub the rumour had spread that something strange was happening. Darby and Crosby said nothing but it was obvious to everyone that the old boys were deeply involved in something unusual.

When the time arrived for the race at the Curragh the pub almost turned violent. The crowd down one end were appealing for the channel to be changed. They wanted to watch a race from Ayr. Darby shouted no and he meant it. He stood and told them they were blow-ins unlike himself and Crosby.

But the crowd down the other end did not take Darby's insults lightly. They had rights, and the race at Ayr was special, not some minor gallop of a mile. Darby was livid. He stood on a chair and he shouted.

'Do yiz not know what meself and Crosby are trying to do?'
The crowd took little notice. Darby shouted again.

'Are yiz men or what?'
One or two put down their drinks and Darby, seeing his opportunity, appealed to the one closest to him.

'It's all for a crippled child,' he said, 'a poor unfortunate crippled child.'

'What's he saying?' said one of them.

'Quiet, listen, let him go on.'

'It's a hard man that'll stand in the way of a crippled child, a hard man indeed. Do none of yiz have families of your own? Well do yiz?'

Some of the crowd looked away. Darby knew he was winning.

'How would any of you feel if you had a crippled child and that child was being stopped going to Lourdes?'

'Lourdes? What's he talking about?'

'Well I'll tell you sir. Myself here and my good friend Crosby are trying to raise the money to send a crippled child to Lourdes and you crowd, yes you crowd down there, are standing in the way of that child being lowered into the curing waters of that grotto.'

The crowd became still. There was some minor shuffling of feet.

'Do yiz not realise that what we are doing is for charity? That everything depends on that race at the Curragh? That the money on that race is for the crippled child going to Lourdes?'

'This is crazy,' said Fay.

'Relax,' said Hackett. 'Just look at them.'

Fay turned to see the whole pub in silence. Darby, who had stood down from the chair,was walking down the other end towards the largest of the blow-ins.

'There's going to be trouble,' warned Fay.

'No, Darby is playing a blinder.'

The veins on Darby's neck were pulsing. He faced the man head-on. The man's face was flushed red. He looked like he was deeply embarrassed. The man leaned across the counter and spoke to the barman. A brown paper bag was produced. The man took the bag, opened it, and dropped in a fistful of coins. He passed the bag around to his friends.

'For the child to go to Lourdes,' he said, and the message was repeated as the bag moved around the bar.

They all watched the race from the Curragh. The atmosphere in the place was electric. Everyone began cheering for the horse. They stood on tables and chairs. As each furlong went by the tension grew. It was neck and neck. They willed the horse on. It was if every man in that pub was in the saddle. They took the jumps, they felt the landings, they could feel the wind in their faces. This was their race. Their horse. The horse to take the child to Lourdes.

When the horse finished first they couldn't contain themselves. They rushed for the bar. No one cared whose round it was. Everyone wanted to buy. The last time the older barmen had seen such an outpouring of emotion was when Ronnie Delaney had won gold for Ireland at the Olympics in Melbourne. But this was better. At least Ronnie Delaney could run, could walk, not like the crippled child going to Lourdes.

After they all had been served, the blow-in approached Darby and presented the older man with a large whiskey. They almost embraced. The pub applauded. They were feeling so good about themselves. Imagine going home and telling the wife that the day in the pub had been suffered for Lourdes?

When Hackett returned from the bookie's he presented the winnings to Crosby. The pools collector had been keeping tabs. And now he was about to do his sums for the last time. It was like election time waiting for the votes to be counted. Crosby took his time conscious that the eyes of the place were upon him. He savoured his sense of importance and power. When he finished his calculations, Darby insisted on a recount, anything that might drag the occasion on and extend their time in the spotlight.

Finally Crosby passed a note to Darby. A hush descended on the place. The television was turned down. Darby put on his spectacles. He rose and stood unsteadily.

'Gentlemen of Fagan's,' he said, 'friends all.'

The blow-ins looked at each other with radiant smiles of inclusion. They had been accepted at last. Darby continued when they settled.

'Gentlemen, all of you will be pleased to hear that we have reached our target.'

Loud cheering burst out. Darby waved his arms and appealed for hush. They calmed. Darby went on. By now a tear had appeared in Darby's eye. He wiped it away.

'Yes, we have met our target. In fact we have overshot our target. The fact is that because of the success today on the course and the generous contributions from you all there is a distinct possibility that instead of sending one child to Lourdes, we may now be able to send two. The final figure comes to forty seven pounds.'

It was an hour later before they managed to leave the pub and head up the road for home. They offered to take Darby but the old boy was basking in the glory and wanted to remain centre stage. It wasn't every day that he had something to celebrate, when everyone in Fagan's wanted to buy him drink.

When the boys reached Fay's house O'Meara and his assistant were waiting. The builder was almost at the point of taking the doors down again. He was having doubts about the money.

After they paid O'Meara they went inside. The place was almost the same as they left it. Fay collapsed into an armchair. He looked up at Hackett.

'Hackett you're a wonder. Thanks, thanks a lot.'
Hackett smiled broadly.

'Any drink left?' he asked.

'Plenty.'

Harry's stock was raided again and a cork pulled from another of Harry's favourites. They poured large measures into two already stained glasses. Hackett didn't care. They lit cigarettes and relived the previous twenty four hours, from the exploits in the shed to the final race at the Curragh. They roared uncontrollably at the memory of it all. It was one of the most hilarious episodes of their lives.

'But you know something?' said Hackett sounding a note of caution. 'With the money that's left we'll have to get a child to Lourdes.'

'Why?' asked Fay.

'Why, I'll tell you why, because Darby and old man Crosby will want to know the details. Those wise old codgers will want to know where the child lives. You don't believe for one moment that they are going to take our word for it?'

'Are you sure?'

'Sure, I'm sure and I'll tell you why. I don't believe they swallowed the story at all. I think they went along with it all for the fun. And if we don't come up with the name of a child we are in deep shit.'

'So what do we do?'

'Simple. We go along and meet my good friend Brother Dominic. I might even bring Brennan along with me. We tell him about the generosity of Darby and Crosby and how they made this wonderful contribution. We don't say anything about the gee gees.'

'But if we do that are we not opening up the fact that only one is going, not two?'

'That's no problem. We tell Brother Dominic that the old boys are a bit simple and they thought that they had enough money for two. We ask Brother Dominic to pretend that two kids went. He'll be so delighted with the price of one that he'll say anything.'

'Do you know something Hackett? You're a genius.'

'Yeah, well we'll know soon enough about that when the exam results come out.'

'Don't talk about that now.'

And they didn't.

Sometime later the bottle was drained. And so were Hackett and Fay.

CHAPTER NINETEEN

While Hackett and Fay had been organising the trip to Lourdes for the crippled child, Brennan was in preparation mode for his date with Fiona the following day.

He had been to Paddy Fallon's barber shop and then took the bus to town. Besides the Gene Pitney record he had decided that it would be appropriate that Fiona should have a photograph of him so that she could gaze at him whenever the pangs of separation afflicted her. He entered a three minute photo booth on Henry Street. It took several attempts to get the photograph right. In the first selection of shots he looked too anxious. In the next the stool was badly adjusted so that when the photos came out all you could see was his hair. On the third attempt he was leaning too close to the screen and while the final selection was the best of the lot the lighting gave him the look of a wanted poster in a film.

He was so taken up with his memory of Friday and his success with Fiona that the hours flew fly. This was unusual for Brennan. Normally he was organised and disciplined, compulsively driven by the clock. But on that particular Saturday time eluded him. It was almost seven in the evening before he got home.

It was usual for Brennan to go out on a Saturday night, but somehow he seemed strangely content to stay in and go to bed early. This change of pattern was not lost on the family.

'I'd say he's in love,' said Maura, the bitch, whose mission in life was to stir the pot of trouble.

'Not at all,' said Mrs Brennan as she drew a hairnet over her plumage of rollers.

'A monk with a haircut like that,' answered Maura, 'and the whiff of him.'

Mrs Brennan hoped Maura was wrong. Ever since Brother Dominic had begun calling, Mrs Brennan had prayed earnestly that her son might one day follow in the footsteps of Saint Francis. But Maura wouldn't let go.

'What do you think, Dad?'

'Think about what?' asked Mr Brennan as he polished his shoes before the fireplace.

'Think about Frank and his new hair-do?'

Mr Brennan looked up from the newspaper he was kneeling on. This was all news to him.

'Just a phase,' he said, 'just a phase.'

'Well, I hope you're right,' sighed Mrs Brennan as she looked up at the picture of the Sacred Heart for consolation.

Sunday was a busy day for Fay. For a start, he had to get the hall door painted. Normally this would be a simple business, but to produce a paint brush on the Lord's Day was something that would not go down well on the street.

He set the alarm for five. Before the first of the mass-goers were leaving the street at seven, he had the door painted. Then he went to the shed. He took down the curtains, removed the mattresses and dumped the bottles.

Hackett called down at ten and they started work on the kitchen. Then the Scout arrived to help. At eleven Rob arrived. This was his first appearance since Friday. Sheepishly he made his entrance. His memory of the party was hazy. He couldn't recall sleeping on the mattress. All he could remember was the woman at the toilet window and the pair of cops jumping the garden wall.

When Brennan arrived the work was complete. He found them all relaxing in the front room drinking coffee from clean cups. All of them wanted to know Brennan's story. They wanted to know about Fiona. Had he done the bold thing? Did he get his way? They kept at him.

'Tell us Brennan, tell us.'

'Go on lover boy, tell us.'

Brennan told them nothing. He didn't have to. His look said it all. They became convinced that the shy, silent, reticent Brennan had succeeded where all of the others had failed.

They spent the afternoon in the shed playing poker. Brennan was careful not to speculate heavily. He knew he had to watch his money. The last thing he needed was not having any money should the chance of another date arise.

Around five in the afternoon the card game came to an end. Brennan went home. He didn't eat much at tea-time. His usual appetite had waned. Other things dominated his thinking, the ifs and buts of the impending date and how he would handle the situation. He stood from the table and went upstairs.

In the bathroom he checked the hot-water cylinder. There was just about enough water for a bath. He turned the taps and the water gushed out. He added some of Maura's bath salts. It was a stroke of good luck that she was away for the day otherwise she would have freaked.

He watched the frothy surface of the water rise. Soapy lemon coloured bubbles grew and expanded.

Slowly he lowered himself into the bath. At first the water was boiling and he had to sit up. Then gradually he allowed himself to slide down until both his shoulders were covered. He moved his knees up and down to create a wash. Mini-waves of water washed over him. He started to relax. He thought of Fiona.

In his mind he pictured her face, those soft lips, her blue eyes, the strands of her long fair hair. The thought of her created a slight stirring between his legs. He looked down to see a swelling of glands. He moved his knees again and the water brushed against his partly erect penis. Then he began to sigh softly. It must be love, he thought, it must be love.

After the bath he stood before the mirror. The surface was covered with steam. He wiped the mirror clean with his underpants. Several flecks of fluff stuck to the glass. He wiped them away before lathering his face with his father's shaving brush. Carefully he drew the razor across his face. He didn't want to miss any stubble. It was essential that the surface of his skin be smooth. Several times he covered the same area with the razor. Then he rinsed his face and looked closely into the mirror. No sign of pimples or the dreaded blackheads. He hated blackheads and would relentlessly squeeze his face until the ugly little beads of dirt were ejected. And, finally, several applications of Old Spice were applied. The spirit stung his face and the smell nearly overpowered him.

He dressed in his small bedroom at the front of the house. Every item of clothing was examined in the mirror. He strained his neck to see from the back and the side. Eventually he was ready.

He left the room and descended the stairs carefully, anxious to avoid all the creaking steps. He turned the lock in the hall door delicately. He pulled the door open and was gone.

At the end of the street he turned left and walked the short distance to Hollybank Road. This was the road he had jubilantly run on Friday night. It was here he had sung out the Gene Pitney lyrics. Oh shite, he'd forgotten the record.

For a moment he considered leaving the record but, after all the trouble he had gone to getting it, he turned back. He prayed that his parents would still be in the back room. He was in luck. No one heard him.

Back on the street he checked his pockets again. Money, cigarettes and the record. Despite the fact that he had plenty of time he moved swiftly. He told himself to slow down but his legs didn't seem to heed the command.

Out of the corner of his eye he saw Rob cycling down the road. He knew if Rob spotted him he was likely to follow and relay the information back to the shed. That could not be allowed to happen. Brennan hid behind a tree and waited for Rob to pass by.

At the top of Hollybank Road he turned right and headed for Mannix Hill. From the top of the hill he could see the park gates and all along Botanic Avenue almost up to where Fiona lived. So far there was no sign of her.

It was almost half past seven. He lit a cigarette. Across in the park he could see a group of children playing football. Their coats were piled in heaps to mark the goals. He walked down the steps slowly. As he pulled deeply on the cigarette he noticed that his hand was shaking. He switched the cigarette to the other hand. It was shaking too.

God, this was ridiculous. First the problem with the words, now the shakes as well. He hadn't been shaking the other night. But maybe that was the effect of Harry's wine.

At the bottom of the steps he stood under a tree and strained his eyes for sight of her. She was not to be seen. It was now half past seven. From now on she would be late. She did say half seven. He recalled the conversation. Every word. But where was she?

He lit another cigarette and began climbing the hill again. Then he stopped and turned back. He looked at his hand. The shaking, if anything, was getting worse. God, I'm a mess, he thought. If she didn't want to turn up she could have sent a message. He moved from one foot to the other. Then the Gene Pitney record fell from under his jacket and clattered onto the stone step. He bent down to pick it up. *Something's Gotten Hold Of My Heart* was okay. Brennan was anything but. It was now twenty to eight. He'd give her until quarter to. Lies, he'd wait forever.

Despair began to set in, a dark brooding sadness, a feeling of acute uselessness, a deep sense of being back to where he came from in that dreadful world where womankind were to be gazed at, but not touched. He didn't want to go back there, to seeing

159

women from afar, in magazines, in windows from dark laneways, women who were objects, stimulants for fantasies, not human or real, not gentle and kind, as Fiona had been on Friday night.

It was now quarter to eight. She was fifteen minutes late. They probably wouldn't get in to the Drumcondra Grand now anyway. It was all a mess. All the trouble he had gone to. The haircut, the photograph and the bloody record. Some signature tune that. No chance of hearing Gene Pitney live now. No point, anyway. No dedication to Frankie and Fiona from Gene.

Another cigarette. He noticed that his fingers were getting stained again. It was the way he held the cigarette. He remembered years before when on the way home from the cinema he'd rub his fingers off granite walls to remove the evidence. Ten Woodbines left a lot of residue. He wasn't troubled by women then. Except his mother and Maura. Maura the bitch. Maura, the one who gloated when he got into trouble. And to think she was a woman. How could anyone fancy her? Imagine anyone looking up at her standing at a window? You'd want to be a pervert.

On Friday he thought that he had come of age. On Friday he believed that he had made the journey of true awakening where women could be friends, companions and even lovers. But now, as he stood on that hill, the pangs of doubt returned. Women were not for him because he couldn't find the words to hold them. And now he had the shakes as well.

He decided to wait until eight o'clock. Then he would go back. His sense of being a new man was gone. Instead he was the prepubescent kid again with all the confusion and misin-formation about sexuality. Primarily he felt great sadness. It was like bereavement. Would he ever feel like he felt on Friday again? His mother would say that good things don't last. How did she know? How did she have a monopoly on wisdom? A woman who had never shown him any physical affection in her life? Brennan didn't remember hugs. He couldn't remember the comfort and warmth of arms holding him. He didn't understand love. His mother stood back, stood away. Even when others proffered affection, a kiss, she held back. It was as if she was terrified of affection. She couldn't take it, couldn't give it. Maybe she thought it was a sin.

Brennan decided to go. He had thought about calling up to her house but no, he wouldn't do that. He'd be afraid the words would let him down. Maybe he'd be left on the step speechless. It would be better to salvage what was left of his self-esteem.

He turned and began climbing the steps again. His head hung low as he watched his feet meet each step, lifting his body upwards and onwards on the sad journey home. At the top of the hill he paused for a moment. Turning towards the park he saw the young children gather their coats. The evening for them was over as well.

As he turned to move on he thought he heard his name being called.

'Frankie! Frankie Brennan!'

He stopped and turned. He heard it again.

'Frankie! Frankie! Frankie!'

She was standing at the bottom of the steps. She was waving and calling out his name.

'Come on,' she said, 'we'll be late, come on.'

As he descended the steps the despair began to lift. When he came close to her he thought he saw a mischief in her smile. It was the look of a child caught with a hand in the biscuit tin.

'Frankie, I'm sorry, I really am. You must think I'm awful.'

'No, I don't.'

'Let me tell you what happened.'

'No, it's okay.'

They walked along Botanic Avenue towards the cinema. She linked him on the way. He grew in confidence and composure at the touch and closeness of her. He was back in the promised land. He could walk beside her forever.

She told him how she had to wait for her father to come home so that he could mind her younger brothers and sisters. Her father had been delayed and she couldn't leave the younger children on their own. Brennan wondered where her mother was. He didn't have to ask. She told him that her mother was dead, taken from life by cancer. One day feeling fine, the next some mild pain and six months later the unbearable journey to the family plot in Glasnevin. He was pleased she told him the story. He saw it as a vote of confidence in their union.

His feeling of closeness grew. He felt drawn by her intimacy. He was her man and she was sharing her sorrow. When she finished her story she brought their walking to a stop.

'So you see,' she said, 'at times it can be hard for me to get out.'

'That's okay, I understand.'

'Do you?'

'Yes, I do.'

'You're not annoyed?'

'No.'

He wanted to tell her how privileged he felt at being brought into her life. This he felt sure was a sign that she must have feelings for him. She didn't have to tell him of the agony she had been through. She could have made up a story. He would have believed anything.

They passed the small park beside the river where a group of elderly people had gathered to say the rosary. Brennan knew the place well. His own mother would sometimes go there.

As they crossed over the bridge they saw the queue for the cinema.

'Do you know what's on?' she asked.

'No.'

'No idea?'

'No.'

'Full of information as usual,' she said before starting a fit of the giggles.

They joined the end of the queue. The usher in his plum coloured uniform marshalled the crowd, guiding everyone to the box office. Brennan was worried that the place might be full by the time he got to pay. He was also concerned that all the seats at the back would be gone.

Sunday night was the one time in the week when the couples came out in their droves, when, in the darkness of the cinema, the game of courtship was played out. What was on the screen was of little importance. What mattered was the progress in the stalls where the object of the exercise was to manoeuvre an arm around the back of a seat and draw the woman closer. This was a delicate operation which had to be taken slowly. No sudden movements, just a quiet yet determined progression. If the arm was rejected, then the night would be a failure. If it was allowed to stay, then the evening held the promise of a deeper intimacy.

Brennan paid for two tickets. Luckily there were seats left near the back of the cinema. As they passed the kiosk he thought about buying popcorn. He decided not to. It would be hard, he reasoned, to encourage any romance if they both had their mouths full with tuck. Then they entered the darkness of the cinema. An usher pointed to their seats with the beam of a torch. There were groans and sighs as they pushed along the row. Those already settled resented the disturbance. Maybe they had already made progress and now they would have to start all over.

They both sat back and watched as Pathe News told its stories. Princess Grace of Monaco was holidaying in Switzerland. Bing Crosby played golf with Bob Hope in Florida while closer to home The Queen was holidaying at Balmoral.

All around them the mating game had begun. Seats creaked as bodies moved. Legs were crossed and uncrossed. Heads moved closer to other heads.

The pair directly in front of Brennan were breathing heavily. Every so often the woman would break away from the entanglement and laugh giddily. He seemed to be nibbling her ear. To his right, a female body was turned towards her partner. She kept whispering while he ran his hands up and down her legs. At one stage she started to moan. Then without warning she stretched out her legs and invaded Brennan's space.

Brennan took out his cigarettes and offered one to Fiona. He had to do something. Fiona said no, not now. Instead she reached over and held his hand. He put the cigarettes away. She moved her thumb across his fingers and stroked his knuckles tenderly.

'All right?' she whispered.

'Yeah.'

'Sure?'

'Sure.'

'I'm glad you waited.'

'So am I.'

Beside him the activity was becoming frenetic. The woman was almost out of her seat. She was almost on top of her man who was relentlessly tugging at her clothes. At one stage there was a snap of elastic. And all the time the moaning went on.

Brennan knew he had to act. Almost everywhere he looked the couples were locked in embrace. Eventually he raised his hand and slid it along the back of her seat. She didn't object. Then he let his hand fall forward onto her shoulder. Again no negative response. He began to massage her shoulder and as he moved his fingers she drew closer to him. The strands of her hair brushed across his face. He could smell that familiar scent, that intoxicating aroma. He was in his element. She reached across and held his hand again. Her touch was gentle. She turned her face to him. She was making all the moves.

With eyes closed their lips met. Again, like Friday, she led the way. She moved her mouth across his, her full lips urging a response. Then she probed with her tongue. All of this desperately aroused him. It was like being in the bath. The kissing went on so long that he thought he might faint. It was overpowering. He had not yet mastered the kissing technique of breathing through his nose. Like in the swimming pool he needed to come up for air. He needed a break. Reluctantly he was forced to disengage.

Gently he pulled back. His heart was thumping. He opened his eyes. He was going through one of the most important experiences of his life. He felt energised. A surge of confidence came to him. He was just as good, as competent, as any of the males in that place.

She pulled him close again. She wanted to do it again, recapture the magic of it all. He looked at her in wonder then sucked in some air. He moved closer and, just as he was about to press his mouth on hers, he observed the row behind. More courting couples. More demonstrations of passion. But there was something else there too. A man, a solitary figure, sitting directly behind him, a man who had obviously been watching Brennan's last deep embrace.

Brennan was sure he knew that face. There was something about it. Then the action on the screen changed. From a night-time sequence it moved to dawn. Searing sunshine filled the screen and lit up the cinema. It lit up the man. But worse, it lit up his eyes and one of them reflected the light like a mirror.

The eye was Gormley's eye, the glass eye, the one that had gazed at the woman at the window all those months before. And now he was gazing at Brennan, perhaps reminding him of the evil path he had walked.

A subdued Brennan walked beside Fiona on their way home. Since seeing Gormley all thoughts of romance deserted him. He couldn't bear the thought of kissing her again in full view of the glass eye.

He knew he owed her an explanation otherwise she might think that he had suddenly gone off her. Maybe she might think that her heavy embrace had put him off, that he was a less experienced lover. And that was something he needed to put right.

He cursed Gormley. He hated the man. What sort of man was he? What sort of man would sit in a cinema and watch as the urges of romance were played out?

As he neared her home he prayed that she might speak. He needed her help in opening the discussion. She slowed when she came near her house. Was this the end? The final farewell? She stopped and turned towards him. She fingered the lapel of his jacket. Then she looked up. In her eyes he thought he saw sadness.

Then as before the Gene Pitney record fell from under his jacket. Originally he had intended presenting the record after the cinema. But the Gormley episode ended that. He went to pick it up but she got there first. Instead of passing it back she took the record out of its sleeve. It was as if she was happy to have a distraction. She looked at the title. Then she looked at him. He *had* to speak.

'It's em . . . It's em . . . for you.'

'For me?'

'Yes.'

'Why?'

'Because.'

'Because why?'

'Just because.'

'You bought this for me?'

'Yes.'

'I don't understand. I thought in the cinema . . . '

'I need to explain something.'

She took him by the hand and led him into the laneway. He put his hand on her shoulder and she wrapped her arm around his waist.

Away from the street and in the confidence of the shadows she stopped and spoke.

'Well, tell me,' she said gently.

He found it hard to begin. Eventually with more coaxing he managed to tell her the story of Gormley. Not the full thing, a heavily edited version. No mention of the woman at the window, the cops in the garden, or Brennan's subsequent relationship with the monk. Gormley, he told her was a dirty old man and he didn't want her to be the object of his lecherous eye.

'But why didn't you say?'

He didn't know what to tell her. Instead he sighed. She smiled contentedly.

'And you bought this for me?'

'Yeah.'

'But why?'

'Because it was the record that was playing when we first danced.'

'You're sounding like an old romantic. I like your hair, it suits you, it does.'

'Thanks.'

'It really does.'

'I got you something else.'

'What?'

He rummaged in his pocket and took out the photograph.

'I'm not sure whether you want it or not.'

She took the photograph from him, held it towards the light that came from a street lamp, then looked up at him studiously. It was like a passport check at arrivals.

'You're better looking in the flesh,' she said.

'Do you want it?'

She nodded and put the photo and the record into her bag before placing the lot on the ground. She raised her head and looked at him closely. He started to become embarrassed. Putting her arms around his waist she hugged him deeply and laid her head on his chest.

The earlier confidence he had felt returned. This was love he told himself. The scent of her perfume was magic. He had imagined love before, but nothing like this. Here he was with his arms wrapped tightly around this special person. A mood of relaxation came over him. He sighed almost with gratitude. He felt himself swaying with her. It was as if both their movements were in concert. They didn't speak. They didn't have to. He probably wouldn't have known what to say.

After a time she raised her head and looked up at him. She kissed him deeply. This time there was no need for her to do all the work. He responded instinctively. It was as if he had been doing it all his life.

As they kissed her outstretched fingers began peeling his shirt upwards. She wanted to touch his skin. Her fingers worked on the small of his back. Brennan was in ecstasy. He wanted this to go on forever. She leaned back her head and looked at him.

'Did you enjoy tonight?' she asked him.

'I did.'

'Really?'

'Yeah really.'

'So? I'd better go in.'

'Okay.'

'Is that all?'

'Sorry?'

'Am I going to see you again?'

'Wednesday?'

'I can't. Remember what I said about it not being easy for me?'

'Then, you say.'

'Friday?'

'Friday is great.'

Shortly after she left him in the laneway and crossed the road to her house. At the gate she turned and waved. A blown kiss and she was gone.

Just like the night after the party, he stood outside tracing her movements through the house as lights went on and off. He fixed his stare on her bedroom window. He thought of her getting ready for bed and undressing. He saw himself being with her, holding her close, drawing in the warm scent of her presence.

He waited until her bedroom light was turned off. Then he lit a cigarette and marvelled at their evening together. It was hard to believe that the Gormley episode had been rescued. The outcome added to his self-confidence and, as he turned for home, he felt good about himself and the new life that was evolving.

But would she turn up on Friday?

CHAPTER TWENTY

When Harry Fay returned home from the country he had the look of someone who had fallen asleep in the sun. Flakes of skin were peeling away from his face and his bushy moustache was almost bleached white.

When he walked into the house he could not believe what he saw. The place was like something you'd see in a magazine. All the rooms had been cleaned. The kitchen resembled an advertising setting for detergent. The hall was immaculate, the two smaller rooms like a feature from *Good Housekeeping*. The pungent fragrance of pine was almost overwhelming.

Harry knew his son well. His immediate reaction was suspicion. What was this sudden conversion to domesticity? What was the younger Fay hiding? Harry couldn't figure it out. Finally he put the whole episode down to the gradual maturing of his offspring. That deduction didn't last long.

The first reason for rethinking was the wine stock. Harry could have sworn that his stock was much larger. It was hard for Harry to be precise about such things. Details were for note takers and accountants. He was a champion of the arts. But even so, he found it hard to believe that he had consumed so much wine himself. He tackled Vincent. His son knew nothing about the missing wine. Indeed, the young lad swore that he had not broken his pledge, that no alcohol had ever passed his lips. Harry didn't believe that. In fact he remembered clearly young Vincent polishing off a half bottle of champagne the previous Christmas. After a few days the issue of the missing wine faded away, but unfortunately another matter, arguably more serious, took its place.

It was the man from the gas company that caused the commotion. As usual he called to empty the meter. But when he opened the meter there was no money there. Not a bob. Not a solitary shilling in the bottom of the metal tray. How did they cook? How did they eat? It was not possible to live in a house and cook without gas. Did they not boil kettles? Did they not drink tea? What did they live on?

Harry listened to the rant from the gas company man. He went on and on. He reminded Harry that it wasn't that long ago before when the same thing had happened. No money in the meter.

Harry called his son. He pointed to the meter. The gas man held aloft the empty tray.

'Well,' he said. 'What have you to say?'

'I don't know what to say.'

'It all seems very fishy to me,' said the gas man.

'How do you mean fishy?' said Harry.

'Well you explain it to me. You tell me how you've been cooking. You explain, because as far as I'm concerned you can't cook without gas. Do you accept that?'

'Do I accept what?'

'That you can't cook without gas.'

'When I was growing up my mother used a range.'

'There's no need to be smart with me.'

'You asked a question, I gave you the answer.'

'And what would you say if I told you that we were cutting you off?'

'Cutting me off? Why?'

'Because you are using gas and as far as I'm concerned you're not paying for it.'

Before Harry could respond there was a knock on the hall door. Harry was delighted with the interruption. Anything to put this gas fellow off his stride. He strutted to the door and opened it ceremoniously. Standing on the step was his old friend Darby.

'You're back?'

'I'm back.'

'What did you do to your face?'

'Burnt to a crisp I was. Are you coming in? We're having a little debate here with the gas man.'

'A debate is right,' said the gas man.

'Are you having a problem?'

'What do you think of that?' said Harry pointing at the gas meter.

'An empty meter?' said Darby.

'Yes an empty meter.'

'What's so strange about that? Has he not just emptied it?' The gas man jumped forward.

'Excuse me,' he said. 'I most certainly did not empty the meter.'

'He's almost accused me of fraud Darby,' said Harry pointing at the gas man. 'Threatening to cut me off if you don't mind.'

'This is a very serious situation,' said Darby. 'Very serious indeed.'

'Well you explain how they can cook for almost two months with no money in the meter. You explain that?'

'Tell me,' said Darby, 'who was with you when you opened the meter?'

'What are you saying?'

'A simple question. Who was with you when you discovered that there was no money in the meter?'

'No one.'

'So you've no witnesses?'

'What are you trying to say?'

'I am saying nothing. I am merely stating facts.'

'Are you saying that I opened it and took the money?'

'I am saying that there are no witnesses to the alleged crime, and if there are no witnesses there is no proof. Am I correct?'

'What are you insinuating?'

'I am insinuating nothing. Did I accuse anyone?' said Darby as he looked at the Fays.

'You said nothing,' said Harry. 'Absolutely nothing.'

'I merely stated the facts, and I would remind you sir that the law only deals in facts.'

'And the fact is,' growled the gas man, 'that there was nothing in this meter.'

'According to you,' said Darby.

'You may be an old man,' said the gas man, who by this stage was almost frothing at the mouth. 'You may be an old man but if you go on with any more of that sort of talk there'll be trouble.'

'Are you now threatening violence in front of these people?'

'Would you go and feck yourself.'

'And bad language too?'

'This is not the last you'll be hearing of this,' said the gas man as he closed his book, turned off his torch and headed for the door.

As he was leaving Darby made another observation.

'If I were you, young man, I would be careful what I say in other people's houses. And another thing, did you ever consider the possibility that the gas company could be at fault? Did you check for a leak? Did he?'

'No he didn't,' said Harry cockily.

The gas man slammed the door. Harry roared with laughter and led Darby into the small front room for a drink. It was then he thought of the wine again.

'Darby,' said Harry, 'there is another matter you might be able to help me with.'

Fay stood at the door listening. He knew if Darby revealed the details of the party he was sunk. As liberal as his father was, Fay knew that old Harry would not be impressed with stories of the ambulance, the cops and the woman who locked herself in the toilet. Fay looked at Darby with pleading eyes. Please, Darby, don't tell. Darby recognised Fay's discomfort. He dragged the process out wondering how many bottles could be missing and which type of wine had disappeared.

173

Fay would have gone down on his knees before Darby. He would have done anything the old man asked. He didn't have to. Finally Darby declared.

'Well I'll tell you Harry, I have a confession to make. When you were away, meself and Crosby called over here one night. I had been telling Crosby about your stock and I took the liberty of showing him your display. Crosby was so taken by it all that I suggested that he take some of the wine and he could pay you later.'

'You took the wine?' said Harry.

'I hope you're not offended.'

'I'm relieved,' said Harry, 'very relieved.'

Fay could have kissed old Darby. He could have sworn allegiance till death. Darby looked at Fay his smile revealing a mouth of missing teeth and winked, not once but several times. Fay's secret was safe.

Fay wondered at Darby's behaviour. Why had the old boy with the red whiskey nose told a lie about the wine? It didn't make sense until he talked with Hackett. His scheming friend had the answer. The reason, according to Hackett, was all down to his old friend Brother Dominic.

The previous day Hackett and Brennan had called to see the monk at the friary. They explained about the money for the crippled child going to Lourdes and how the old boys who had collected the money thought there was enough money to send two. The old boys in question were, according to Hackett, quite advanced in age and forgetful.

Brother Dominic listened to the story. Any lingering doubts he may have had were immediately dispelled when Francis Brennan declared that the story was true and that he knew the two men personally. Brother Dominic was so relieved that he agreed to do as he did before and call to see the benefactor. And so the following day the small man with the brown flowing habit called to see Darby. Not alone did he thank the old man, he also presented him with a framed photograph of Saint Francis. Darby was particularly pleased when he discovered that, as far as Brother Dominic knew, the money had been raised by Darby and Crosby themselves during the previous Lent when both of them had given up the drink.

When Brother Dominic left, Darby was on cloud nine. He believed that his generosity would unquestionably guarantee himself and Crosby a seat in the front row of the assembly on high. There was also the on-going adulation in the pub.

'There's the man who organised the fare for the children to go to Lourdes.'

Later when he met Hackett he could hardly contain himself. His praise for Hackett gushed out. What a genius Hackett was to think of the Lenten Sacrifice.

'Well I could hardly tell him that you won it on a horse, could I?'

'You could not son, you could not,' said Darby, before heading down the road to share the good news with the locals.

175

CHAPTER TWENTY ONE

As the weeks of summer went by it seemed that the boys no longer had the same appetite for madness. A certain order took over. Hackett got a job as a messenger boy with a pork butcher's in Dorset Street. Brennan, through the influence of his old man, became a helper on a van for Clery's, Fay got relief work as a porter in the gallery where his old man worked. The Scout continued to deliver telegrams and Rob Finnegan spent his summer days ministering to the sick, delivering his tonics and tablets.

Maybe it was the physical work that sapped their energy for fun or, as one of them remarked one night in the shed, perhaps they were getting old.

There were no more parties in the shed, no excursions to Kilmartin's and no more visits to Brother Dominic. The crippled child went to Lourdes and Darby and Crosby had a mass said for their intentions. The mass card was displayed in a prominent position in Fagan's to remind those present of the important collection that had been made. Often Darby would be asked about the child and, as always, he would allow himself a few moments of indulgent reflection. He would put on his sad look and tell whoever asked that the child was progressing nicely. If, in the course of the discussion, Darby was invited to partake in a drink, the pools collector would say yes and toast the health of the child.

Brennan continued to see Fiona over the summer though they gave the local cinema a miss. He didn't want to have the glass eye cramp his style again. He was moving on and the less reminders of the past, the better.

On more than one occasion his sister Maura saw him with Fiona. She couldn't keep it to herself. She blurted it out over dinner one evening.

'Guess who's got a girlfriend?' she teased, but instead of sending up flares of alarm her parents simply nodded. Somehow, they knew already.

Brennan knew as the relationship developed that he would have to come clean. He dreaded the prospect of telling his mother, but he knew before long that the news would be common knowledge.

Brennan devised a plan. During one of Brother Dominic's visit he asked to see the monk. It was a delicate matter and he needed the counsel of the cleric. Brennan explained how he had been praying hard for a vocation. He was looking for direction from the Lord. And, as he said to the monk, God works in mysterious ways. He told Brother Dominic that he had met a girl, a lovely girl, who had lost her mother to cancer. Brother Dominic nodded in sympathy. Brennan continued by explaining that over a period of months he had become fond of her. He asked Brother Dominic was there anything wrong with that. The monk said no, the feelings Francis had for the girl were natural.

'And what about the vocation, Brother?'

Brother Dominic sat back and smiled.

'Now Francis, I think you and I both know that the vocation hasn't been foremost in your thoughts lately.'

'I know, but I tried.'

'Yes I know you did.'

'It's just me parents, they were expecting me to be a priest.'

'I know that, but you don't have to a member of a religious order to do the work of the Almighty.'

'Yes, but what do I say to them?'

'Leave it to me Francis, I'll talk to them.'

'And what about the girl, Fiona? What will I say about that?'

'You say nothing. I'll tell them that having a girlfriend is the most natural thing.'

Brother Dominic stood to leave the front room.

'Mind Francis, remember to respect the girl.'

'I will, Brother.'

'Remember both of you are temples of the Holy Spirit.'

'I'll remember,' said Brennan as he reddened slightly at the thought of himself and Fiona down that back lane and she with her probing fingers.

'I'll remember,' he said again.

'And I'll sort out your parents. Don't worry I know how to handle things,' said Brother Dominic. And handle them he must have done, because when Maura tried to draw the wrath of his parents down upon Brennan her plan didn't work.

This new licence to associate with members of the opposite sex added to Brennan's sense of self-worth. No longer did he have to keep it all a secret. Regularly he would stroll with Fiona in the park or in the Botanic Gardens. He began to feel more mature. His sense of always being hunted fell away. The constant feelings of guilt diminished. He was developing a rational capacity to evaluate things. The emotional side of his character had more balance.

Brennan and Fiona became inseparable. They saw each other several times a week. Sometimes, because of Fiona's domestic responsibilities, their meetings were brief. But it didn't matter to Brennan. Seeing her, even for a short time, was enough.

On several occasions he helped her mind her siblings. Though he wasn't much use himself, he played football with her brothers in the park. He also got to know her father, a commercial traveller for a tobacco company. Fiona's father had always been wary of whom his eldest daughter might eventually bring home. The early death of his wife made him sceptical. He dreaded the prospect of some layabout entering their world. But Frankie

Brennan wasn't like that. Initially Fiona's father thought him distant and remote, but after a time he realised it was shyness. But that changed too. Brennan became more comfortable and outgoing. He became less flustered when having a conversation. He offered opinions and views. This gave him more confidence. It was as if Fiona had opened a door and shown him his own potential.

In their quiet moments together Fiona realised that her boy-friend had changed. He had opened up and blossomed. No longer had she to do all the work. Sexually too, he had grown. The vice grip of guilt no longer restrained him. He was much more relaxed about it all. Earlier urgencies dissipated. He was content to hold her and kiss her, and enjoy the intimacy they shared. Going all the way no longer seemed that important. Much as he may have desired the fulfilment, he became content to wait. I think we should wait, he said to her, because somewhere deep down he feared that the ultimate act might be their last.

CHAPTER TWENTY TWO

Neither the Scout nor his family had ever been on the receiving end of a telegram. And that's the way he wanted to keep it. He had seen too many trembling fingers open those small green envelopes. Too many times had he witnessed the horror and the sadness. Telegrams were bad news.

Mrs O'Neill, the Scout's mother, was sitting in the kitchen when she heard a knock on her door a little after seven. She was alone in the house at the time and expecting Mrs Fenton to call. She rose from the table and went into the hall. She pulled the door open.

The young man, wearing the same uniform as her son handed her the small green envelope. She took it warily. She looked at the face of the young man, not much older than the Scout. She thought of how often he would have stood on steps like her own waiting for the messages of gloom to register. The telegram boy stood looking at her as if waiting for a reaction. Did he do this with everyone? Did she have to sign for it or what? Oh God, what was happening?

'Do you want me to stay while you open it?' said the young man.

'Sorry, what?'

'Do you want me to stay? I know you're Mick's ma.'

'Do you know what's in it?'

'No, Mrs O'Neill, I don't.'

Opening this envelope was something she didn't want to do. As long as she didn't know its contents, life would go on as before. But that wasn't true. Something had changed, something profound and the details were in the envelope.

'Do you want me to stay?' the young man said again.

Mrs O'Neill managed a smile of gratitude. The envelope in her hand was now crumpled. She knew it would have to be opened and as she began to straighten it she realised that her hands, her whole body, were trembling.

Slowly she prised the gummed envelope apart and took out the telegram. She read the message, folded the telegram and put it in the pocket of her apron as if dismissing what she had seen. After a moment or two she took it out again and studied each word. Then she looked upwards as if some other-worldly power could help in some way. As her eyes began to fill she looked at the young man and mouthed a *thank you*. He was only doing his job!

She didn't cry out. Instead, quietly, she let the water from her eyes flow down her cheeks. All her heavy make-up dissolved. She wiped her face with her apron.

'Can I do anything, Mrs O'Neill?'

'Do anything?'

'Do you want me to do anything for you?'

'There's nothing can be done now.'

She closed the door and walked into their small front room and sat on the arm of a chair facing the china cabinet. Before her the framed photograph of their wedding. Her husband and herself on that special day. She walked to the cabinet. She took up the wedding photograph and held it close. Things would never be the same again. She began to cry again. At first deep mournful sobs, then as her body began to shake a slow painful wailing came from this woman full of love. All those years of marriage. All those years apart with him away working in England while she raised the boys in Drumcondra. And yet she suffered the separation in the sure and certain knowledge that there was always Christmas or Easter to look forward to. Now she could only look back. All that was left were the memories, the picture book of the mind. She would live out her days never again knowing the sound of her house singing out in reunion. She would stand no more on the North Wall Quay watching the M.V. Leinster steam down the river. Her separation from her husband was now final. It ended the previous day in Islington when the walls of a trench fell inwards killing him and a labourer from Cork.

She sat in that room for ages. There was nothing she felt like doing. She wanted to be alone, to allow the words become real in her mind. This was her time, her space to be with the recollections of the man she had taken for better or worse, the one who was so like his son in looks and temperament.

She remembered how they met. A dance in a Dublin temperance hall. She fell for his smile, the roguish look, the way he swirled her on the maple dance floor. That was twenty five years ago. A quarter of a century that seemed like a drop in the ocean. Now time would grind on slower. The hours and days would be marked with anguish.

The sound of the hall door opening and closing stirred her. She heard her son go up the stairs. How was she going to tell him? He called out her name. He seemed excited. He called again. Then she heard his footsteps coming down the stairs. The door opened and he walked in.

As soon as he saw her sitting there a light went out in his face. He loved his mother. If she was upset, so was he. Her eyes were red from crying. He knew by her look that her heart was full of trouble. She tried to talk, to be brave for him, but her grief held her back. She took the telegram from the pocket of her apron and offered it to him. He looked at it in horror. He knew what those envelopes meant. Day after day he had seen the effect of their content.

He didn't take the envelope.

'Is it Dad or Fergus?' he said.

'It's your father, son.'

'No, no, no,' he screamed.

She stood from the chair to hold him, but he pulled away. Her embrace would confirm the news and the sadness. He ran from the room, climbed the stairs and threw himself on his bed. She followed him upstairs and sat on the bed while he sobbed. Just like old times, she thought, the times when he'd run in from the street when the world was against him. She would console and comfort him and send him back. Once a boy, always a boy. He turned his head to look at her and she remembered that look, the pleading one, hoping that mammy would make it better. But this time there were no motherly cures. No amount of hugs and kisses would ease the devastation. This was something beyond both of them. All that remained was darkness.

The news spread along the street. As always the neighbours rallied. There was something about death, its finality, that put things in perspective. Petty squabbles were put aside.

They poured into the O'Neill's house. The Fays, the Brennans and the Hacketts. Darby came too. Most of the women gathered in the front room to comfort the new widow. They spoke in hushed whispers. How had she heard and how had it happened? And wasn't it only a month since he had been home? It was such a cross to bear. You know not the day nor the hour.

In the back room and the kitchen the men gathered. Old Harry Fay arrived with a crate of wine and Darby came with the whiskey. At first there was almost a reverential sipping of drinks. Their voices were low, almost mournful, but as the drink went down the volume of conversation went up. They told stories, not alone about the departed, but also of others who had gone before. The boys stood among them. They watched the ritual of their elders; how people coped with loss.

After several rounds of whiskey, Hackett was sent home by his father. Another bottle was needed. And if there was any port or sherry left over from Christmas he should bring that as well.

As the evening wore on more people arrived. The swelling of numbers diluted the atmosphere of gloom. There was almost a sense of joviality. Maybe that was their way of coping.

Finally Mrs O'Neill decided to circulate. She left the small front room and went into the men. She was there to say thank you, to acknowledge their presence. She had known most of them for years.

As she entered the back room the place went quiet. The men felt awkward and challenged. It was hard to know what to say. Women were best at talking to women.

It was Harry Fay who surprised them all. He approached the woman with tears in his eyes. He too had know the loss of a spouse, when his own wife had left. He knew about grief. Harry put his arm around Mrs O'Neill and held her tightly. She began sobbing again and Harry gently told her to cry on, to let it out, it was what she should do. She did and Harry comforted her with soothing words. The other men watched this display and felt deeply embarrassed. They could not have behaved like Harry.

Standing looking on was the Scout. The boys had persuaded him down from his bedroom. He watched the agony of his mother and tears gushed from his eyes. Then Harry paused for a moment. Gently he released Mrs O'Neill. Then he called the Scout over. He brought the young man into a circle of arms before retreating himself, leaving mother and son clinging to each other.

Brennan watched what was happening. He looked over at Hackett and was relieved to see that his friend, like himself, had tears in his eyes.

All through the night there were callers to the door. They'd just heard the news. They had come as soon as they could. All of them brought food or drink. Everyone was there. Even O'Meara, the builder, came. Darby's friend, Crosby, had heard the news in Fagan's and couldn't pass the door without calling. The Mulligans, the Finnegans, the O'Briens were there. Old Mrs Hickey, Fay's neighbour, brought a freshly baked brack.

The night wore on. The earlier atmosphere of mourning was gone. Yes, there were still tears, but laughter began to dominate. The men told stories, tall tales of their youth. They spoke like lads again. Even old man Brennan told of a misdemeanour. The boys listened intently. They laughed too. Even the Scout had a snigger, helped in part by the glasses of beer which Hackett had smuggled from the kitchen. Hackett was glowing. So was Fay. And Brennan, at one stage, had to throw up in the garden.

Just before one o'clock the merriment was brought to a halt. Mrs O'Neill was going to bed. The back room fell silent. She looked at them all with gratitude. She wished her husband could have been there to enjoy the company of such neighbours. He would have loved it all. They were not to go home, she told them. She wanted company that night above all, to feel that others were there, when in the bleakness of night she might feel alone. Then she went to bed.

As soon as she left the women began to clear up. Tomorrow there would be more callers and they would need clean cutlery and delph.

The men sat up until dawn. They talked the same talk of the finality of it all, the random unfairness of selection. They told stories of disease and affliction. They smoked and drank all night.

By seven in the morning there was little left to say. It had all been said and over the next few days, the same words would be used over and over in futile attempts to make sense of it all. It was the only way they knew to cope.

The following day the body was flown to Dublin airport. From there it was taken home by hearse and, as the black Mercedes turned into the street, every blind was down. The place was still. Not a child was seen playing in the street.

Outside the house a number of people were waiting. Some of them went forward to carry the coffin inside. Slowly, carefully they carried the coffin into the hallway. This was the first stage in taking the body upstairs. Mrs O'Neill wanted her husband to spend his last night in their bed. But manoeuvring the coffin up the narrow stairs and around the landing would be a problem. So, they laid the coffin down in the hallway and the undertaker came forward to loosen the bolts and take off the lid. Then the men came forward again and, with a tender dignity, took the body of their neighbour and friend upstairs to his bed for the very last time.

In the double bedroom at the front Mr O'Neill was laid between freshly starched sheets. Mrs Hickey supervised things. She took time in making all the preparations. Mr O'Neill was a special neighbour and everything had to be right. Sheets were straightened, covers turned down. She lit a candle and placed an old family rosary beads between the rough fingers of the dead man. He was now ready for God and anyone else who cared to see him.

Some hours later Fergus arrived home from the Royal Navy. He was lucky that he was ashore in Plymouth when the news arrived.

When Fergus appeared he was ushered into the front room where his mother and brother were waiting. They spent some time together going over things, not in any order, just the fragments of information they tried to cling onto so that they might try and make sense of it all.

After some time in the front room Mrs O'Neill led her two sons upstairs to the bedroom. Together they stood in silence looking down at their father and husband. Then, as she would have always done, Mrs O'Neill walked forward and adjusted the fringe of her husband's hair. At the sight of this the Scout broke down. It was all too real. He cried uncontrollably and soon his elder brother was equally moved. Mrs O'Neill told them to cry out, to grieve, to mourn, to stay as long as they liked with their father. Then she blessed herself and turned and walked out of the room. Suddenly the boys felt alone. This was not their father, the man they had known, the man they had loved. This was a man who looked like their father. Where were the smiles, the winks and the laughs? Why were the jokes gone silent?

Fergus walked to the head of the bed. He looked down at the pale yellowed face. He ran the outside of his hand against the cold cheek and felt the abrasion of stubble. Then he nodded to his brother to come forward. The younger one was reluctant, scared. Fergus urged him on. Slowly the Scout moved towards the head of his father.

'Touch him,' whispered Fergus, 'touch him, go on.'

The Scout reached out his fingers and laid them on the cold brow of his father. This was the man he had adored. Then he pulled his hand back, covered his face and ran from the room.

Later that evening the priest called. Those in the house were asked to join in the recitation of the rosary. Everyone climbed the stairs. The family went into the room first and knelt around the bed, the Scout beside his mother. The rest knelt wherever they found room. There were no formalities to tragedy.

The theme that night was the Resurrection, that chapter in the life of Christ when he returns to the world after three days in the tomb. But those that cared to listen to the priest knew that there would be no coming back for the one they prayed for. Never would he be seen again in Drumcondra.

Hackett, Brennan and Fay knelt as close to the door as they could. All of them were shattered by the brutality of it all; how could a man they knew well and admired be cut down so easily.

When the rosary ended, everyone filtered down the stairs for refreshment. Mrs O'Neill had ordered crates of stout for the men and bottles of sherry for the women. Tea was in plentiful supply.

Most of the men were in the front room where the empty coffin lay. Neither Hackett nor Brennan wanted to go into that place. They needed no more reminders of death. But Darby, who had just come out of the room, insisted that they comply with convention. Weren't they men now? And hadn't they been with him in Fagan's? A question he posed with a large wink, a sign to keep it all confidential.

Brennan pushed Hackett first. The room was choked in smoke. Standing in a large circle were the men holding court, holding glasses and incessantly puffing tobacco. Harry Fay had a large cigar in his mouth which he had held over from Christmas. And Hackett's old man was devouring his Capstan Full Strength. Rob Finnegan's old man was asleep in the corner propped up against the coffin.

Fay, who had already been in the room, came over to Hackett and Brennan with a bottle of wine under his coat. He poured a glass for the boys.

As more people came into the room the crowd had to move forward and make space. This meant that Brennan was heading for the coffin. He didn't want that, but he had no choice particularly when old man Gormley fixed him with a look and told him to 'move on for God's sake' and he did.

Brennan was now jammed against the coffin with Rob's slumbering father. Some macabre fascination drew Brennan to look into the coffin. He saw the soft lining, the resting place of Mr O'Neill. He wondered what would happen if you were trapped alive in that thing. What would you do? What could you do? Nothing. He shuddered at the thought and immediately muscled his way through the throng and made it to the door.

The three boys searched the house for the Scout. They tried every room but there was no sign of their friend. Finally they found him out the back in the small yard and garden. He was sitting beside the outside toilet on a box they kept for sticks.

He didn't look up when he heard the back door open and close or the footsteps on the concrete. Fay walked over and put his hand on his shoulder.

'Do you want to do anything?'

'Do what?'

'You say.'

'I just want to sit here.'

Fay looked at the others and shrugged. They all hung about and smoked cigarettes with their friend. Fay produced more wine and they slugged gulps from the bottle. No words were spoken. There was nothing meaningful left to say. They were awkward in their muteness. They were not used to the dialogue of death, the mouthing of words to fill silences. Their parents had this vocabulary, the ability to express what was required.

They sat outside for over an hour. Fay left and returned with more wine and beer. They all drank deeply. Having a glass or bottle to your mouth meant you didn't have to speak.

During one extended period of silence the awkwardness was broken with the sound of the back door opening. They were all relieved to see Darby.

'There yiz are. Big queue on the stairs for the toilet. This one still working? Well?'

The Scout nodded and told him it was. Darby went into the darkness of the small brick outhouse muttering to himself. He was playing two roles in some sort of conversation, asking questions and answering them. At one point he was arguing quite loudly with himself. The boys were enthralled. Even the Scout lifted his head to listen.

Suddenly the discussion halted and, after several seconds of silence, a large groaning noise came from the toilet before what sounded like a hose being discharged in the bowl. He must have been bursting because it went on for ages. It was like a waterfall in the Botanics. Fay thought it was hilarious. He started to snigger. Then the others joined in. Even the Scout had to laugh.

'Do you know what it's like?' said Fay, 'it's like a horse pissing on the street.'

And it was. Darby must have drunk a gallon of porter. When they heard the chain being pulled they went quiet. Darby emerged and buttoned up his trousers. What a relief, he said and walked over to the Scout. He patted the young man's shoulder.

'It's time you were all inside,' he said. 'It's getting cold now. Come on.'

They took the old man's instruction and followed him back inside to mingle again with neighbours and friends, to listen to the same people try and make sense of it all and, in the end, to concede that it was not for them to reason why.

Two days later they buried Mr O'Neill in Glasnevin. It was the first time that old Harry and his son had been back in the church since the men's retreat. The steward Monroe was there looking officious, but once he saw Harry his demeanour became sullen and even more so when the younger Fay blew him a kiss.

The church was packed. The young curate said predictable things about the dead parishioner he had never met, the one forced by circumstances to spend his working life in England. He extended his sympathy and asked for prayers for those left behind.

After the coffin had been blessed and circled by the wafting of incense, it was carried down the centre aisle to the hearse. Inconsolably the family walked behind. Mrs O'Neill and her two sons sat in the mourning car. The boys stood in a group near the hearse. They looked towards their friend whose eyes were red from crying.

On its way to the cemetery the hearse passed the door of O'Neill's. It stopped briefly then carried on to take the Scout's father on his last journey. Later he would be placed in another trench, only this time the earth was meant to fall on him, and allow him to lie still in the ground forever.

After the funeral Fergus decided to extend his leave and stay at home a little longer. His mother was delighted. It would give her time to let the tragedy sink in. She took time off from Lemon's and the Scout had a week's leave left over from earlier in the year.

This period together gave them time to talk, to look through the mass cards, read the letters of sympathy. They got on well as a family. The love that was bestowed upon them as children always came to the surface. The boys rarely argued even when they were smaller. They seemed to have this unique ability to let the cares of the world pass over them. Contentment seemed to radiate from them and, though they rarely had a lot, they always had enough.

But this change in their world shook them to the core. Neither of the boys seemed to cope. Fergus spent an increasing amount of time in the 'men only' bar at Fagan's while the Scout rarely left his room after tea-time.

The boys would often call over. Sometimes the Scout would come down the stairs and join them in the front room. But there was little conversation. None of them knew what to say. Occasionally Fergus would join them. The boys loved hearing his exotic stories from far-away places. But the best stories were about women. Fergus would have told them about Singapore and Hong Kong and places you'd never have heard of. And in all those places the ports and the bars would be crammed with the most delectable creatures imaginable. And in the midst of it all would be Fergus, debonair, silver tongued Fergus, as he charmed them all into his bed.

But this time there was no talk about women, no talk of film star cocktails in bars that were made from mirrors. This time there was no talk or mention of sex.

Instead Fergus spoke of his career and prospects, how joining the navy was the best thing he ever did, how he was better off away and out of Ireland.

The boys listened to what he had to say. They too wanted to get on in the world. They wanted a slice of prosperity. Though deep down they knew that Fergus was a bragger, it was hard to ignore the gold watch and identity bracelet, the fashionable

191

clothes and the gear. They were impressed by Fergus, the way he spent money, the way he flashed a wallet which was always crammed with five pound notes.

The Scout didn't want to go back to work yet his mother convinced him that it would be the best thing to do. It would take his mind off things. But she was wrong.

On his first day back at the General Post Office the Scout reported to his boss. The man was full of sympathy for the young telegram boy. He said he understood the pain the lad was going through. For the first few weeks they would ease him back into the job. The deliveries he would be given would be local.

The first telegram he was given was for a Corporation housing scheme on the North Wall, one of several blocks of flats constructed to house the dock workers in the port. It was close to the GPO and would take barely ten minutes to travel there on his bike. The Scout took the envelope and stowed it in the leather pouch he wore around his waist. Then he left on his first delivery.

The traffic on O'Connell Street was light. He turned onto the Quays, down past Butt Bridge and along by the Custom House. As he moved towards the North Wall memories of his father came back, those days of contrasting emotions, the great excitement and fun when he arrived, the dull emptiness when he left.

From the Quays he turned into Mayor Street. Ahead of him he saw the block of flats, a four storey building with outside walkways and balconies. At the entrance he asked a woman pushing a pram where sixty two was?

'Are you all right?' she said. 'Your eyes are all watery. You look like you were crying?'

'Just the wind,' said the Scout.

The woman said she'd mind his bike. She knew the woman who lived in sixty two. He'd find it on the third balcony.

The Scout ran up six flights of stairs. At the top he paused and checked the door numbers. Sixty two was the fourth door along the balcony. He looked over the parapet wall. The woman minding his bike was looking upwards. He walked on trailing his hand along the top of the wall. At the door he stopped. From all his days delivering telegrams he had learnt a lot about doors, the way they were kept, the way the brasses were shined, what it said about those living within. This door was tidy and clean.

The door was opened by a woman in her mid-thirties. Two small children still in their night clothes stood beside her. One clung onto her apron, the other sucked on a soother.

The Scout opened his pouch and took out the envelope. The woman watched his motion with anxiety. He handed the telegram over. She held it in her hand and, as he turned to walk away, she called him.

'You open it,' she said.

'I'm not meant to.'

'Open it please. For God's sake I'm on me own here.'

He wanted to lean over the balcony and call the woman with the pram.

'Please son, please.'

Slowly he separated the paper from the gum. He took out the folded message and straightened it to see the words. She searched his face for a clue. Without saying anything he looked at her.

'What is it? What is it? Is it bad news? Is it Richie? Is it? For God's sake tell me.'

He couldn't say the words. Without speaking he handed her the telegram and turned and ran the full length of the balcony. He took the stairs several steps at a time. Down on the ground the woman with the pram was waiting. She looked at him. She could read what the telegram said by the look on his face.

'I don't know how you do that job,' she said. 'Honest to God I don't know how you do it.'

Back at base the Scout threw up in the toilet. He stood over the bowl as the perspiration ran down his face. What was happening? Up until then he had delivered thousands of telegrams. He had handed over the envelopes in a detached sort of way. What was inside did not concern him. It was none of his business. But since handling the telegram that had brought the news about his father, he had begun to realise that he couldn't go on doing this job. And now this morning the same thing, over and over.

He left the cubicle and went to wash his hands in the sink. In the mirror his eyes were red, his face ashen. His mouth stank with vomit. Not since childhood had he felt so ill. The smell, the taste, brought back all the nights he had held his head in a basin. Chickenpox, the mumps, maybe measles. He hated that smell, that reminder of vulnerable childhood when only a mother could make it better.

He tidied himself up and returned to where the other telegram boys waited for their envelopes. They laughed and joked and smoked cigarettes. Some ran around the corner to the bookies. Though the Scout was popular they all were hesitant to talk to him. Like him, they were young and innocent when it came to talking about death. A couple came over and jabbed him affectionately. That was all they could manage.

He left the room and slowly walked the long terrazzo covered floor to where his boss had his office. The corridor echoed with the sound of his shoes. As he came closer to the door he made up his mind. No longer could he go on delivering the same green envelopes that had destroyed his life.

The boss was sympathetic. He'd see what he could do. But there were no vacancies in other departments. Maybe in a few months? Who knew? He'd do his best. A clerk? Eh, no, he didn't have the educational qualifications. Hadn't he left school early?

Time, his boss told him, was a great healer.

But time for the Scout was running out.

CHAPTER TWENTY THREE

Counting down the days to the opening of school was worse for Hackett than Chinese torture. At least the torture would end, but school went on and on like eternity. In June, when the holidays arrived the eight weeks stretched out like a never ending menu of fun. But now, as the first day approached, he was losing his will to live.

Brennan didn't mind the prospect of going back. It was part of life, he'd say, an attitude that Fay agreed with totally.

But Hackett was miserable about it all, the dreaded prospect of sitting on those hard wooden seats for another two years of boredom. He had spent the summer working for a pork butcher with a Hungarian name he couldn't pronounce. The work was laborious and repetitive but it was far better than learning useless tripe about gobshites that got killed on some foreign battlefield, fighting for some nancyboy who dressed himself in silk stockings and wore a wig.

All during the summer he put the exam out of his mind. But now as the leaves began to fall from the trees and the light was leaving the evenings earlier, Hackett could not get the exam out of his mind. He visualised derision and disgrace and it was something he didn't look forward to.

The results came out on a Wednesday. By that stage the boys had been back in school for almost a week. For Hackett those first few days confirmed all his negative thoughts. There were new teachers, new books, a daunting syllabus that made no sense whatsoever. It all looked like a life sentence.

Brennan and Fay tried to cheer him up. They told him the time would pass quickly, that he wouldn't feel it until he was working in a decent job that paid well. He liked the notion of money. It was the waiting that gave him the problem.

The dean of studies stood at the top of Hackett's class on Wednesday morning at nine. In alphabetical order he called out the names. Each boy rose from his seat and went forward. Hackett watched them go up and return giddily to their desks. It was interesting to watch their reactions. Some couldn't wait to open the envelope. Others prised the flap back hesitantly as if what was inside would awaken suddenly. But predictably, the ones like Fogarty beamed triumphantly when they read the news. It was like he had performed another miracle.

Hackett stood up and walked to the top of the class. The dean gave him the envelope. Hackett nodded, took the envelope and returned to his desk where he sat. He fingered the envelope anxiously. Then slowly he opened it. His mind had been conditioned for disaster, but still there lingered the vain hope that something magical might happen. He straightened the page and scanned the detail. Then he looked at each subject individually. In total he had taken seven subjects. He was looking for the miracle. Perhaps some ancient saint might have interceded, put in a word, and upped his score. But that didn't happen. It was worse than the disaster expected. Even the imploring letter to the history examiner didn't work. So much for Christian charity – the bastard!

Out of the seven subjects he passed three. It was, the dean commented later, the worst result the school had recorded in years. There however, he went on to say, extenuating circumstances.

It was the tradition on results day that the boys, once they knew their fate, could return home and share the news with their anxious parents.

Hackett didn't linger in the school yard like the rest. He had no wish to hang around in the swoon of mutual praise or be

196

subjected to the gloating sniggers of Fogarty and his tribe. He hated them all. Swots and licks, the lot of them. Could any of them have organised that trip for the crippled child to go to Lourdes? They could in their arse. Fogarty would have rung a travel agent!

He left the school and walked onto Parnell Square. He turned for home. He would take his time. A lot of thinking needed to be done, thinking and planning, scheming really, for the challenging interviews that lay ahead.

At home he knew his parents would be waiting. His father would be pacing the hall in a cloud of Capstan Full Strength. His mother would be quietly fingering her beads.

His father had taken the day off in the quiet expectation of having to take a trip to convey the good news to Granny Hackett. She was expecting great things. Why wouldn't she? She had a grandson who had won so many academic prizes.

The dilemma that Peter Hackett faced was one of the most challenging yet. There was little room for scheming. The paper in his pocket said it all. Three passes. Art, English and Latin and not an honour in sight.

He passed the pork butcher he had worked for during the summer holidays. For a moment he thought of asking for his job back. But that wasn't a real option. The winter was coming and there would be no joy in pushing that heavy bicycle up and down hills in biting wind and rain.

At Binns Bridge he looked up the canal, the scene of so many days when he had mitched from school. Those were the days when he had won so much money playing cards. Now? Now he was very much a loser. The hand he had been dealt was unplayable.

Normally he had the inner capacity to keep separate the individual aspects of his life. He thought of it like the biscuit tins at Christmas where each variety was kept in a separate section. Custard Creams in one, Kimberly in another. The biscuit tin philosophy meant that he could concentrate on one thing at a time and not be distracted. But that sort of thinking didn't work now. All his thinking was consumed by what he carried in his pocket.

As he passed under the railway bridge and headed towards the Bishop's Palace he kept his head down, not out of any desire to hide, it was just the way he was feeling. In his head he tried to figure it all out. He knew he wasn't thick or stupid. It was just . . . just that he hated school and saw no point to it. It bored the ass off him, bored him to death. It was, for him, moronic. Then a voice jolted his meanderings.

'Well?' said Darby Maguire. 'Well, how did you do?'

'Not great.'

'Oh, I thought you were the brainy one?'

'No, that's Brennan.'

'Ah well, sure we can't all be scientists.'

'No, I suppose.'

'And did you pass or what?'

This was the first test for Hackett. What he said next was crucial. He hesitated. Darby seemed to understand.

'Is it that you don't want to say?'

'I don't know what to say.'

'So it's bad news?'

'You could say that.'

'Well, sure what about it? What about it?'

'Can I ask your advice, Mr Maguire?'

'You can, Peter, you can.'

'What would you do if you failed?'

'I'd put it behind me and carry on.'

'Yeah, but what about me parents and all?'

'Well,' said Darby with a genuinely concerned tone, 'well Peter, you either tell them the truth or you tell them a lie. And if you lie they can check it out easily.'

'They're going to be really disappointed.'

'They'll get over it. It's life.'

'So I tell them the truth?'

'That's my advice. Just walk up the street, sit them down and tell them.'

'Sounds so easy?'

'And it is. At least you'll have been straight with them. If you lie then you'll have to live with it and anyway they'll find out, they will.'

'Thanks, Mr Maguire.'

'Thanks for nothing, son.'

Hackett left the old man and walked on. Darby called after him.

'Remember Peter, we can't all be scientists.'

'I'll remember.'

Hackett's parents were waiting for him. As he approached the house he could see the net curtains move in the window.

They were all gathered in the front room. His mother sat on the edge of an armchair twisting the corner of her apron. His father stood and stole glances at himself in the oval shaped mirror over the mantelpiece. He lit a cigarette, then another.

'Well?' the old man said.

Hackett took out the envelope. The eyes of both his parents darted in the direction of the paper.

'Tell us, love,' his mother said.

'I failed.'

His father drew in a cloud of smoke.

'Failed? Failed what?'

'Failed the exam.'

'You can't be serious?'

'I am.'

'There must be a mistake.'

'There isn't.'

'Show me that,' demanded his father as he reached out and grabbed the results.

Hackett watched his old man's face begin to pale. It was like a blood transfusion working in the opposite direction, a draining process as the source of life was taken from the man.

'This can't be right. You failed French? What about that gold medal you won?'

'I didn't win any gold medal.'

'You mean you were telling lies?'

'Yes.'

His mother held her face in her hands. The poor woman didn't know what was happening.

'Peter, Peter,' she sighed.

'And,' his father went on, 'and I suppose your cousin passed with flying colours?'

'Probably.'

'Is that all you can say? When I think, when I think of all the money your grandmother spent on your education.'

'I tried.'

'You did in your arse.'

'Language John, please,' pleaded Mrs Hackett.

'Well if he tried he would have passed.'

'I'm sorry.'

'You're sorry? You're sorry? Is that all you can say? And what, what do you mind me asking do I tell your grandmother?'

'Tell her what you like.'

'Do you hear that? The cheek of you. That poor woman spent all that money.'

'I didn't ask her to spend the money.'

'She gave you a chance of a wonderful education and that's all you can say. Where's your gratitude? Well? Where's the gratitude for everything she did for you? I can't go there to Griffith Avenue and tell her that her grandson who won all those medals is a fraudster, can I?'

Neither Hackett nor his mother answered the question. Hackett had never seen his old man so annoyed. His face was grey and his cheeks were sunken and the smoke was pouring out of him like an exhaust.

'If I tell my mother that you failed the woman could die of heart failure. What then?'

Hackett felt like telling him to go ahead. At least if the old woman died his father would inherit a few bob. And he wouldn't have to go into that darkened room with its smell of cats.

Mr Hackett looked at his wife.

'I can't tell her that he failed, can I?'

'I don't know,' said Mrs Hackett who was hopeless in a crisis.

'Are you sure there's no mistake?'

'There's no mistake.'

'This is a fecking disaster.'

'John, please.'

'Well, what else is it only a fecking disaster? And I suppose Brennan and Fay sailed through it?'

'I don't know.'

'A disaster. How the hell did it happen? You mustn't have done a tap of work.'

'I tried.'

'You did like hell.'

'I tried. I really did.'

'A son of mine coming home with a result like that. God Almighty, it's unbelievable. What were you doing up there in that room every night?

'Studying.'

'Don't give me that.'

'I was.'

His father lit another cigarette. Chain smoking at eleven in the morning. The man was in some state. He looked like an emaciated greyhound in a refuge centre.

'And what's to happen now,' his father went on, 'what's to happen now with your education? If the woman knows that her money has been wasted she'll stop paying the fees and we can't

201

afford to send you to that place. That's of course if she survives hearing the news. The woman could be gripped by a seizure and drop dead. Oh God, this is terrible.'

'I'm sorry.'

'Is that all you can say?'

Hackett wondered if crying might help. Supposing he began to sob, to weep, to cry out in long bursts of emotion, like that play he had seen in school when everyone in the village was drowned. He decided against tears after the next salvo from his old man.

'Are you thick or what?'old man Hackett thundered.

Hackett wasn't sure he heard right.

'What did you say?'

'I asked you were you thick?'

'No I'm not thick, I'm as smart as the next guy.'

'Smart, is it now?'

'That's what I said.'

'And a lorry load of cheek as well.'

'I tried the exam. I failed. I'm sorry. I'm sorry I let you down, but that's it. It's over now. I'm sorry you'll have to go and tell Granny Hackett what happened.'

'You can tell her yourself,' barked his father.

'I'm not going near her.'

'You'll do as you're told.'

'I'm not going near that dive.'

'You're talking about the home I grew up in. It's no dive. How dare you?'

An hour later the discussion was still going on. His mother by this stage had chewed most of her apron. His father's rage had subsided. His main preoccupation now was meeting his mother and delivering the news.

Hackett began to feel sorry for his father. He knew that his old man would be totally humiliated, particularly when the story spread around the relations. He could visualise their laughter and all the questions about the gold medals.

Old man Hackett sat down. He was drained. He lit another cigarette.

'Oh God,' the old boy said, and kept repeating. 'Oh God, oh God, oh God, oh God.'

Hackett looked over at the man. His father's pallor had paled even further. The front of his jacket was covered in ash. He had the look of an undernourished waiter carrying a tray of despair.

Eventually his mother, the one who by general consensus had little to offer to any debate, was the one to make the most sensible comment.

'John,' she said, 'there's no point in going on and on and on, with this oh God thing.'

'Oh that's easy for you to say. What do I tell me mother?'

'Tell her nothing.'

'Don't be stupid, woman.'

'Tell her lies. Tell her he passed the exam with flying colours. How will she ever know?'

Hackett thought that a flush of colour began to creep into his father's complexion. His mother stood for the first time, and went to the window. She pulled the curtain back and opened the window. A pall of smoke was released.

For a woman who was regarded as dull with little to contribute, Mrs Hackett's suggestion was regarded as inspired. Old man Hackett was delighted it had come from her. It meant that it wasn't he who had suggested deception. And the more he thought about it the greater merit the idea seemed to have. He convinced himself that it wasn't deception at all. Instead it was life saving. It would avert the danger of his mother having a heart attack. And that, after all, was the number one priority.

Mr Hackett began to perk up. All they needed to do now was to come up with a new set of results. Father and son conspired together and came up with adjusted percentages. Now they were ready for the visit to Granny Hackett. The woman deserved to know that her outlay on Peter's education had been worthwhile.

Mr Hackett seemed to look forward to the meeting. It was as if he too was truly convinced of his son's academic triumph. He left the house in buoyant spirits. To the exterior world he was the father of a scholar, a model student that had brought distinction on himself and his family. His humour improved as he walked along Drumcondra Road. It was only a white lie, a slight exaggeration of the truth, a tactic whose only purpose was to extend the life expectancy of his mother. It would make the old lady's day. She would glow with pleasure as she reached for her bottle of port to toast the achievement of her gifted grandson.

While the pilgrimage was making its way to Granny Hackett there was other rejoicing on the street. Brennan had arrived home with a table of results which created ecstasy. His mother, a woman not given to any physical displays of emotion, actually hugged her son.

Mr Brennan could hardly speak. It was the first time that Brennan saw his old man lost for words. John Brennan beamed. It was the sort of news he wanted to spread. His son, his own flesh and blood, had got honours in every subject.

Brennan enjoyed being the centre of attention, watching father and mother pay homage to the brains in the family. He particularly revelled in the moment when his father passed the results to his sister Maura. For once the bitch had nothing to say.

Down the street in Fay's, Harry was jubilant. His son had passed as well. Harry was not a man who placed great store in honours. For him education began the moment you left school. Harry spoke continually about the university of life. He regarded himself as one of its finest graduates.

To mark the occasion Harry produced a bottle of wine and insisted that his son join him in a celebratory glass or two. Fay was a little reluctant given his assurances about the pledge, but Harry insisted and they sat around the table till late rambling on about things most people wouldn't understand.

Across the street in the Scout's the atmosphere was anything but jovial. Leave for Fergus was almost at an end. In three more days he'd be gone.

This was a parting that Mrs O'Neill had been dreading. For almost a month her eldest son had brought life into the house. His personality and good humour made the widow's life almost tolerable. She still desperately missed her husband, particularly at night as she lay in that bed. She tried to sleep thinking of the pleasurable memories, the good times they had together. But sleep rarely came. Its promise of serenity evaded her. Instead she would lie awake listening to the night-time sounds of the house, the creaking of boards, the dripping of taps, the clock downstairs. It was as if the house itself was unable to rest.

As the day of Fergus's departure arrived the anxiety became intense. Another member of the family to take the boat. Another empty bed. Another free place at the table. It was so hard to bear. But of equal concern was the state of her younger son.

The Scout had not settled back to work. She had been sure that delivering his telegrams would take his mind off the death of his father. But it hadn't. Indeed, the young man seemed to be growing morose. He was also losing weight. He told her he hated the work, that he wanted a transfer. But so far nothing had come up. It wasn't easy without any academic qualifications. His boss had been sympathetic, but there wasn't a lot he seemed able to do.

Mrs O'Neill was consumed with worry about her son. She tried to draw him out, but he said little. Each night she prayed for her son. She prayed that some force might intercede and guide him in a new direction. But sadly, the young man seemed to regress rather than improve. And this his mother found deeply upsetting.

Before long, there would be worse to come.

CHATPER TWENTY FOUR

As father and son turned into Granny Hackett's driveway the first thing they noticed was a gleaming new Ford Cortina. Clearly the Southside cousins had arrived, not alone to present the academic achievements of the pimply faced Bob, but also to show off the material supremacy of his father. As Hackett passed by the brand new motorcar he could feel a welling up of hatred. It wasn't the wealth he objected to, it was the way they flaunted it, the way they tried to make his father feel the lack of it.

The hall door was opened by the maid. She barely smiled before ushering the two of them into the darkened room. Granny Hackett sat in her usual chair. Beside her on a circular table was her range of medicines and a tall-stemmed glass of port.

Standing to her right was pimply faced cousin Bob and his father. Everyone smiled broadly and nodded. It was the ritualistic game of family which was always played when they met.

'And how are you?'

'Good, and you?'

'Never better, and all the family?'

'Great, really great.'

And then the pause while everyone prepared themselves for the inevitable.

'Well,' began Granny Hackett, 'how did young Peter get on?'

'Not as well as he expected, Mam,' said Mr Hackett.

'Oh,' said the voice from the chair.

Hackett noticed that the pimply faced one was smiling.

'No, sad to say, not as well as he expected.'

'And what did he get?'

'He only got five honours.'

At the mention of five honours the one with the pimples froze. This was not part of the script they had expected.

207

'Five honours,' Granny Hackett repeated.

'He's very disappointed. Aren't you, Peter?'

'I'm sorry, Gran. I did me best.'

'*My, my* best, not me.'

'My best Gran.'

'That's not a bad result, Peter. What do you think Bob?' said Granny Hackett addressing the question to her other son, Bob the father.

'Not a bad result at all, Mam,' answered Bob, almost choking.

'Have you the results with you?' asked Granny Hackett.

The pause which ensued was terrifying. Mr Hackett in his new found delirium of result creation did not expect to have to produce documentary evidence to support the fiction. The only solution was to divert attention. He turned to his son.

'Did you bring the results, Peter?' asked Mr Hackett.

'No,' answered Hackett.

All eyes were now focused on Hackett. The pimply faced one and his father suspected something sinister. They looked at each other in hopeful anticipation. Would this be the undoing of the honours student?

'And why not, Peter?' probed Granny Hackett.

'It's embarrassing, Gran.'

Mr Hackett was perspiring heavily.

'What's embarrassing Peter?'

'The whole thing, the exam results.'

'For Heaven's sake Peter, what have you to be embarrassed about?'

Uncle Bob and cousin Bob were now gleaming almost as brightly as their Ford Cortina outside. They were sensing triumph, the final snaring of the Northside smart ass.

Hackett drew breath and took a step forward.

'It's embarrassing because Father Osborne, the dean of studies, asked me not to talk about it.'

'What do you mean?'

'He said he'd prefer me not to talk about it.'

'I am your grandmother. I demand to know.'

'Father Osborne is disappointed with my results. He felt I should have got seven honours.'

'Seven honours?'

'Yes, Gran.'

'And where are the results?'

'Father Osborne took the results sheet. He's demanding a recheck. He told me to forget about the results because according to him they were wrong. He wants to get to the bottom of it.'

'And can I ask why is Father Osborne so insistent?'

'Because the honour of the school is at stake.'

'I don't follow.'

'Because if he's proved right our school wins the gold medal.'

'The gold medal for what?'

'The gold medal for the best academic results in a Jesuit school in Dublin.'

'You mean you could win another award?'

'Another gold medal, Gran.'

The door opened and the maid entered carrying a tray of tea and cakes.

'Not now Alice, not now,' cried Granny Hackett as she reached for her glass of port.

'Another gold medal,' cried Granny Hackett. 'Another gold medal. My God you have to hand it to the Jesuits. What do you think of that Bob?'

The elder Bob muttered something incomprehensible while his son looked down seeking some solace in the shine of his shoes.

Granny Hackett told the maid to forget about the tea and bring in another bottle of port. They would all have a glass. It wasn't every day that a member of the family had achieved such academic distinction.

Michael Harnett

The Bobs were growing seriously uncomfortable. It was one thing to be beaten in a contest, but the thought of having to drink a toast to someone as despicable as Hackett was something they found impossible to do. Besides, there was every possibility that Hackett was lying. They would have to leave, make some excuse and get out. An important engagement with some merchant prince would be an appropriate excuse. But before they left, the matriarch had a request.

'Do you not think, Bob, that it would be a nice gesture to give your nephew something to mark his success?'

'Eh, yes, yes indeed,' grumbled Bob.

Hackett watched his uncle reach into his pocket and produce his wallet. Slowly he opened it and produced a ten pound note. He would have chanced five, but he knew his mother was watching.

Hackett took immense pleasure in accepting the money and, as the Bobs left, Hackett smiled sweetly at the pimply one who left the room with his head bowed and his thoughts confused.

'You see them out,' Granny Hackett instructed her son and old man Hackett left the room.

As soon as she and Hackett were alone Granny Hackett reached for her bag. She was delighted with the news. Her faith in her grandson had been justified. With her long narrow arms she fished about in her handbag and recovered an enormous purse. Opening a side flap she peeled away several notes from a pile.

'Come here,' she said as she beckoned to Peter and the potential winner of yet another gold medal moved forward. All that was missing was the playing of an anthem.

'You know something?' she said. 'I'm delighted you won, that you did better than that other twit. He thinks he's the bee's knees so he does, the spider's ankles. Here, give your Gran a kiss.'

For the first time in his life Hackett thought he loved his Gran. He bent down to kiss her, allowed his lips brush against the powder-caked cheek. She held his arm tightly. And as he drew in her various smells of soap and perfumeries Granny Hackett looked him in the eye.

'Tell Father Osborne not to bother with the recheck.'

'But why, Gran?'

'Because I like the story as it is and you wouldn't want to disappoint an old lady. I backed you as a winner and that's the way I want it to stay.'

'Whatever you say, Gran.'

'Because, Peter, we all have our secrets, don't we?'

'Yes, Gran.'

There was a mix of emotions as they left Granny Hackett's. Mr Hackett was elated. The scheme, as far as he was concerned, had worked. He had seen off the challenge of his brother and for some strange reason had won the affection of his mother.

Hackett wasn't so sure how he felt. He enjoyed the pleasure that his scheming had brought to his Gran. But at the back of his mind he knew he had lied yet again. Another award. Another gold medal. He just couldn't help himself.

And yet, when his Gran looked him in the eye and told him not to bother with a recheck he wondered. Why did she say that? What was at the back of her mind? Did she know the full truth? Had she known all along? Had she realised that all the gold medals were fake? Maybe she herself was the queen of the schemers. Maybe she, in her dark room, spent her days plotting. Hackett would have liked that, to know that behind that dark exterior was a trickster, that perhaps through some strange genetic conduit his ability to scheme had been handed down.

And what had she meant by everyone having their secrets? What was hers? Could she have been that woman being led from Kilmartin's, the bookie's, to the car with the darkened windows?

211

CHAPTER TWENTY FIVE

The following evening at seven a taxi pulled up outside O'Neill's to take the family to the North Wall to watch the departure of Fergus.

A small group had gathered on the street. Everyone was sad to see him go. They felt especially for his mother who would now have to face the double difficulty of her first winter as a widow. For themselves too it was moving, because seeing Fergus leave was a reminder of all those they had known who over the years had been forced to go.

Fergus put on a brave face. He knew that if he let his mask down, grief would be the winner. And his mother couldn't cope with that. He chatted with the neighbours who kept him going. Old Darby wished him well. Mr Brennan shook his hand and Mrs Hickey came across the street with a brown paper bag of Hafner's sausages. The sausages in England never tasted the same. Then Harry Fay came over with some wine. Just before the taxi pulled away, Mr and Mrs Hackett joined the group and offered their best wishes.

The boys stood nearby watching the adults go through the ritual of parting. It was like the funeral all over again, only this time it was a wake for the living.

They all stood quietly in a group until the taxi left. They said little. It had all been said before.

The boys felt the sadness too. They were particularly upset for their friend. Since the funeral the Scout had been different. Rarely did he leave the house and when he did sadness covered his face. His humour too had changed. The laughs and jokes were gone. He had come to hate his job.

The boys tried to offer advice but the Scout didn't want to hear. He was in a place that had taken a grip on him. He seemed to be in a cocoon of despair.

On many evenings they sat in the shed and talked about how they could help their friend. But no solutions came. The sadness was contagious. It was hard to believe that they were sitting in the same place where there had been so much fun and enjoyment. Now it was dull and desolate. Their own world was beginning to crumble and even Hackett had no thoughts or schemes that might hold it all together.

Hackett had no appetite for schemes anyway. His most recent one with Granny Hackett had backfired spectacularly. Whether the old girl believed him or not, she had agreed to continue paying his fees. And while this news brought relief to his father, for Hackett it was the equivalent of a prison sentence and this awful realisation was made plain during his second week back in school.

He was sitting at his desk trying to look interested when a knock came to the classroom door. Someone wanted to see him. He stood and walked out to the corridor. A boy about the same age told him that the class tutor wanted to see Hackett in his office. Hackett followed the boy through a maze of corridors until he stopped and knocked on a door. A voice inside told him to enter. Hackett walked forward and stood before the tutor. He was invited to sit.

Hackett knew from the serious expression on the priest's face that this wasn't some frivolous chat about how he had spent the summer. And when the tutor opened his mouth Hackett's hunch was confirmed.

The tutor didn't want to open old wounds or make life miserable, but he reminded Hackett that the results of his exam were well below par. Hackett was told that there were two years left before the Leaving Certificate, two years during which the tutor would take an extra interest in Hackett. The Intermediate exam was one thing, the Leaving was something else.

There were, according to the tutor, more issues at stake than Hackett's performance. The reputation of the school for one! It didn't want any more failures, particularly from someone like Hackett, a young man with buckets of ability to pass. And so, to make sure that Hackett did well, study time and homework would be thoroughly supervised. And he meant thoroughly. The school authorities would leave nothing to chance. Instead of doing his homework at home, Hackett would be required to stay back in school each evening. And depending on his progress, Saturday mornings might form part of the programme.

Hackett pictured all too vividly the horror of his life before him. The bastards were treating him like a convict. A two year sentence with his own personal jailors. This wasn't living. This was hell.

Hackett related his story to the boys. He was expecting sympathy but none came. Fay and Brennan were unimpressed. Maybe they too were won over by study. They told him that he was smarter than most, that passing the exam was easy. It was only two years and was worth it. At the end of it all he'd have a job, a proper job. Did he want to end up sweeping the streets or as a nipper making tea on a building site for the men? Hackett told them that they were talking just like his parents.

'We're only telling you the truth,' said Fay.

'You asked for our advice,' added Brennan.

'You have to study to get a job.'

Hackett looked at the two of them. He couldn't believe that they were siding with the school, siding with his parents. Where was their loyalty? Where was their spirit? Where had their rebellion gone? Hackett sensed that a new chapter in their lives was being written. Their carefree existence seemed to be at an end. He knew Brennan was a swot but what about Fay, the mad guitarist, poet and womaniser? Was he too becoming sensible?

'The pair of you are sounding like me oulfella.'

'All we want is a good job,' said Fay.

'With decent money and a future to look forward to,' added Brennan.

'So for the next two years it's all about study?'

'We don't have a choice,' said Brennan.

'And what about here? What about the boys? What about all the fun we had?'

'We'll still see each other, have a laugh,' offered Brennan.

Hackett looked closely at Brennan.

'And how often have we seen you since you took up with that woman?'

Brennan's face turned red. Hackett wasn't finished.

'And when we do see you, it's Fiona this and Fiona that, Fiona all the bleeding time.'

'Ah here,' said Fay, 'that's not fair.'

'Maybe not fair, but it's the truth.'

Hackett could see that he had touched a nerve. Brennan wasn't happy. But what Hackett had said was the truth. They had hardly seen Brennan at all since Fiona came on the scene. It was one thing to have a girlfriend, but did Brennan not know that the boys came first?

'Things change,' said Brennan.

'Yeah, I've noticed,' said Hackett sulkily.

'We'll still have fun,' added Fay.

'Yeah once a month if we're lucky.'

'For God's sake Hackett, we have to start taking things seriously,' said Brennan.

'Yeah, well you do that.'

'I will.'

'And when's the big day? When are you getting engaged?'

'Fuck off.'

'No, you fuck off.'

'If I want to go out with Fiona, that's my business.'

'Yeah and forget all your friends?'

'I'm forgetting nothing. Just because I've got a steady girlfriend?'

'Well, stay with her.'

'Yeah, I will.'

'Would the pair of yiz shut up,' said Fay.

'Just because he failed the exam he's taking it all out on us,' pleaded Brennan.

'No I'm not.'

'Yes you are. All myself and Fay are trying to do is put you straight, that's all, nothing else, and you start all this crap about me and Fiona.'

'Yeah, well I spoke the truth.'

Brennan didn't reply. He had heard enough. His evaluation of the situation told him there would be no winners to this argument. He wasn't angry, maybe sad. He stood, nodded at Fay and left the shed.

Fay lit a cigarette and took several pulls before speaking.

'You were over the top with Brennan.'

'Was I?'

'His first real bird and you're jealous.'

'I'm not jealous.'

'You are, you know.'

'Brennan is breaking up the boys. Can't you see that? The gang is falling apart.'

'It's not Brennan's fault.'

'Then whose fault is it?'

'It's life,' said Fay taking upon himself his philosophical mode. 'It's just life, Hackett. Things change. The Scout's old man dies. The Scout changes, he's in bits. There's no getting through to him. Brennan meets a bird, the first real bird ever. He changes. That's the way things happen. Nothing is for keeps. Brennan wants to study. Maybe me too. You don't. That's your decision. It doesn't mean the boys are gone. It means that the boys are growing up. Getting older. Things can't stay the same forever. Nothing does. You can't keep living in the past. You have to move on.'

'Yeah, well maybe I will then.'

Hackett left the shed. Fay followed him through the house to the hall door. Hackett didn't speak as he opened the door and left.

On the opposite side of the street the Scout and Mrs O'Neill were walking towards their door. They had got the bus home and vacantly watched all the familiar landmarks flash by the window. They only had eyes for what they had watched earlier; a son and a brother sail down the Liffey out of their lives for what seemed like an eternity.

Hackett hardly slept that night. The lives of the boys were in turmoil. A summer which had started so well had ended in grief. The boys who had been so united in June were now in chaos. They were no longer a cohesive group. Their friendship had fractured. Hackett knew in his heart that what he had said to Brennan was wrong. He should not have mentioned Fiona. Like the episode with the gold medals, he couldn't shut up. He had to go on. It was as if another side to his character took over. He knew Brennan had a disastrous history with women and yet he couldn't leave it alone.

As he lay awake Hackett tried to connect with his feelings. He wanted to discover what was behind his anger towards his friends. Was it his failure in the exam? Was it his need to see nothing change in the gang? Did he want everything to go on forever?

Deep down he knew he was bright enough to pass the exam. But he didn't really try. And why was that? Was it really because he hated the subjects, saw them as irrelevant and ridiculous? Or was there something else? He didn't know the answers.

In his mind he mouthed words, carried on conversations. Often he would do that. He wanted to try and understand what was happening to his young life. He thought of the way he had fooled Granny Hackett, or had he? Had the old bird had the last laugh? Had she been behind the new study regime in school? Had she made contact with the school?

What was he to do with his life?

Scheming was the thing he enjoyed most. He loved nothing better than organising deception. The rescue of Brennan, the child for Lourdes, the awards for study, these were the things that made him come alive - not study, not Caesar's Gallic Wars or complex questions on trigonometry.

But why should it be like that? Why should he crave the excitement of things not ordinary? Why was that? Why did he need the satisfaction of scheming? He didn't know. He didn't understand.

Before he slept he made two decisions. First he would talk to Brennan. He would try and put things right. Brennan, despite his peculiarities, had been his friend for years. He shouldn't have hurt him. It was wrong. It needed to be put right.

His second decision was to have more far-reaching effects. He would not spend the next two years of his life in the prison of school. Nor would he subject himself to the humiliation of supervised study. Instead he would get out. He would find a way to extricate himself from it all. He would get a job, something that paid well and no amount of persuasion would change his mind. And then he slept, but not soundly.

CHAPTER TWENTY SIX

The following morning Hackett rose early and descended the stairs for breakfast. As he sat at the table he had little to say. He wasn't in much humour for eating. His mind was still going over what he had decided last night. It was business as usual for his parents. The anguish with Granny Hackett was over and the school fees were secure for the next two years.

Hackett pulled the hall door behind him. With little enthusiasm he ambled down the street towards the bus stop. On his way he saw the Scout on the opposite side, head down, carrying a bag of messages for his mother. Hackett crossed over.

'All right, Scout?'

The Scout nodded.

'What's up?'

'Not much.'

'Are you working or what?'

'Meant to be, but I'm not.'

'Just hanging around, yeah?'

'Something like that. You going to school?'

'Meant to be.'

'You're better off going.'

'What if I take the day off? We could go up the canal for a bit of a laugh. What do you think?'

'Hackett you should go to school.'

'Yeah and you should go to work.'

Hackett arranged to meet the Scout at the second lock on the canal above the bridge. The Scout seemed pleased to have something to do. Hackett began to feel better about mitching from school. Now he was involved in an act of Christian charity to cheer up a friend swamped in grief. How could that be wrong?

As he left the street Hackett checked the bus stop. He didn't want anyone to see him pass by. He walked down along Drumcondra Road and as he neared the bridge he could feel a sense of freedom coming over him. It was like old times on his own heading for the canal bank, those grassy verges where the further he walked the more the city sounds faded. This was where he was happiest, away from the regime of school and the droning voices of the bored.

At the second lock he stopped to wait for the Scout. He looked down into the neglected chamber now a dumping ground for discarded rubbish and debris. This was once a proud waterway, a commercial artery along which goods were carried in flat-bottomed barges. Now it had fallen into disuse.

When the Scout arrived they walked on. They passed beneath the shadow of the walls of the prison. It was here that Hackett had played poker and won money, funds which were later donated to Brennan's release.

Hackett noticed that as they walked the demeanour of the Scout seemed to change. It wasn't what he said, which was little. It was his body movement, his head no longer hung low.He reached several times for stones to lob into the canal. His pace quickened. He wasn't as lethargic or bored.

They stopped to smoke a cigarette and leaned against the railway wall. They looked down into the twin-track culvert of the permanent way, a rail line that ran to the other side of Ireland. A diesel engine came out of the tunnel, behind it a long string of open carriages heaped with gravel. As the train passed beneath them the boys tried to land stones in the centre of the open carriages. None hit their mark and they watched the long snake of metal fade from view and enter the tunnel at the other end. When the noise subsided Hackett spoke.

'So, how are you doing anyway?'

'Poxy.'

'Poxy?'

'Yeah, poxy.'

Then Hackett recalled what he had been thinking about last night, how he had wondered what he'd do with his life.

'Tell us something?' he said.

'Tell you what?'

'If you'd one wish, one wish in the world, what would you wish for?'

'What sort of a question is that?'

'Go on tell us. What would you wish for?'

The Scout looked at him almost with contempt.

'I'd wish me old man hadn't fucking died. That good enough for you?'

'I'm sorry Scout, I really am. I shouldn't have asked such a stupid question.'

They smoked some more. Then the Scout surprised Hackett.

'But if I had another wish, what would you think it would be?'

'Don't know.'

'Guess.'

'I don't know. Tell us.'

'I'd wish,' the Scout said, 'I'd wish I was out of this kip.'

'You mean Drumcondra?'

'Yeah, Drumcondra, Dublin, the lot.'

'And where would you go?'

'Anywhere.'

'And what about your job?'

'I don't give a shit about me job. I hate it. It's a dead end job anyway.'

'But it's a job.'

'I'm not going back, Hackett.'

'And what are you going to do?'

'I'm leaving.'

'Going to England?'

'Why not?'

'And what about your old lady?'

'She's the only reason I'm not gone already.'

The Scout confided in his friend. He told him about delivering the telegram and the effect it had had on him. He described everything in detail, how he had felt when he handed over the small green envelope to that woman in the flats. Hackett listened intently. He was impressed by the way the Scout analysed his situation. It became clear that the telegram boy had to get out.

The Scout also told Hackett that he had discussed it all with Fergus before his brother went back to the navy. At first Fergus, like his mother, tried to convince the Scout that time would ease the pain. But, as the conversation was repeated, Fergus came to see that there was only one solution to the problem, his brother would have to leave.

When the subject of England came up Fergus was less supportive. Life on building sites was hard. Isn't that what had killed their father?

As the Scout spoke Hackett kept thinking of himself. He too was trapped. He hated his life in school and the prospect of two more years was unimaginable.

When the Scout finished Hackett told his story. Part of him wanted to empathise with the Scout. But another part wanted to hear himself say the words he had been thinking, as if hearing them would help make what he felt seem real.

The Scout could not believe that Hackett had failed the exam. He found it incredible that a genius for invention like Hackett could fall down when it came to putting down words on a page. What was education for if it didn't harness the potential of the brilliant?

When Hackett finished the Scout summed up the position.

'So you're in the shit as well?'

'That's the way it seems.'

'So what are you going to do?'

'I don't know.'

'You'll have to do something.'

'I know.'

'You could join the navy like Fergus,' suggested the Scout.

'And what? Spend me day with me head in a bucket puking up me ring?'

'Yeah, I'd be the same. Have you ever thought of the army?'

'The Irish army?'

'The British army.You want to get out of this place, don't you?'

Hackett had never thought of anything beyond getting out of school.

'It could be shite.'

'Could it be any worse than here? I've been thinking about it.'

'Really?'

'All you have to do is go to Belfast and join up where Fergus went to join the navy. It's simple.'

'And what happens then?'

'Then you're sent to Germany or Hong Kong or wherever. It's better than hanging around here and the pay's okay.'

'You serious about this?' asked Hackett.

'Never more serious in me life.'

They spent the rest of the day idling around the Royal Canal. At times there were long silences. Each of them realised that they had explored something new and exciting. There was also the question of honesty, how each of them had spoken intimately about what was making their lives so difficult. Each was trying to understand the other. There was no one there to mock or deride. Their openness and frankness brought them closer.

Hackett thought about the suggestion of the army. Was it not another regime like school? You did what you were told. There was no room for scheming or self-expression. Your job was to toe the line, polish your kit and assemble each day beneath the fluttering flag of one's country. But the Union Jack was not the flag of Hackett's country. How would he feel about that? How would he feel about 'God Save The Queen.' He might not feel so bad if he was paid to do it. It had to be a better option than school?

'Do you know where the place in Belfast is?' asked Hackett, 'the place you sign up?'

'Have the address at home.'

'And the pay's good?'

'That's what I've heard. And anyway you don't really have to spend any money. The grub's paid for. You can save a packet. Fergus is worth a mint.'

Hackett visualised the stuffed wallet that Fergus would wave before them, the gold watch too and the clothes, the fashion. There were also the women, droves of them, and all of them making themselves available for all the guys in uniform.

'So what do you think?' asked the Scout.

'I don't know.'

'Maybe it's worth a try.'

'Maybe.'

'Well I'm going to try it,' said the Scout. 'I'm going to try it because anything is better than here.'

'And what about your Ma?'

'I think she'll understand. And what about you?'

'I wouldn't say anything until I was gone.'

'You'd run away?'

'I couldn't face them, Scout. I couldn't.'

And he couldn't, but later that evening he had to.

Earlier that day Mr Hackett took a phone call in his office. It was Peter's tutor, the one who was taking a special interest in the boy. Just keeping in touch was how the softly spoken cleric put it.

'Just wondering how he is,' said the tutor.

Mr Hackett decided to kick to touch.

'Very nice of you, Father.'

'It's just that he wasn't in school today and I wondered how he was.'

The bastard, thought Mr Hackett.

'Well I left very early Father, so I'll check when I get home and ring you tomorrow.'

'That's great because we don't want any more failures do we?'

'Oh you're so right there, Father.'

Mr Hackett left the office early. He would be home to meet the little bastard when he came through the door. He would eat the arse off him. Only a few days back and he was up to his tricks again.

When Hackett arrived home later in the day the hall door nearly flew off the hinges. A red faced man glared at him.

'Get into that room,' he roared, 'get in!'

Hackett walked into the small front room. His old man charged after him.

'Where were you today?'

And before Hackett could trawl his mind for something to say his old man went on.

'No, don't answer that, don't say a word because I don't want any more of your lies. You little bastard. You're up to your tricks again. After all that we've been through you're still mitching from school.'

'I can explain.'

'I don't want to hear.'

'But I have an excuse.'

'You have no excuse, none in the wide earthly world. I'm fed up to my back teeth listening to your lies. For as long as I can remember you have been feeding us with your lies. But no more, never again will I believe a word out of your mouth, never. I tell you what I'm going to do. From now on you will take the same bus as me into town. I'll make sure you go to school. And when I get to work I'll ring the school to check that you didn't come down with a bout of Asian flu as you walked in the gate. Is that clear? Is it? Do you hear what I'm saying?'

Hackett wanted to tell him that everyone on the street had heard.

'Do you understand?'

'Yes.'

'Do you?'

'Yes.'

'Now get up those fecking stairs to study. Go on, get going and you'll be told when it's time for tea.'

'Can I say something?'

'If you open your fecking mouth. . .'

Hackett left the room. In the hallway he saw his mother standing at the kitchen door. She had been listening to it all. Hackett tried a softening-up smile. It didn't work. She turned away and closed the kitchen door.

They were all against him. All of them. He was on his own. He climbed the stairs and went into his room. He closed the door and sat at his desk. He felt trapped. His old man had it all worked out. There was no escape and no room for any more excuses or scheming. They were going to watch him night and day. He would never be able to take a day off again. And worse, every hour he spent in school would be monitored by that prick of a tutor.

He walked to the window like a prisoner gazing at freedom from his cell. Across the street he saw the Scout heading his way. Then he heard a knock on the door. He couldn't make out what was said. It couldn't have been much because the door slammed almost immediately. As he crossed the street the Scout turned and looked up towards Hackett's window.

Hackett turned from the window. He sat on the edge of the bed. He began to think over his last day as a free man, how he and the Scout had shared so many secrets. He recalled how his friend had described Hackett's situation.

'So, you're in the shite as well?' he had said.

And Hackett knew that there was no more eloquent way of putting it. He was in the shite and, in no uncertain terms, up to his neck in it.

CHAPTER TWENTY SEVEN

It was not until Friday evening that Hackett had a chance to talk to the Scout. All through the week his movements had been watched, from his journey on the bus to school with his father, right through his supervised homework and after school too as a curfew was imposed restricting his movements. Instead of instilling a respect for discipline this strict regime had the opposite effect. By the end of the first week Hackett had decided to rebel.

On Friday evening his father relented and allowed Hackett some free time. He called for the Scout and together they walked through Griffith Park along the banks of the Tolka. They stopped at the pedestrian bridge and looked down at the dark coloured water as it made its way towards the bay. Hackett lit a cigarette. Then, with his eyes still focused on the river, he spoke.

'I've decided to go,' he said.

'Go where?'

'Go where we were talking about, Belfast, to join the army.'

'You sure?'

'I have to get out. They're driving me mad. Are you still on for it?'

'When do we go?'

'Straight away.'

'You mean tomorrow?'

'Yeah, tomorrow. Saturday's best for me. Any other day during the week they're watching me all the time. Anyway, why hang about?'

They decided they would leave the following day. Another week would be an eternity. They needn't take much, just a small bag for odds and ends. And of course money. Hackett had saved quite a bit from his summer job.

On the way back home they made their plan. They would pack a bag and leave in the morning. But they would have to talk with Fay and Brennan first.

They gathered in the shed. Brennan had been reluctant to attend. He had not spoken to Hackett since the incident over Fiona. And the longer it dragged on the more defiant Brennan became. But when the Scout told him it was important that they meet, Brennan agreed to be there.

'So,' began Fay as he lit a cigarette, 'to what do we owe the pleasure?'

'Myself and Scout have something to tell you.'

Brennan sat forward. Fay took a long drag.

'Go on,' said Fay.

'We're leaving.'

'Leaving where?'

'Leaving here, leaving Dublin.'

'Going where?'

'England.'

'To work on building sites?'

'No, we're joining the British army.'

Initially Fay challenged them, but as the argument went on and their serious intent became plain Fay held back. He had been particularly moved by the Scout's story of his telegram delivery. Then Fay stood.

'I'm going to see if Harry has any fresh stock.'

While Fay was searching for wine Brennan talked with the Scout. He asked sensible questions, typical Brennan questions about how they would survive and other practical details. He did not engage with Hackett.

Fay returned with two bottles of red and a handful of glasses. He pulled the first cork and poured.

'Well here's to you, lads.'

They drank in silence. Hackett sighed loudly. It was like the sounding of relief now that the story was no longer a secret. No one really knew what to say. Fay filled the void by topping up glasses. It was hard for them to understand what was happening. They had grown up together, shared the same experiences and discovered their individual quirkiness and personalities. They had learned about life through each other, from the madness of the summer just gone to the awful reality of the death of one of their fathers.

Now it seemed that a vital chapter in their lives was over. It would never be the same again. Individually they knew that at some stage they would go their separate ways, but none of them expected it to be so soon. It was like growing old, something that happened in the future, something that happened to others.

Hackett lit a cigarette. He stroked his forehead, he scratched his head. A feeling of discomfort came over him. He looked towards Brennan, then looked away. He sighed again loudly.

'There's something I'd like to say,' he began, 'something that's been bothering me. Something that I feel really bad about. I know I should have said it earlier, but things at home and in school. . . things, things haven't been easy. What I want to say is that I was out of order with you, Brennan. I shouldn't have said those things. I'm, I'm sorry.'

The ice was broken and Brennan responded.

'Thanks, Hackett, thanks a lot.'

'Doesn't mean that we don't want to know how you got on with her,' said the Scout.

'That's right,' said Fay, 'the boys have to know all the details.'

'Did you go all the way Brennan, did you?' probed the Scout.

'No secrets, Brennan.'

'Tell us,' said Fay.

And Brennan surprised them by talking. At first he was tempted to spoof, to tell them what they were expecting, but then he thought better of such a plan. What if stories spread about the woman he loved? What if the stories got back to Fiona? This was the woman who had transformed his life, changed his knowledge of women. It was she who had given him confidence.

'When I left here that night I walked her home. We kissed and that was that. And since then, since then it's been really good, really nice, and no, no we didn't go all the way.'

None of them had been expecting an answer like that. They would have been more comfortable with fiction. They wanted exaggeration, detail they could challenge, even mock, juicy stuff about panting and grappling. They wanted to be able to slag and confront. Brennan had robbed them of every opportunity to gloat. And their silence said it all.

After lighting another cigarette Fay summed up.

'She's a nice girl Brennan, really nice.'

'Yeah,' agreed the Scout, 'she is, she really is.'

As they made their way through the second bottle of wine and the finality of what was about to happen their friendship dawned, they took refuge in nostalgia. They told stories of old.

'And do you remember. . .'

They laughed at their innocence, of the times they had been caught robbing orchards, the times they exploded stink bombs in church, the dud fireworks they'd been sold. They were looking back at their childhood as if they were they fifty, but that's how they dealt with the imminent parting.

Several times Fay tried to get them to change their minds but at each attempt the resolve of Hackett and the Scout became stronger. It was the only way forward for them. And as they went over their reasons for leaving it was clear that the decision was final.

As one story ended, another began. There was an instinctive need to keep talking, as if the babble of conversation would keep the reality at bay. None of them wanted silence. Long pauses were fertile ground for sadness. It wasn't just the thought of parting, it was also the friendship they would miss in the future. Throughout their lives they imagined staying together as a gang growing older, even wiser, but most of all adding depth and meaning to their friendship. Never before had they talked of leaving.

They were reluctant to draw the evening to a close. Among them was a wish that this moment could be frozen and preserved, that their warm glow of friendship could remain. In some ways they were closer now than they had ever been and in the years to come they would look back on this time with deep fondness.

Hackett knew that he had a bag to pack, but he too was reluctant to leave. He knew that once he walked out of that shed he would be closing forever a unique chapter in his childhood. And yet he knew he had to go. He looked over at the Scout and, despite the effects of the wine, it was obvious that the telegram boy was hurting. His head hung low. Maybe the full realisation was making its mark, the thought perhaps of having to tell his mother that he was walking out of that house for good.

And yet they were all frightened of parting. It wasn't just the separation; it was how they would behave and what they would say. There was also the question of intimacy. What do you say to someone you have known all your life? Do you express how you feel? Or do you, like most adults you know, let words fall from your lips like loose change from a purse? And what about the physical? Do you shake a hand or slap a back? Do you offer a hug?

Finally it was Fay who took control.

'Lads, it's getting late. You pair have things to do. So we'll see you tomorrow. We'll go with you to the station, won't we Brennan?'

'Sure.'

They all stood and left the shed. It was dark outside and they were glad of the lack of light. It meant facial expressions were hidden. Awkwardly they stood in a bunch. Then the Scout spoke.

'What about your woman?' he said pointing to the window on the far side of the lane.

'She's still at it,' said Fay. 'In fact if you hang about I'd say the show is about to commence.'

They moved towards Fay's back wall. They stood on the old tea-chests. Across the muddy laneway a light shone down from the window. Then the woman appeared.

They were glad of her presence, not that any of them had any interest in her performance, her appearance diverted their thinking. They watched for a while, but it was now like a film they had seen several times. It was Brennan who spoke for them all.

'Come on lads, we've seen enough.'

The four of them walked towards Fay's house. The back door was open and they made their way through the familiar debris that lay all around. The kitchen had once again become a health hazard.

They stood at the hall door then parted in silence.

Sleep would not come easy that night.

CHAPTER TWENTY EIGHT

Before he lay on his bed that night Hackett sat at his desk. He decided that he would write a letter to his parents, having dismissed the prospect of telling them face to face.

In the letter he tried to explain his position. No one was to blame for his departure. All he wanted to do was make a new life for himself. He would write often and spend his holidays in Drumcondra.

To let them down lightly he lied again. He told them he was taking up an apprenticeship in the army in the complex world of electronics. This was a discipline which would serve him well later in civilian life. He would have a marketable talent and would have no problem getting a well-paid job after the army.

Hackett read the letter several times. He thought it made convincing reading, he was even beginning to believe it himself. He licked the gum and closed the envelope.

Across the street the Scout was scribbling away. Despite repeated attempts to put down his thoughts the words would not flow easily. He found it impossible to say what he felt. He wanted to tell his mother that he had no choice, that the turmoil he was feeling was driving him mad. And yet he didn't want to upset her. He tried to tell her how much he loved her, that he wanted to go but he hated to leave. He knew that she would be heartbroken, that the sight of another envelope would be a catastrophe for her. In desperation he tore up all the letters. His head was a mire of confusion. Then he did what he had been dreading. He stood and walked down the stairs.

His mother was sitting reading a magazine. At first she didn't hear him come into the room. He stood there like he had done so many times, the naughty boy waiting for mammy to deliver her scolding. She must have sensed his presence. Lowering the magazine, she looked over at him. Instinct told her that something was wrong.

'Something the matter love?'

He lowered his head as he always did as a child.

'What is it?'

And he told her. Her face slowly registered the anguish of the news. Her worst fears had been realised. The third man in her life was leaving, taking himself out of her life forever. Yes, he said he would come on holidays, but that was a vague hope, a pipe dream, poor consolation for such a loss.

She started to cry. She didn't want to show her torment so openly but she couldn't hold the emotion back. The tears ran down her face. She tried to wipe them away. He came forward with a tissue. He sat down on the arm of the chair beside her. She could hear a slight whimpering, a sniffle and then a clearing of his throat. He too was hurting. She knew him so well, the softer of the two boys, like her husband in so many ways, outwardly manly but behind the exterior a softness, a gentle sensitivity to all that mattered in his world. Never in his sixteen years had he brought real trouble home, boyish, rogue-filled devilment yes, but never anything vindictive. He was a special child.

She tried to talk to him of alternatives, of new ways of looking at his problems. But he couldn't see beyond the walls that were trapping him. He wanted to go, to get away from a world that was causing him endless pain.

Reluctantly she accepted his decision. Better that he go with her blessing than have him walk away carrying the burden of a mother's angst. She stood and put her hands on his shoulders. Still sitting on the arm of the chair he leaned towards her. She held him against her breast and stroked his head as she had done so many times before. He may have been the size of his father but he was still a young boy in her arms.

Gently she told him it was bedtime and he stood and left the room to climb the stairs for the very last time.

Hackett found it almost impossible to sleep. His mind played flickering images like a silent movie. Image after image presented itself and in these pictures he saw a career stretching out before him, not a traditional military one. There was no drilling or marching in formation on a barrack square for Hackett. Instead he was a man of strategy, planning campaigns in the bunkers of war, standing, looking down on enormous maps of the world, moving battalions of men, convoys of armoured vehicles, fleets of destroyers and all around him officers with epaulets and honours turning towards him, waiting, wondering what General Hackett would do next. Intermittently a red telephone would ring and somebody would answer and tell the Prime Minister that the General was busy and would call back later.

When Hackett wasn't directing operations in his bunker he would be travelling the world incognito. Fleeting images of this extraordinary Irishman would be seen in exotic back street bazaars as he did his business with spies. When not crossing borders or dropping from planes, Hackett could be seen at the gaming tables of Monte Carlo and, as always, a bevy of exotic creatures would be vying for his arm.

Sometimes, when his busy schedule allowed, he would write a brief postcard to his friends from magical parts of the globe. He would, as always, sign himself 'H' for security reasons, of course.

CHAPTER TWENTY NINE

Old man Hackett was surprised that his son was up so early on a Saturday morning. Normally the young fellow had to be prised from his bed. His mother also found it strange, particularly the sound of taps running in the bathroom. Up so early and having a bath as well! Maybe the dressing down his father had given him had worked. Maybe Peter was growing up at last. She certainly hoped so, and when she heard that his reason for rising early was to head for the Franciscan Friary for a prayer meeting, Mrs Hackett felt that her own prayers and petitions to Saint Jude of Hopeless Cases had, at last, been answered. Hackett was tempted to add more details of the intended penance but he stopped himself short. He had told enough lies. And there were more in the letter he held in his pocket.

Hackett sat at the kitchen table. He didn't want any breakfast but, as always, his mother was insistent. She wanted him to eat. He couldn't. Instead, he sipped tea. And though his mind was a sea of preoccupations, he lingered at the table watching his parents. He didn't know why but some strange impulse gripped him; his mother at the gas rings, manoeuvring her rashers and sausages on a spitting pan, his father sitting there, a mug of tea in one hand, a Capstan Full Strength cigarette in the other.

If Hackett had space in his head he might have felt sadness for them. But already his mind was full up with images of departure and train journeys and a place called Belfast.

He excused himself and went upstairs. In the toilet another bout of diarrhoea hit him. He had been to the toilet several times already. He wasn't sure whether it was Harry Fay's wine or nerves. Eventually, when he felt that all the liquid had left his system, he washed his hands in the sink and looked into the mirror. The eyes, he saw, were hollow and his complexion was waxy and pale.

Slowly he descended the stairs. At the hall door he wondered if he should call out and say goodbye. He didn't. Instead he walked towards the kitchen. Both of them were sitting at the table. His mother looked up. He saw those tired and compassionate eyes. She smiled and for an instant he felt huge regret for all the suffering he had caused her. And yet he could do nothing now. It was all too late. His father nodded and sipped his tea. In their own way they seemed happy. But for how long? How would they feel after it became clear that their only son had left? Hackett didn't like to think on those things. He turned and walked towards the hall door. He didn't see the looks that his parents exchanged, those hesitant expressions of curiosity and concern, looks that masked minds full of hope that their only child might reform his ways and make life less of a trial for them all.

The Scout's parting was less solemn. His mother had decided that she should make it easy for him to go. She wanted him to be full of good feelings. Countless times she had seen her husband leave, Fergus too, and she knew the burden of hurt they were carrying. She didn't want her youngest to feel any pain even though she knew that he, more than any of them, would deeply feel the wrench of parting.

All morning she had kept the banter of conversation going. She talked of how it would be an adventure for him, a rare opportunity to see the world. And he nodded, knowing that his mother was doing what she had always done to protect him from the harsher things in life. Then it was time to go.

She wanted to go with him to the station but he prevailed upon her to stay. It would be bad enough leaving her now without having to wave from a window on a train.

He waited in the hallway as his father and brother had done. She took him in her arms and drew him close. Though he was choking with emotion he managed to tell her that he loved her, and she didn't reply, she couldn't, because if she opened her mouth she knew she would wail.

It was she who pulled away first. She wiped her face, looked at herself in the oval shaped mirror and walked to the door. She turned the latch and pulled the door open and he, eyes streaming, walked slowly into the early morning light of the street.

She closed the door after him, stood for several seconds resting her face against the door. Her face was wet, her heart pumping. She wanted to cry out, to blame someone, to castigate those who had ruined her life. She wanted someone to explain, to tell her why she had been selected to receive more than her share of sorrow. It wasn't fair. It wasn't right. Why had she lost her husband and her family? Why was she consigned to a life full of grief?

With the heaviness of all she was bearing, she walked slowly into the front room and stood before the china cabinet with its array of photos on top.

When Hackett got to the corner of the street Brennan and Fay were already there. Their greetings were wary and restrained. None of them knew how to behave.

'All right?'

'Yeah, all right.'

'Here,' said Fay who handed Hackett a bag he had been storing overnight, a bag that contained the few things that Hackett would take with him on his journey. Hackett took the bag and dropped it on the ground. Then they went silent.

Fay flashed a packet of cigarettes and they all lit up. They were grateful for the void the smoking filled. They all drew deeply and released the smoke. Fay tried puffing rings. Hackett alternated between his mouth and his nose and Brennan let the smoke trickle out slowly.

All about them the street was coming to life. O'Meara the builder was piling planks on top of his van. Mrs Hickey was cleaning her downstairs windows. Rob Finnegan's old man was heading for an early opening pub in the city.

Then the image of the Scout appeared. He was walking slowly towards them carrying a blue duffle bag. There was nothing jaunty or exciting in his movement. He seemed downcast and restrained. Inwardly they all recognised the signs.

When he came up to them he nodded. He tried a smile but it was obvious he had no feeling of joy. His eyes were red and one of his cheeks was stained with his mother's mascara. Fay offered him a cigarette and he took one. He drew on it anxiously in short sharp drags almost as if he didn't want to be seen.

Then Darby Maguire appeared.

'Not another prayer meeting I hope?'

'How did you guess?' said Hackett as he laughed when he thought of the excuse he had given his parents.

'You're a gas crowd, I'll tell you that,' said Darby, who became convulsed in laughter.

'What's so funny?' said Hackett.

'Yeah,' said Fay, 'tell us.'

Darby tried to explain, but each time the words almost came out another seizure of laughter came over him. The boys watched as Darby's face grew redder. The normally heightened colour of his nose made him look like a cartoon character. The man was gripped in a fit. And then suddenly he stopped. His expression changed. The laughter drained from his face. Pointing at the bags, he spoke.

'What's all this? I hope none of you are thinking of doing anything stupid?'

The boys glanced at each other. Then the Scout spoke.

'I'm leaving Mr Maguire, me mother knows.'

Darby nodded. Then he looked at Hackett.

'And you?'

'Just going to the station with him.'

'Sure?'

'Yeah, sure.'

'You're certain your mother knows?'

'Honest to God,' said the Scout.

'Well take care of yourself,' said Darby, as he turned to move off, 'yeah, take care of yourself. Your father was a good man, a man I really respected.'

'Thanks, Mr Maguire.'

Darby smiled and began walking up the street.

'Tell us,' said Hackett, 'what were you laughing at?'

Darby paused and turned to look back at them. His face lit up again.

'When I said you were a gas crowd. Do you not get it? Gas? A gas crowd. Gas.'

And then he started to laugh again and walked on. They watched as he continued up the street and saw him stop several times to draw breath between bouts of hysterical laughter.

'He knew all along about the gas meter,' said Fay, 'the old codger knew all along.'

At the booking office in Amiens Street Station Hackett and the Scout bought single tickets to Belfast. The train was due to leave at eleven. They stood under the giant clock and watched the hands move slowly.

'I hate this waiting,' said the Scout.

'Yeah, me too.'

The Scout strolled over to the platform and looked through the gates at the Belfast train with its string of carriages.

'Is he going to be all right?' asked Fay, looking over and nodding towards the Scout.

'He'll be all right once we get going,' said Hackett.

'Yeah, he'll be okay,' said Brennan.

'What do you say we try and get a drink?'

'You're mad,' said Brennan, 'they won't serve us.'

'It's worth a try. What do you say, Hackett? You've got a ticket and all.'

'Why not?'

They called the Scout over and the four of them walked into the bar and sat at a table. The place was strangely empty. A few people with suitcases stood in a group sipping drinks. Beside them an American couple was talking loudly about Killarney. They were drinking water. The boys argued about who would approach the bar to try and get served. Eventually it was Hackett who stood and walked towards the counter. As he moved between the tables he tried to take stock of the barmen. He was trying to decide which of the three would be less discerning about underage drinking. It was hard to figure out. All three of them had that crusted look that comes with experience and that practised ability to arch an eyebrow when doubting a statement.

'What age did you say you were?'

The closer he came to the counter the more he believed that his mission would be a failure and he would be reluctantly forced to return to the boys empty handed. His final scheme would have to be a success. He would have to think of something.

He rested his elbows on the counter. In the frosted mirror at the back of the bar he saw his reflection. He tried to look serious and grave. He furrowed his brow, pouted his lips. Then a voice broke into his concentration.

'What can I get you?' said the barman, a man about the same age as Hackett's father. Hackett knew instinctively that in normal circumstances this man would say no. Something different was called for.

Hackett looked at the man intently then pointed at the tap which dispensed beer and held up four fingers. The barman looked at Hackett and shook his head.

'What age are you?'

Hackett pointed at the breast pocket in the barman's uniform. The barman looked down at his pocket and turned his gaze to Hackett.

'What are you on about?'

Hackett pointed again and mouthed the word *pen.*

'Pen, is it?'

Hackett nodded and the barman placed the pen on the counter. Hackett took up the pen and on the back of a beer mat wrote out a message. He told the barman that they were out for the day, the four of them, released from a home for young men who had difficulty speaking. All they wanted was a pint of beer. And yes, though they may not look it, all of them were eighteen. Hackett passed over the beer mat.

While the barman was reading the message, Hackett wrote another note. In this one he said that one of their group was leaving today to join the missions. In all probability, this drink would be his last before reaching the searing heat of Africa.

They nearly missed the train. Hackett's final scheme had produced not one round of drinks, but three. But the drink came with more than a monetary price. For a start they couldn't talk. If any of them were caught speaking, the scheme would have been seen as a scam. And so, for the duration of their time in the bar, they communicated using a mix of sign language and beer mats. It was hilarious. The laughter was loud and raucous. Even the Scout seemed to emerge from his earlier gloom. It was like old times, the boys together full of fun and antics. And predictably it was this respite from their sadness that made the final parting all the more poignant.

They left the bar in a hurry and ran to the gates at the platform. The final moment had arrived. They stood looking at each other wondering what they should say. It was Brennan who spoke first.

243

'We're going to miss you lads.'

'We are,' added Fay.

'We'll write,' said Hackett, 'and maybe send you loads of French letters.'

'What?' said Brennan in alarm, before realising that Hackett was up to his tricks.

'See yiz,' said the Scout as he turned to walk away. All of them could see that the hurt was returning to the Scout, that his eyes were filling up again. They let him walk on. Then Hackett stuck out his hand and Brennan and Fay grabbed it. They didn't speak. They nodded and forced a smile. Then Hackett produced the letter to his parents. He passed it to Brennan without explanation. Brennan would know what to do.

Hackett followed the Scout along the platform. They didn't look back to see the faces of the others. They boarded a carriage near the front, found two seats and threw their bags on the rack overhead.

Almost immediately they felt the shunting movement of the carriages. The journey had begun. The diesel engine sounded its hooter and slowly as the steel wheels gained purchase on the track the train moved forward, out from under the cover of the giant canopy of the railway station and into the morning sunlight.

Along the embankment the train moved gathering speed, picking its way through the tapestry of track, heading northwards on its journey.

Their eyes blinked as they looked out the window. They were glad of the distraction of seeing into the back gardens of strangers, of where they lived and the jumble they collected. They took a childlike satisfaction in recognising landmarks, but it wasn't long before the familiar scenes fell away. They were entering an unfamiliar world.

The sight of the greenness of the countryside confirmed in their minds that this was no ordinary train journey, no day-excursion to the seaside. This was a one-way journey, a single ticket to the unknown.

CR

Michael Harnett